READERS LOVE THE OTHER PART OF HER

"Powerful! Impeccably researched and emotionally enriching."
-Commander Gary Forsberg, US Navy

"This page-turner of love, honor and duty compelled me to laugh, cry and cheer unlike any book read to date. It begs to be reread and to be gifted to those most dear to us."
– Dr. Connie Sitterly, EdD, Author

"Love letters transport readers and the English language."
– T. Vardell, English Teacher for Gifted Writers

"Reading this book is as comfortable as snuggling under a blanket with a cat. All the characters come to life, and the story glides through each transition."
– P. Hirst, High School English Teacher

"This captivating tale touches on every human emotion."
– Genny Smith, Mgr. Manpower

"For readers who appreciate beautiful love stories with twists and turns, and delightful characters guided by courage and faith, you will be undoubtedly pleased that you took the time to read Kay Turner's book, The Other Part of Her."
-Peggy Syrus, High School English Teacher

THE
OTHER PART OF HER

Kay Aline Turner

Trenton, Georgia

Copyright © 2024 Kay Aline Turner

Paperback ISBN: 978-1-958892-73-2
Hardcover ISBN: 978-1-958892-74-9
Ebook ISBN: 979-8-88531-733-7

All rights reserved. No part of this publication may be reproduced, stored in a retrieval system, or transmitted in any form or by any means, electronic, mechanical, recording or otherwise, without the prior written permission of the author.

Published by BookLocker.com, Inc., Trenton, Georgia.

BookLocker.com, Inc.
2024

First Edition

Library of Congress Cataloging in Publication Data
Turner, Kay Aline
THE OTHER PART OF HER by Kay Aline Turner
Library of Congress Control Number: 2024908731

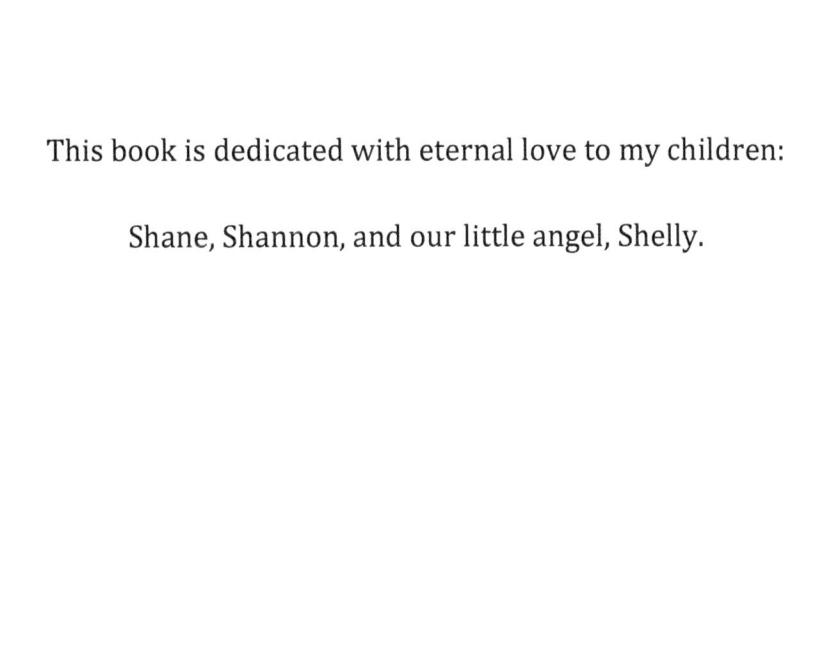

This book is dedicated with eternal love to my children:

Shane, Shannon, and our little angel, Shelly.

ACKNOWLEDGEMENTS

Gary Forsberg, Military Advisor. You have my deepest gratitude for breathing authenticity into this book and for your exemplary military service.

Dr. Ed Lowe, Professor of Creative Writing, Boulder, Co.
Your words of encouragement inspired the writing of this book.

Kris Arnett, Editor. Thank you for patiently wading through endless drafts. Your incredible persistence helped make this book into a reality.

Dr. Connie Sitterly, Award-Winning International Author, Consultant, Professional Coach. Thank you for your constant encouragement and enthusiasm! Because of you, this book is crossing the finish line.

Peggy Syrus, Proof Editor. My deepest gratitude for your expert knowledge, and all your hard work. You transformed this love story into a book for the ages.

Brenda Bernhardt, Photographer. Your beautiful images tell silent stories.

Craig McGraw. Your love and encouragement refresh my soul daily.

THE OTHER PART OF HER
Kay Aline Turner

PROLOGUE

June 1970

"The pledge of love is not written in my clenched palm, nor etched in a monument. It's stitched into my soul where tear-stained notes on monogrammed paper, faded photographs, and letters perfectly scripted, line the heart like wall portraits hanging."

- Hope Madison

A thousand yesterdays consume my mind. In particular, the vision of a man dressed in a Navy uniform. Years have passed since our last encounter, but I remain deeply affected by him. By his charm. By his words. By his betrayal.

Was there ever a time when I didn't desperately search the magazines and newspapers for him? Or look to the stars and pray for his return? How do I close the door on the past when every plane soaring in the sky is a reminder of him?

My frustration inches to the surface like a caterpillar hiding venomous spines under its soft hairs. The room is silent, except for a brass clock swinging its long pendulum and chiming once. My teeth grind. My jaw stiffens. I check the calendar and will myself to forget today's date; the same date that is buried in my bones. The day he vanished. As if I had forgotten. I haven't. Not for a moment.

Beads of perspiration dot my forehead. I dab them with a tissue while surveying my new photography studio. Slightly tinted walls showcase framed portraits of clients. Large photo albums line the shelves. The clang of a loud rattle, persisting from an old window air conditioner, screams for attention. For a moment, I stand motionless in front of the sputtering machine while cool air travels across my face. Eventually, I twist the knob that brings it to one last shudder, one last breath.

I pause briefly and twist my neck from side to side. Drew Bartlett stole my sleep in the night and grief has buried an old ache into my shoulders. Fear rips through me. Would I recognize his gleaming turquoise eyes? His wide shoulders and chestnut hair? Would I be able to recall the distinctions that made him the only man to totally capture my heart?

Suddenly, my heartbeat accelerates and my spirit plummets. This is typical when he appears so vividly in my memories. I must admit there's no denying the effect he has on me, but I quickly grab my suitcase, along with the pile of camera gear, before turning to close the door. My heart pounds at the sound of brass keys rattling. I insert one into the lock and twist.

Dread consumes my body. Fear chases my steps. Not forgetting. Never forgetting. And I should.

'Eliminating the burdens of the past would increase the quality of your remaining time on earth,' a counselor once instructed.

I can't. Not yet. Not without an explanation. Eleven wasted years have come and gone.

My eyes squint, as they do in the summer sun, and again persistent questions pummel without warning. They're always the same, yet choices have been made.

First his. Now mine.

ONE

1959

Hope Madison yanked on the black silk dress crawling up her long legs, as the funeral procession inched toward the church. Pangs of grief scaled her body like a mountain climber.

Her grandfather. Her pilot. Her hero. Heart Attack. Gone.

Exhaustion, the crowd in the limousine, plus reality, overwhelmed her. She closed her swollen eyes while leaning her head on her father's shoulder as Riley, her older sister, powdered her face for the photographers lining the sidewalks.

"By the way, Hope," Riley whispered. "Your best friend, Sarah Whitmire, called while you were in the shower. She wants you to return her call after the funeral."

Hope stared ahead, confused. "Sarah Whitmire? Did she say what she wanted?"

"No, but she said it was urgent!"

The conversation ceased as the church steeple edged into view along with a crowd of people, as thick as a bed of ants. Men in uniform were standing rigid, as they saluted. Their hollow eyes were scarred by war. Non-military men removed their hats, placing them over their heart. Women were filled with memories of how he had touched their families' lives. Some whispered amongst themselves, while recalling their first plane ride with her grandfather, or how he had thrilled them with acrobats, wing walkers, and landing in the middle of the main street in Tyler, Texas. All were touched by the loss of the East Texas pioneer, Colonel O.C. Palmer. A legend, the "local Lindbergh," they said on this warm, spring day in May.

The limousine halted and Hope sat upright. Her hollow eyes stared ahead, as she exited the car.

****

Hope slowly hung up the phone while Riley, standing impatiently in the doorway of their grandparent's home, twirled her long brown hair around her finger.

"Well, what did Sarah say?" Riley asked.

"She wanted to know if I could have lunch with her, as soon as I return to Boulder," Hope stated, numbly.

"Why would Sarah spend so much money on a long-distance call for the single purpose of asking if we could have lunch? We ALWAYS have lunch after I return home from school."

"Did the operator break in?" Riley's eyes glowered.

"Yes. She uttered in a condescending tone, as she always does, 'Your three minutes are up.' The line immediately went dead. We didn't even get to say goodbye."

"Cheer up, Hope. You'll be in Boulder tomorrow. You can see her then."

"The wait will be agony."

"Perhaps, she has a new boyfriend," Riley teased.

"That's quite possible. One blink and they're gone."

"Write and tell me all about it," Riley ordered.

Hope studied her sister, uncertain how to respond. Riley's sudden interest baffled her. In a downcast tone, Hope mumbled, "I will, but I doubt there will be anything to share."

"We never know what God has planned for us, Hope."

An unrelenting grin stretched across Riley's face, into her brown eyes.

TWO

Hope rushed into Boulder's popular restaurant, Timber Tavern, promptly at noon. Fifteen minutes later, she was still pacing near the front door and nervously checking her watch while an overflowing lunch crowd, mostly comprised of University of Colorado students, grew louder. Hope wondered if they were competing with Elvis Presley, as he belted his latest hit from the brightly lit jukebox in the corner.

Suddenly, Sarah Whitmire appeared in the doorway and every head in the restaurant swiveled at the sight of her and the red dress molded to her curvaceous body. Hope grimaced, realizing the spotlight shone on her, too. She was the tall one, the one in a crumpled yellow dress. The one who dropped her shoulders a bit, but she still stood a head taller than Sarah. Anxiety tightened in her throat.

"You look great, Sarah," Hope mumbled.

"Thank you. So do you."

A handsome college waiter approached, unable to turn loose of Sarah with his eyes as he pointed to a booth, "Feel free to take that one by the window. I'll be there to take your order."

Moments later the young man appeared with menus and two glasses of water. Sarah flashed him a smile, waved away the menus, causing him to fumble with the pen in his hand. Hope nervously edged into a corner, before addressing Sarah.

"I know you want me to meet your brother's best friend, but I can't," Hope stated firmly.

"Of course, you can. We'll double date like we did in high school."

"Sarah, I refuse to go out with someone I don't know, especially to an important event." Hope's face turned tomato red as she adamantly rejected the offer. Sarah waved off the outburst, but Hope refused to be ignored.

"I can't. He'd be miserable."

"Hope, you don't even know who it is. It's my brother's best friend, the one I've been talking about for years."

"Are you referring to the guy you idolize? Drew Bartlett?"

Hope's face suddenly became as white as her napkin.

"Yes! His date cancelled at the last minute. I'm going with my brother's other friend so the four of us can double date. Think of the fun we could have."

Hope's best friend was proficient in ripping down the guard that she had carefully erected. And they both knew it.

"The guys leave for the Navy in a few weeks." Sarah continued. "Right after their graduation." She lowered her head and in a pleading voice continued. "I wouldn't ask you if I didn't think you'd have a great time."

Hope tried to summon a grain of self-confidence, however, it dimmed against the unbridling of Sarah's beauty and relentless persuasion. She listened to Sarah's ramblings with one ear, while nervously glancing outside, then shifted in the booth, turning her head toward the window to absorb a broad line of purple, snow-capped mountains. A meadow of green was bending like a dancer in the gentle breeze.

Sarah continued selling Hope on the idea of a double date, but she didn't need to sell Drew. Hope knew him to be handsome from the photos Sarah had shown her, and she even thought he might be an enjoyable date, until Sarah said he had a bashful side. That made her throat as dry as a cracker.

The Other Part of Her

Hope felt anticipation and dread tumbling together, but suddenly along with the feeling of obligation, the thought of waving his picture in front of her college sorority sisters filled her with excitement and a burst of confidence.

"Sarah, you've talked about Drew since the first day we met. It appears, from his picture, he could have any girl he wants. I'm not the one to accompany him. Besides, you know I don't date."

Hope felt better for speaking her mind, until a sudden surge of guilt caused her palms to sweat. Sarah had been nothing but kind, and now she was disappointing her. Remorse silently polluted the conversation, but Sarah prattled on, as if Hope had agreed.

"Do you need anything else?" the waiter inquired of Sarah while placing the pepperoni pizza in the center of the table. Sarah smiled graciously at him as she swept a lock of hair from her forehead.

"No, thank you," she purred.

He retreated, reluctantly.

The smell of pizza, mingling with Hope's deflation, floated between them while Sarah spoke about the formal dance in detail. Dancing to a live band gave Hope reason to consider the invitation and briefly, her spirits lifted, until she realized that she'd be dancing with Drew Bartlett the entire evening; then her stomach lurched. It was a preposterous idea to entertain.

Sarah's star-like radiance continued for the next hour and Hope continued to shrink under her glow. After the server filled their glasses for the third time, each time ignoring Hope, Sarah began applying red lipstick to her full lips while Hope dipped the corner of her napkin into a glass of water and dabbed at the pizza stains on her wrinkled dress.

"Want to try?" Sarah extended the gold tube of lipstick across the table.

Hope shook her head. The thought of bringing attention to her mouth, or to any part of her body, sent shivers down her spine.

"Okay, I'll go," Hope mumbled through clenched teeth. "But if he's as shy as you say, I know I won't be able to think of one thing to say. His evening will be ruined."

Sarah's bold, red lips stretched into a grin the size of the Mississippi River.

"Oh, don't be silly. Just be yourself, like you are with me. In fact, why don't you come over to our house for dinner on Friday night so you can meet him? Mother is having an early graduation celebration dinner for my brother, Ken, and of course, Drew. I can't believe they graduate from the university in a few weeks."

Hope, the studious one, the one who preferred spending time at the library, immediately regretted accepting the invitation. But thoughts of how envious her friends would be, when they saw his picture, calmed her frazzled nerves.

Sarah swiftly launched a plan. "You and Drew can meet at my house tomorrow night, but on the night of the ball, let's get ready in your luxurious bedroom and private bath," she said excitedly. "I can even fix your hair in one of those new upswept hairstyles, like the movie stars wear."

Sarah's determination ricocheted like a bullet bouncing off steel when she tried to convince Hope that her long, silky hair could be tamed, an achievement that her own mother, had not yet accomplished. And considering how Kathryn Madison controlled everything within the walls of their home, Sarah's idea created a lingering smile. Hope imagined her mother skittering across the floor, joyfully thanking the angels for the special young man who would soon be at their door. In Mrs. Madison's mind, the time for Hope to find a suitable husband had arrived.

Hope had ignored her mother's desperate pleas, and, at times, she had accomplished the feat with a degree of success. But she couldn't ignore the hurt when her mother would trill in a sing-song voice, "You need to find a husband before the bloom is gone from the rose." The phrase made Hope vow she'd never insist her own daughter, should she be blessed with one, feel her worth, intelligence, and beauty depended on having a man.

In truth, though her mother wouldn't admit it, Hope knew she didn't understand her. It was Riley, her older sister, who was the carbon copy of Kathryn Madison, both in looks and personality. Hope, on the other hand, was told she exited the womb with the same coloring and temperament of her father, including his tall frame and love for adventure. On one occasion, Hope overheard him boasting about her athletic prowess, especially at golf, and how she could throw a football farther than any of the neighborhood boys in junior high. His words had warmed Hope from the inside.

Now, after waiting for years, the upcoming dance would present her mother with ample fodder for her next church luncheon, bridge group, book club, and garden club. But first, her mother would notify Miss Bain, her personal shopping assistant at Neiman Marcus, that a shipment of white dresses, matching Drew's white uniform, would arrive soon.

Hope bid good-bye to Sarah then turned her convertible toward home while marveling at the breathtaking view. Regardless of how long she was away, she frequently visualized the mountains and continued to be amazed, even today. "God's perfect handiwork," she declared quietly.

On the short drive, she determined the first person she'd tell, about her upcoming date was Odie B, the Madison's housekeeper, her closest friend, and ally. Their bond was tighter than any of

Hope's familial connections since they had celebrated large and small triumphs from the time Hope was three years old.

"Can you believe it, Odie B? I'm going to a dance with a graduating senior!"

Odie B's face, as bright as twinkling lights on a Christmas tree, brought encouragement to Hope and together they shared the excitement. Odie B, her ears warm with the likes of Drew Bartlett, began dancing around the kitchen stretching her hands high in the air.

"Thank ya, Jesus! Thank ya!"

Hope stood alone in her bedroom that evening, staring into the mirror at her long, slender legs, round bust, narrow waist, and smooth hips. The explanation of her figure became the subject of her mother's annual report to their personal shopper at Neiman Marcus.

"She matured early," her mother would say, as if Hope had a disease. Judging from the sneer on Miss Bain's face, Hope would have welcomed the alternative.

It was true. Her figure had blossomed into one of a woman by the age of fourteen, making her the target of jealous girls and gawking boys. She also reached her full height the same year. "As tall as a giraffe," they'd say. Very few boys could meet her at eye level. Awkwardness prevailed.

Hope couldn't help but compare herself to her sister, Riley, diminutive in stature and not too curvy. Riley's flawless olive skin, dark hair, and chocolate-brown eyes trimmed in thick lashes were perfection in Hope's opinion. The contrast had provoked Hope to approach her mother for encouragement, following her first day in high school.

"Mother, why can't I be beautiful like Riley?"

Mrs. Madison, sitting at her mahogany desk with reading glasses perched on her nose, glanced up and studied her youngest daughter's face.

"You're unusual," she said in a flat tone, then returned to the checkbook.

The invisible scar remained.

THREE

Dreams paraded across the mirror, one by one in radiant splendor, while Hope turned from side to side, checking her reflection. Her new hairstyle, moving like a butterfly lightly brushing her shoulders, offered no indication of her pounding heart, wet palms, and jittery nerves. Floating in the air was one question: why had she relented to Sarah's request? Regret plagued her.

"Not much longer until the favor is granted, then I can go about my summer," Hope mumbled while glancing at the crimson sun sinking behind the mountains outside her bedroom window.

"Are you ready, Hope?" Irritation could be heard in her mother's voice as she yelled up the stairs.

"Coming, Mother." Hope imagined her standing in the foyer, pursing her lips, checking her watch.

Hope nervously slipped into a cornflower-blue dress before clasping a strand of pearls around her neck. Next came the challenge she faced with every date, especially a blind date. Her height.

Hurriedly, she tried on several pairs of shoes before finally deciding on a pair of low heels. She then raced down the carpeted stairs with a white wool jacket flung over her arm.

"I'm ready," she announced in a breathless tone.

"Your father is pulling the car around," her mother replied coolly while draping a cashmere wrap around her shoulders. "I told you we could go in one car, since our dinner parties are a block apart, but we must be punctual, Hope."

"Yes, Mother." Hope's nerves stretched to the tipping point when she heard a page from her youth return, but once again, she let the rebuke slide, as she always did.

"You look beautiful, Hope." Tennessee Madison murmured while opening her car door.

Hope smiled and planted a light kiss on her father's smooth-shaven face, before slipping into the back seat. The scent of his pipe tobacco and the familiar splashes of Old Spice cologne clung to her, as did the comments from her friends, "Your father is such a dignified gentleman," they'd say. She'd grin with pride knowing he captivated the youngest, the oldest, the least, and the greatest with his charm and twinkling eyes.

Tension and silence curled together like a tight ball of yarn. Only the hum of Mrs. Madison's new Cadillac could be heard. Ten minutes later, Hope began taking several deep breaths before exiting the car. There was Sarah eagerly waiting at the window of her home. Hope's knees weakened as she stepped into the entry.

"I can't believe this, Sarah. I haven't even been home twenty-four hours." Hope's eyes stretched wide. She knew it wasn't anything out of the ordinary for Sarah to plan dates faster than a rainbow fades, but she needed time to prepare for such an occasion. Lots of time.

Sarah smiled, dismissing the sight of Hope's ashen face while brushing aside the dark curls falling on her forehead.

"In a few minutes, I'm going to step outside and wait for Drew on the porch. It's what I always do."

Sarah's eyes were full of merriment, as she took out a coat hanger from the coat closet. Hope handed the jacket to her, and as Sarah placed it inside the small space, Sarah eagerly explained,

"If Drew weren't like a member of our family, I'd be going to the dance with him. Instead, I'm setting up my best friend with the greatest guy I know. I can't believe his date cancelled!"

"Sarah, I appreciate your attempt at finding him a date, but I clam up around guys, as you are well aware." Hope felt her palms growing wet like a lawn layered with dew.

*****

Across town, Drew Bartlett carefully selected a handful of small river stones from the rocky banks of Boulder Creek while two red-tailed hawks circled above him. The creek beckoned him to where he now stood, where he stood every day at this time. He liked to come to the place where he could free his mind amidst a kaleidoscope of sights and sounds found only in nature. Today, the stream's foamy bubbles, swiftly flowing across rocks like a spilled bottle of champagne, filled him with melancholy. He rolled his tense neck from side to side, silently counting the remaining days until his imminent departure.

Nostalgia vanished as fast as a meteor's tail when he realized in four weeks, he would be a commissioned Naval officer with a degree in Aeronautical Engineering. His lifelong dream of being a pilot in the US Navy, the diamond he had been mining since he sat in Mrs. Spencer's third grade class, neared at the age of twenty-two. A cool spring breeze blew, as the dwindling daylight caught his attention.

Quickly, he began sprinting across the University of Colorado campus. The Whitmires expected him in twenty minutes, and he had yet to shower and dress.

Racing up the dorm stairs, taking two at a time, he reached his room and turned on the shower before applying white dollops of shaving cream to his dark, facial stubble. A few swipes with the razor erased all traces of the shadows and he then stepped into the cool water, washing away sweat and fatigue.

The comment previously made by Mrs. Whitmire, "It would be a more formal dinner than usual," popped into his mind as he stood, staring into his closet. Hurriedly, he chose a pale-blue dress shirt, gray slacks, and a lightweight wool sport coat before splashing a few drops of Old Spice cologne on his face. He then ran a comb through his short chestnut-colored hair, glancing at his watch as he did.

Drew then galloped toward the parking lot, jumped into his sports car and pressed on the accelerator. He was aware he was exceeding the speed limit when he turned toward the Whitmire's neighborhood, but nothing, he vowed, would diminish his punctuality record. Not now, not ever!

Sarah would be on the front porch, that he knew; however, the tradition would close this evening. A mix of emotions swirled, as he hastily parked in the usual place, in front of the Whitmire's white stately mansion, but a knot bulged in his throat when he saw Sarah shivering in the cold. He jumped out of the car, checking his watch as he did, and smiled to himself. His record for punctuality remained intact.

"Your warm welcome is appreciated, Sarah, especially with this chilly breeze." His voice hinted of the emotions the night would hold. The Whitmires were as close to having a family as he had ever experienced, other than his grandmother. And this was their final time together, prior to graduation.

"I always want the first hug," Sarah said, smiling.

He tenderly put his arm around her shoulder and together they strode into the entry where Hope stood unmoving with the Whitmire's dog snuggled in her arms. Tongue-tied and shy, Hope began frantically searching for a corner in which to hide. Then she tried to hide behind Sarah who was happily chirping the introduction.

"Drew, I'd like for you to meet my good friend, Hope Madison." Immediately, Hope jostled the dog and extended her hand, though she found it hard to keep her mouth from dropping open like a fish.

"It's a pleasure to meet you, Drew," Hope mumbled in a nervous, high-pitched voice, while trying to avert her eyes from looking directly into his. Her height made it almost impossible. He was over six feet tall, and with her low heels, she could tilt her head slightly, and stare directly into his face, which she was doing now. Drew flashed her a side-grin, his eyes snapping of amusement.

"The pleasure is all mine, I assure you." His voice was as smooth as a coat of honey while gripping her hand. Hope was not aware that her large, sapphire-blue eyes were taking him on a journey, one he didn't want to end.

Hope found his appearance immobilizing, especially his turquoise eyes. They were so intense they almost overpowered his slender build, olive skin and rich chestnut-colored hair. She quickly glanced away, unable to linger on his face. That's when she noted his expensive clothes and shoes.

Irritated that Sarah had purposefully withheld information about him, including his affable manner and finely chiseled features worthy of Hollywood films, Hope searched for a corner in which to hide. Until she realized he still had hold of her hand.

When Mrs. Whitmire entered, Hope felt his grip gradually surrender, as if he were reluctantly pulling away.

"Dinner is ready," she announced. "We'll be eating in the dining room tonight, in honor of Ken's and Drew's upcoming graduation." Hope noticed Mrs. Whitmire's eyes watering as Drew stepped toward her with his arms open. A quick hug had them both wiping their eyes.

Hope headed for the long dining table draped with linens, china, crystal, and freshly cut daffodils. Drafts of cool air, creeping in around the windows, was a reminder that summer had yet to arrive, as it had in Texas. An oversized marble fireplace with crackling flames warmed her.

Mrs. Whitmire pointed to an empty chair by Sarah. "That one is for you, Hope." She then seated Drew opposite the girls.

Hope felt dread snaking through her body. Her tongue went lifeless. Conversing with the guys about football, of which he and Ken were stars, along with his destined career to be a Navy pilot, were topics out of her realm. Yet something about him intrigued her. Under his handsome veneer, she sensed a genuine vulnerability.

She also thought him capable of breaking her heart, so she shifted her focus to the candles flickering in the center of the table. It was while studying the flames, she determined Drew to be a foreign entity. He was the direct opposite from the guys in her study group, the same group that comprised her social life at Texas Christian University. Suddenly, she felt strangely excited. Sarah's idol appeared to have the same desire to squeeze enthusiasm into every moment, as she did, and her grandfather before her. But Drew, she noted, also carried a layer of vulnerability in his eyes.

Drew noticed her stealing quick glances at him. He found himself doing the same with her, even at times, almost staring, more frequently than he felt appropriate. Her poise and beauty in the glow of the crystal chandelier captivated him. For the first time, he found himself unable to concentrate on Sarah's friendly banter, until thankfully, Mrs. Whitmire placed large bowls of beef stroganoff, buttered noodles, and fragrant bread on the table.

"I'm sure going to miss your cooking, Mrs. Whitmire."

"Drew, how many times have I told you to call me 'Doris'? After all, you're part of our family."

Drew sent her a lopsided grin, while twirling the pasta. "I'm not sure my grandmother would approve, but I'll try."

Hope silently engaged in the conversation until a tall, antique clock, standing in the corner, chimed eight times. She welcomed the sound, knowing Drew's presence would soon end. Then, to her surprise, Sarah launched into stories of when Drew came into their lives. Immediately, Hope recalled the conversation when Sarah first mentioned him.

"Drew was denied the bond of a family, at least, the kind he longed to have, after his mother died when he was young. His grandmother raised him and now, during college, our home has been his refuge. He's like family."

Sitting across from the one who had dominated many of Sarah's conversations, Hope felt a connection. Drew knew obstacles. A hole in his heart, he knew. Erecting imperceptible walls were a natural part of his life, as it was hers. Her eyes quickly filled with a glimmer of acknowledgement, and she sat up straighter.

Unaware the room had grown quiet, Hope suddenly realized all eyes were focused on her. She blinked. Then blinked again. Now, she imagined herself invisible. But they continued holding her with their eyes. Finally, she responded,

"I'm sorry. What was the question?"

Mrs. Whitmire graciously repeated the inquiry,

"What are your plans for the summer, Hope?"

"I have no definite plans. I'd like to play golf with my dad and do a considerable amount of pleasure reading. School doesn't allow much time for either."

Hope's face turned as hot as a tropical rain forest when she realized the shallowness of her response. The guys would soon depart for the Navy. The Vietnam War threatened. Playing golf at the country club sounded inappropriate, at the very least.

Drew's deep voice shattered the quiet.

"What do you like to read?"

"Stories about World War II. My grandfather was an Air Force pilot. His handwritten postcards from foreign lands began arriving when I was four years old. I still have them."

Tears formed in her throat with the memory. She swallowed hard, as she covered her trembling hands with a napkin. Mrs. Whitmire rushed to fill her empty tea glass.

Drew leaned back and stared at her, surprised that she found stories regarding the war interesting.

"Did he make it home?"

"Yes. From both World Wars. He didn't talk about them, except to say he enjoyed training pilots on the Flying Fortress, his favorite airplane." She lowered her head, and her voice became a whisper.

"He retired as a Colonel."

"That's a great plane and legacy you have."

"Thank you." She murmured, desperately wishing to reserve the tender topic for a private meeting.

"I'm very proud of all the men and women who serve," she whispered. "Plus, those who keep their families intact while their loved ones are away."

Her hands continued to shake when she met his eyes.

Hours of silence passed, or so it seemed, before Mrs. Whitmire and Sarah cheerfully entered the room, carrying the dessert on a large silver tray.

"Ken and Drew, your favorite dessert, Baked Alaska," Sarah proudly stated while slicing the elegant finale to the delicious meal they had served.

After Drew's second serving, he checked the time. Almost three hours had passed. Pushing his chair back, he unfolded his long legs from under the table and began to assist Mrs. Whitmire as she cleared the table. She immediately ordered him to sit down.

"Sarah and I will clean up, Drew. You're our honored guest, even though we think of you as our son."

The Other Part of Her

Drew's emotions climbed to the surface when he thanked the lady who had lovingly provided a second home for him during college.

He then turned to Hope, before standing to pull out her chair.

"Do you need a ride home?"

"My parents said they would pick me up after their dinner party. They're down the street."

"I'll be glad to drive you," he insisted.

Flustered by the swirl of emotions flowing through her like a sailboat being tossed on crashing waves, she felt her face warm from the blush.

"I'll check to see when they are leaving."

Hope went to the telephone in the hall and began dialing while Ken delivered Drew a silent message, the same message he sent all the guys who talked about their girlfriends, especially the seniors in the Naval Reserve Officers Training Corps Unit, of which they were both a part. "We're leaving for the Navy soon and you're going to meet women all over the world," he'd say. "Don't tie yourself down. Focus on your goals."

Drew acknowledged the silent message to be true, but Hope was different. And he was not going to shy away from getting to know her because of his upcoming departure, regardless of Ken's opinion on the subject.

Hope returned bearing a tenuous smile, while nervously nodding at him. He rushed to help her with her jacket and together they walked in silence toward the car. When he opened the passenger door on his new red convertible, she gasped.

"Corvettes are my favorite sports car, Drew. It's beautiful."

He smiled and quickly slid behind the steering wheel.

"Thank you. It's a graduation present from my grandmother."

Drew twisted the knob on the radio, lowered the volume, and turned on the heater. Hope observed the fluidity of his movements. Graceful and effortless, she thought.

"Where in Texas did you live?" She could hear his warmth in the dimly lit car.

"Fort Worth. I lived there all my life until we moved to Colorado at the beginning of my senior year. That's when I met Sarah. Now, I attend college in my hometown…just completed my sophomore year."

"A move during your senior year in high school sounds challenging."

"It was. I didn't know anyone until Sarah introduced herself, but it wasn't long before she included me with all her other friends. I can't imagine how the year would have been without her," she murmured.

Drew drove slowly through Boulder's tree-lined neighborhoods, sharing a similar story of how he and Ken met in the football locker room at the University. Eventually, she pointed to a large, rambling house.

"That's my home on the corner."

He parked under the streetlamp, distracted by thoughts of the future. Thoughts he never expected to entertain. Especially one. *Could he transition to the Navy easily, if they were to become involved prior to his departure?*

Hope felt her nerves unwinding, as he stared out the window. Convinced he was searching for how to gracefully decline the invitation to the dance, she thought about hastily bolting from the car. Perhaps, she could mutter a few words of gratitude before racing toward the front door.

Drew broke the silence with a deep sigh of resignation. There was no choice. Not for him.

"I have something I wish to say. I realize Sarah mentioned my needing a date for the dance, but…" He paused and cleared his throat.

Hope flinched. The unspoken topic dangled between them like icicles in winter.

She had taken deliberate steps to avoid him for most of the evening, an act that prompted elbow nudges from Sarah and an occasional kick.

Now Hope waited, biting down on her bottom lip while gripping the door handle until her knuckles were white.

"I would like to offer my own personal invitation. Hope, would you do me the honor of being my date for a very special night in Denver? It's a graduation celebration with my Navy buddies."

What made Drew *want* to take her? He could have any girl of his choice. *Why her*? She felt her body grow rigid, angry that she had fallen victim to Sarah's insistence as she began repeating the words in her mind. The words she knew from memory. The words that would hurt him. The words that had to be said. Always.

"Drew, I'm not the one you should be taking."

He turned toward her, a frown creasing his forehead. "Do you like to dance, Hope?"

"Yes, I do. But I've made it my goal not to date until I'm out of college."

His mouth hung agape. "Have I offended you?"

"No. Drew, I'm not cut out for dating. All the ups and downs. Broken hearts scattered on the floor. I told Sarah this, but she wouldn't listen."

"Do you have someone else in your life?"

Avoiding his eyes, she shook her head.

"This *can't* be my final time to see you, Hope. Think about it. Please."

Drew slowly exited the car, wondering about the words that had slipped off her tongue, almost as if they had been memorized. No expression. No regret. Did she take pleasure in saying, "No," or had she repeated them so many times rejections had become rote? Confused, he raked his short hair in frustration, prior to opening her car door.

Still, his eyes couldn't turn loose of her while they stood on the porch of one of Boulder's most prominent homes, the home he had passed hundreds of times during his years at the University.

"Hope, I pray this won't be the last time we see each other. You have something very special, something I've not found in other girls, though I tried. It is my belief that we could have a wonderful evening."

"Then what, Drew? You leave for the Navy, and I go back to school?"

Drew felt the sting of her retort.

"Hope, I believe our meeting was orchestrated. Not by Sarah. She was merely an instrument. I'm not sure of the reason, but I trust it was no accident. I pray we will see each other again. I leave Boulder in three weeks."

She lowered her head, shocked by the trace of disappointment in his voice. He took a step off the porch, then quickly spun around to face her again.

"Hope, can I call you?"

She stared at him, realizing that soon, those mesmerizing turquoise eyes would be halfway around the world.

"Hope, let me prove to you who I am. If you don't like what you see, I won't bother you again. But please give me a chance."

"Drew, I don't want a long-distance relationship. Ever. And that's what we would have." Her words sparked of pain and her tone was resolute.

His arms hung loosely, his voice a whisper. "Trust me, Hope, and the loving God who brought us together." His eyes stayed glued to hers.

She glanced down, as she twisted the door handle.

"I'm glad to have met you," she said quietly.

"You didn't answer my question. Can I call you?"

She tipped her chin and stared at him. "Think about it, Drew. Think long and hard."

"Not necessary, Hope. Are you going to give me your phone number?"

An impish smile tugged at the corners of her mouth. "Trust your instincts, Drew. I'm quite confident that being a pilot requires the refinement of such."

His lips curled into a grin. "I'll get your number from Sarah."

Amusement flickered in her eyes, an uncontrollable sparkle in his.

FOUR

Drew Bartlett hurriedly placed his feet on the floor, shortly before sunrise. Thoughts of Hope Madison had kept him awake all night, but he hoped a Saturday morning bike ride would expel her from his mind.

Grabbing a pair of jeans draped over the back of the desk chair, he slipped them on before pulling a sweatshirt over his head and running a comb through his short hair. He hurriedly grabbed a snack and stuffed it into his windbreaker. Taking the dorm steps two and three at a time, he vowed to banish Hope's lingering presence.

Twenty miles of climbing hills and battling strong winds didn't alter the situation. She remained in his thoughts. Relentless questions remained. The need for answers remained. Dance or no dance, he would visit Hope, after a quick shower.

Drew's nerves stiffly stood at attention when he pressed the Madison's doorbell. Hope raced down the stairs. Irritation was clearly written across her face, when she flung the door open.

"I apologize for arriving unannounced," Drew said, shyly, "but I tried calling."

Hope nervously ran her fingers through her ponytail while gripping the brass door handle.

"I was on the phone with Sarah. Is something wrong?"

She thought he appeared slightly ragged and wondered as to his purpose. Had he changed his mind, or had he accepted her refusal? Confusion swirled.

Drew lowered his head, shoved his hands deep into his jean pockets, cleared his throat, then stared into the most beautiful eyes he had ever seen.

"Would you like to join me on a trip up Boulder Canyon? I thought we could grill hot dogs by a stream."

"When?"

"Now." His face turned as red as the geraniums flanking the front door.

Hope stared at him, feeling guilty she had exaggerated the truth when they were together earlier. It wasn't that she didn't date, though that's what she had told him. She just didn't date anyone who interested her. Not since the time she had been in love long ago. Something had shifted inside her years earlier. Something she couldn't get back even if she tried. Now, an invisible barrier kept her from men like Drew, even if he appeared different from all the rest.

He braced himself for a second rejection; then the resistance faded from her eyes.

"I'll get my shoes and leave a note for my parents." Leaving him standing outside, she turned to run upstairs, finding it difficult with rubbery legs and a quivering body, but she could hear a long exhale escaping from his lips.

Hope, reeling from her impulsive response, suddenly remembered the rules of southern hospitality and returned to the door. "Please, forgive me. I didn't mean to be so rude and leave you standing outside. Won't you come in while I collect my things?"

"Thank you." His obvious relief appeared visible which caught her attention. His shoulders were no longer pinned up around his ears with tension, and his side-grin appeared to match his smiling eyes.

"You'll need to bring a jacket, Hope. It's cool up in the mountains, especially after the sun fades." Catching her breath, she was captured by the idea of being with him at sunset, a thought she had yet to entertain.

She dashed up the stairs, silently scolding herself for letting her heart take the lead, but there was something about him. Or, perhaps, it was everything about him: his humility, his courage, his longings. So much she didn't know. But if she were around him in a setting other than sitting around a dining table, she might see another side. A side that wasn't charming, polite, and thoughtful. Yes, she reasoned, it's better to know now.

She quickly took down her ponytail and ran a comb through her hair, letting it fall beyond her shoulders before applying her favorite shade of red lipstick. After slipping on tennis shoes, she returned to the front door carrying a jacket, emblazoned with her college monogram.

"Drew, do you want me to get some items from the kitchen? Chips? Drinks?"

"It won't be necessary. I thought optimistically and grabbed a few things at the store." His face reddened again.

Hope hurriedly jotted a note for her mother. A large grin appeared on her face, one she couldn't hide, when she dropped the message on the entry hall table. Drew opened her car door, before settling into his seat, adjusting the radio volume, and slipping on aviator sunglasses. A few minutes later, walls of towering trees welcomed them to the canyon.

Drew felt relief until doubts crept in. *Was this a one-time exception to her non-dating rule?* He'd know soon. For the moment he joined Elvis singing on the radio. Hope beamed at his bass voice as she recalled Sarah telling her of Drew's passion for music, and that he was a member of a male chorus at the University.

Drew's smooth-as-butter tone continued up the mountains, and so did her unstoppable grin until the radio lost its frequency. Then Drew would begin to point to sights while yelling various names and descriptions over the wind noise.

The last steep curve suddenly placed them on top of the mountain at the very moment the brilliant orange sun lowered to their level.

Ribbons of persimmon and cobalt blue were swirling across the open sky, above the swaying evergreens. A roaring stream rushed at their feet. Drew, hearing her gasps, smiled to himself while parking the car on a patch of grass.

A torrent of emotions filled Drew, as he rushed to open her car door. She smiled up at him while unfolding her long legs. Questions pummeled his brain. He had to know why this beautiful girl would not date. It was the same query that had lingered throughout the night, even accompanying him on the bike ride, and even now as he busied himself with the removal of a small hibachi grill and a bag of charcoal. Hope, unaware, followed him, carrying sacks of food while he placed the briquettes in the portable grill. He glanced at her and she grinned. He took a deep breath. For now, she was with him. For the moment, that was enough.

He reached for a matchbook in his back pocket while Hope calmly unpacked the groceries. After a few minutes of fanning the flames, he called her name, struggling to be heard over the roar of the river. She turned to see him pointing to a tree across the stream, "Do you want to carve our initials in that aspen tree?"

Hope nodded, reminding herself that such an experience, though not typical for a Texan, was common for a guy like Drew. She speculated he had carved his initials with countless girls during his four years at the university.

Drew continued stoking the briquettes while reminding himself to go slow with Hope, not wanting to hurt her or himself. After a few briquettes began turning red, he took her hand and began gingerly leading her across the slippery rocks. Once they reached the tree, he dropped her hand, pulled out a pocketknife and turned toward her.

"Do you wish to do the carving? Or do you want me to?"

"You can," she said, still shaken by the tucking of her hand in his, then the quick release.

Drew began diligently digging into the bark with the small blade, tediously sculpting their initials into the white tree trunk. Upon completion, he stepped back to gauge his efforts. He twisted his head from side to side then moved back to the tree, still holding the knife. "I think we should carve the year, don't you, Hope?"

She nodded. After a few minutes, he stepped back again.

"That should last a long while," he stated matter-of-factly. Then, as natural as a bird warbles in spring, he gripped her hand, leading her step by step back across the slippery rocks.

Shades of evening began wrapping around the two while they sat side by side on a fallen log, roasting hot dogs, sharing stories. Trees swaying in the gentle breeze created a soft whistle in the air.

Hope spoke of her love for books; he shared his dream of being a Navy pilot, while reaching in the grocery sack for a plastic bag. After tearing it open, he began threading plump marshmallows onto a wire coat hanger. He handed one hanger to Hope, then repeated the process for himself.

Darkness settled. The campfire roared. And Drew was no closer to understanding Hope's philosophy about not dating than he was twenty-four hours ago. It was clear she enjoyed their time together. He could see it in her eyes. He could hear it in her voice. But he had to know the reason for her rule. Their futures were at stake.

He swallowed hard. He cleared his throat. His lip twitched. He took a deep breath.

"Have you ever had a serious relationship, Hope?" Drew heard a tremor of nerves in his own voice, and grimaced.

"Yes, in the fifth grade. His name was George," she responded softly.

Drew chuckled and grinned. "Can you talk about it, or is it still too raw?"

Hope hesitated, smiling at his question, before leaping into a part of her history. In a quiet, melancholy rhythm, she shared a chapter that no one knew, not even her family.

"George was a loner and sat directly behind me in Mr. Milam's class. The kids teased him because he was a bit unusual, but I found George interesting. During lunch, he would come sit next to me, open his satchel, and pull out the latest issue of National Geographic magazine while eating a bologna and dill pickle sandwich, lathered in mustard. He'd turn the dog-eared pages and speak about his plans to be an African missionary. Occasionally, he'd use the back of his hand to swipe the yellow streaks of mustard from his face.

"As we talked, I determined that my faith, along with my dream to photograph tribal people in Africa, merged perfectly with his goals. To seal our fate, I gave him a homemade chocolate chip cookie.

"A few days later, while we were outside for recess, he picked a bouquet of lavender wildflowers growing next to the school's chain-link fence. Gallantly, like a knight on a white horse, he ignored the jeers from the boys and the giggles from the girls, as he marched over to me. With dirt clumped under his nails, he bravely presented the straggly bunch. That night I pressed the flowers in my Bible, next to the photo of a child from his National Geographic. The dream for my life was clear and purposeful.

"A week later George wasn't at school. Days went by, still no George. A few weeks passed before I could summon the courage to ask the teacher if she knew of his whereabouts.

"He's moved away," Mrs. Cobb said in a matter-of-fact voice without ever looking up from the papers she was grading. She relayed this with such a flat tone of voice and expressionless face, as if George had never existed."

Hope glanced down at the marshmallows, unwilling to reveal the tears forming in her eyes.

"He took his satchel and my dreams with him." The words faded into a whisper.

Drew sat up tall, attentive to each word.

"I quietly soaked my pillow in tears for eleven nights and dragged through each day like a boat without a sail. Finally, a plan emerged. My decision was made. I would not marry unless the man promised never to leave me."

Drew could hear her pain. Now he understood the reason for her cocoon of protection, the one that enveloped her broken heart. He reached out, wrapping her, and the hurt she had carried from childhood, into his arms.

"Have you ever told anyone that story?"

"No. You're the first."

"Thank you for sharing it with me. I, too, am familiar with heartbreak at a young age. It's real, regardless of what people might think."

Drew realized that her childhood pledge, buried in her subconscious, was a part of her life, as natural as breathing. He let out a long sigh. How could he possibly establish her trust when he, too, would be leaving?

Despondency draped about his shoulders like an invisible cloak. Quietly, he buried the hot coals near the creek's rocky edge while she sacked the food. Silence lingered on their drive home. Once he parked the car, he reached for the warmth of her hand.

"Would you like to go to church with me tomorrow?"

Not thinking twice, she said, "Yes. I'd like that."

The certainty in her voice evoked an audible sigh of relief to escape from his. Maybe she would continue seeing him, he thought to himself, or maybe she didn't care so much that the absence wouldn't affect her. How was he to navigate this weighty issue? Should he stop seeing her altogether, or wait for her to break it off in a few days? Clouds of uncertainty continued, as he spoke.

"Good. I'll pick you up at 9:15. I normally teach the high school class, but I resigned a few weeks ago, so that I might prepare for final exams. We'll go to the college class then the worship service if that's okay with you."

In a hushed voice, Hope said, "I look forward to it."

On that cool evening in 1959, Drew Bartlett initiated his first solo mission, breathing life-saving oxygen into a heart Hope so carefully guarded.

FIVE

Mrs. Madison scurried to the front door, eager to meet the person who had developed an interest in her youngest daughter.

"Hello, I'm Drew Bartlett. Hope is expecting me."

"Yes. Please come in. I'm Hope's mother," she said, warmly, while eyeing his expensive suit, starched white shirt, and the aquamarine silk tie perfectly knotted.

"What church do you attend, Drew?"

"First Baptist. Been going there since I was a freshman. Now they're like family. It's going to be hard to leave them."

Mrs. Madison smiled. "I know they'll miss you."

Drew glanced at the palatial entry, and the magnificent stairway with its mahogany railing and carpeted stairs. He thought the entire space, in a soothing tone of jade, was almost ethereal, along with the spacious living room.

Hope gathered him in with her eyes while descending the staircase in a silk, fitted dress of royal blue with a companion jacket. Perched on her head, a pillbox hat of the same color. His thoughts were of awe, as if she were a blend of royalty and Hollywood. Hope smiled inwardly, as he had no idea how much trouble she had getting the campfire smell from her hair, in the pre-dawn hours. Three shampoos later, and after sitting under a cumbersome dryer, her hair now flowed in soft waves past her shoulders.

"Hi, Drew. I see you've met my mother."

"Yes, I had the pleasure just now."

"Are you going to be home for lunch, Hope?" her mother asked, stiffly.

Drew glanced at Mrs. Madison, then at Hope, quickly realizing he had a choice to make. Either be assertive or forever regret the outcome.

"I thought we would have lunch in Estes Park, unless I'm interrupting your plans," he stated politely.

Hope glanced at her mother, standing erect with her chin pointing toward the ceiling, as she mulled over the consequences: Accepting Drew's invitation would interrupt their standard routine, having Sunday lunch at the Boulder Country Club, and she would also be usurping her mother's plans.

Suddenly, the cordial environment catapulted to electric tension. Mrs. Madison continued to signal displeasure. Her arched eyebrows formed a narrow line of annoyance.

Hope glanced back at Drew and smiled,

"I would love to go to Estes Park with you, Drew."

"Wonderful. I thought we could have lunch at the historic Stanley Hotel then we could do some exploring. Shops are closed on Sundays, but there are beautiful areas I'd like to introduce to you. In fact, you may want to grab your camera, along with a change of clothes. I put mine in the car, just in case."

Hope dashed upstairs then quickly returned with the camera bag swinging over her shoulder, and clothes stuffed into a canvas bag. An awkward silence greeted her. Drew took the items from Hope, as he uttered a proper goodbye to Mrs. Madison. The room was as cold as a mausoleum when she waved goodbye to her mother.

Drew laid the camera and the change of clothes carefully into the trunk, then he opened Hope's car door. Once he was assured by the smile on her face, he sped away.

"I'm sorry, Drew. Mother isn't accustomed to changes in routine, especially mine."

"The important matter is how it affects you. What are your thoughts on a change from tradition?"

"I'm discovering that I may have a slight streak of rebelliousness, but I think it's time I exert my own will. After all, I am twenty years old!" Her smile landed between each word.

Two hours later, when they stepped outside following the church service, Hope could still hear Drew's bass voice singing the familiar hymns. It had sent chills up her spine, as she sat on the wooden pew, beside him so close his jacket rubbed her arm. And it completely eradicated the tension regarding her mother.

Hope felt a flush of warmth flowing through her. She finally knew her place in the world. It was beside Drew Bartlett.

Hope stood on the church steps, where his friends of all ages gathered following the worship service. After he introduced Hope to the eager crowd, handshakes were extended, backs patted, and shoulders swatted in the same manner as when Drew scored a touchdown in the last ten seconds of a game. The jovial crowd resembled a victory celebration, and to her surprise, she and Drew were the celebrants.

Hope stood poised, greeting each one, while they unabashedly eyed her up and down. Drew received high praise for having chosen such a beautiful girl; their comments flowed with great enthusiasm. "She's a beauty." "It's about time!" "She's perfect for you, Drew."

One of his football buddies, with eyebrows raised, leaned over to mumble in his ear, "Drew, she looks like a movie star. Elegant, beautiful, poised. Reminds me of Grace Kelly. Don't know where you found her, but don't let her get away."

Drew, standing tall and proud, uttered a quiet, "Thanks."

"I mean it," the teammate said, firmly. "She's the most beautiful girl I've ever seen."

Drew understood why his friends would recognize Hope's beauty, but he had already discovered even more desirable traits since they had met. He was eager to discover more. If only he didn't need to think about a separation, one that was too painful for him to entertain.

A frown creased his forehead until she glanced at him. Holding her with his eyes, he winked at her. With an air of confidence, she suddenly felt as if she'd been born into the limelight as she turned to a group of giggling, older ladies standing a few feet away. One lady, with silver curls and bright pink lipstick, both on her mouth and on her plump cheeks, boldly stepped forward with a twinkle in her eye. The others eagerly waited, like cats licking their lips.

"Are you and Drew engaged?" The lady's whisper could barely be heard. Hope's face reddened.

"No ma'am." Hope's southern drawl caught the lady's attention.

"Where are you from?"

"Texas."

"No better young man will you find. Not even in Texas," she declared firmly while shaking her finger at Hope.

Hope, fearing her heart might burst as she listened to these ladies praising Drew, nodded in agreement. Drew stared in awe at her unflinching poise.

A pretty, young mother, carrying a whimpering baby girl, approached. Hope, at once, patted the baby's blond curls, instantly soothing her.

"Hi, I'm Kate. Don't let all these people scare you. To some, Drew is the son they never had, and to others, he's the husband they long for."

"Kate, thank you! To tell you the truth, I feel honored to be standing here. Your kind words will be held close."

Drew checked his watch then came to Hope's side and grabbed her hand.

"I think I better rescue my fair lady. After unknowingly throwing her into a lion's den, I have some making up to do." His side-grin and smiling eyes brought chuckles from the group.

"You have a lovely girlfriend," one said. "We hope you'll both visit us again."

"Thank you, we will." He squeezed Hope's hand, as he silently recalled his time there.

The church had been his sanctuary, and the loving group was like family. Members, both young and old, had invited him over for Sunday lunch through the years. He had gladly accepted their love and encouragement. They had buoyed his spirits, but now he felt a lump forming in his throat. The reception today was more than he had ever dared to dream.

Hope pondered the shocking attention her presence had garnered, as they strolled toward the door, plus the unquestionable love and praise they felt for Drew. But it was the queries, by one group of young women that touched her.

One college girl had asked, "Are you two going steady, or are you engaged?"

"Neither. Drew and I are new friends," Hope responded warmly.

The older ladies had twinkled with merriment; the younger ladies had beamed with optimism. The high school and college girls had teetered with ambivalence, as they listened to every word Drew uttered.

"I'm so sorry you had to go through this, Hope. Please know it wasn't intentional. I had no idea the people would respond in such a manner." He stopped next to the car before turning to face her. His eyes held her motionless. "It's hard for me to comprehend what just happened. I had no idea the congregation, and the ministers, would react that way."

Hope absorbed his tone, sensitive words, and his humility. As she listened to all the praise being given to Drew, she realized he was more concerned about her, than lapping up the affectionate glory bestowed on him.

"It was an honor, Drew. I could see you glancing at me through the throng of people, and for some reason, I felt connected to you. Your strength and composure fueled mine."

"Hope, I felt the same. Maybe that's a good sign for what lies ahead."

Her breath caught, as she slid into the car. Something set Drew apart from the other guys, something she didn't want to lose.

He slid in behind the steering wheel, taking her hand into his; then turning toward her, he uttered, rather apologetically,

"I never entertained the idea of inviting a girl to church until I met you."

"Really?" She fidgeted with her purse, while her eyes widened in surprise.

"Yes." That first night, when we were sitting in the car talking about the dance, I knew before the evening ended, I wanted to share this part of my life with you, to make it part of our experience. I sincerely appreciate the skill with which you handled the crowd and their curiosity. As surreal as the situation was, your diplomacy and graciousness were stellar." He lowered his head. "I'm grateful and proud to have you by my side, Hope Madison."

"Thank you," she whispered. "It's my honor."

They rode up the mountain in silence, each processing what neither had expected. Thirty minutes later, he pulled into a long gravel driveway.

The Other Part of Her

"Here we are," he said. The Stanley Hotel. I love this place and the large green lawn. It's one of my favorite places in Colorado."

"I agree. Each time I return, I'm fascinated with the majestic setting and the lavish edifice." She pointed toward the west. "Look at the mountains under the cloudless sky. What a glorious day it is!"

He took her hand, as they ambled toward the historic white structure.

"It's hard to believe this place was built in 1909. And here it is fifty years later, still glistening in regal majesty, surrounded by beautiful snow-capped mountains!"

They climbed the steps, leading to the expansive veranda where rows of white chairs lined the porch. Well-dressed tourists, sitting in wooden chairs, turned to gaze at the couple. An older man with gray hair, dressed in an expensive suit, had found his place near the entrance, where he leaned up against a white pillar, puffing on a cigar.

"Welcome to the Stanley Hotel," he said in a distinct New England accent. "You from here?"

"Yes," Drew stated. "Boulder."

"Hope you enjoy your time." A coughing frenzy took the man's breath.

"Thank you, sir."

The front door flew open and a young boy, proudly wearing a red uniform with a matching bellboy cap, greeted them. His contagious smile made the sun appear dim.

"May I help you?" he inquired with brown eyes lighting up his face.

"Yes." Drew shook his hand. "We have reservations for the Sunday Brunch."

"Certainly. Come with me," the boy directed in an authoritative voice.

Drew speculated the lad knew the hotel, along with all the guests, so he inquired of the boy.

"Do you know who the gentleman is on the porch, standing by the pillar? He looks familiar."

Proudly, the boy said, "Yes sir, I sure do. He's from back East, part of a well-known family, the Kennedys. It's rumored that his son, John Kennedy, will run for President of the United States in the next election."

"Thank you for enlightening us." Drew reached into his pocket until his fingers felt a quarter.

"What's your name?"

"Johnny, sir."

"Well, Johnny, you're doing a splendid job. Maybe one day you, too, will run for President of the United States."

Drew slipped the quarter to him when they reached the dining area.

"Thank you, sir. Thank you!!" Johnny's smile was as bright as a big city skyline.

A dignified Maître d', standing by the entrance into the formal dining area, couldn't seem to tear his eyes away from Hope, until he realized he must. Then he turned to Drew with embarrassed eyes.

"Do you have reservations, sir?"

"Yes. Drew Bartlett."

The man perused a list of names, then made a grand gesture, as he picked up their menus.

"Follow me, please." He led the way as he discreetly brushed lint from his black tuxedo.

The brunch crowd, in their hats and finery, filled the red-carpeted room. Women appeared with cinched-in waistlines, full skirts, elegantly fitted suits with matching hats, and pencil dresses that sheathed their trim bodies from bodice to mid-calf. Big hats to small

The Other Part of Her

pillbox styles dotted the room. Young girls rustled their starched petticoats.

***

Drew eyed the men sporting well-tailored suits, white shirts with French cuffs, silk ties, and wingtip shoes. Each would remove their hat at the entrance, placing it on a hat rack before entering the dining room. A few Stetson hats revealed southern men to be present, especially Texans who identify with "the bigger the better" philosophy.

Towering oak columns and floor-to-ceiling windows sparkled. Whispers trailed like dogs on a foxhunt when Hope strolled by.

The Maître d' approached a table draped in white linen. Subtly, he removed the reservation card with Drew's name scrawled across the front.

"Does this meet with your approval, Sir?"

Drew nodded, as he pulled the chair out for Hope. "Yes. Thank you very much."

Hope stared at Drew sitting across from her. A boyish grin spread up to his eyes as he leaned over the table.

"I guess you're wondering about the reservations."

"Yes, I am," she teased.

"I called yesterday, prior to our trip up the canyon. Was I being too presumptive?"

"Not at all. I like your positive attitude. Did you request a table by the windows, as well?"

"Of course." That playful grin again! She ducked her head, trying to hide growing emotions, stirring in her mind.

"Hope, did you notice the stares when you walked in the room?"

Her face flushed, as she stared into his eyes.

"It's my height. I'm tall when barefoot, and with heels, I soar into the stratosphere. 'How's the weather up there?' is the question I've been asked many times since the eighth grade. I wish my classmates could have found a better way to address my height, but since I towered over them, that question seemed to fit their need to be witty."

"You're kidding! That's rude!" Disgust was flashing from his eyes.

She leaned back, shaking her head.

"Hope, the stares are not restricted to your height. You have a presence that radiates. I realized it when we first met at the Whitmire's. Then I saw it yesterday at the river, and this morning at church. God has graced you with an abundance of grace and humility which makes your beauty, inside and out, captivating."

"Thank you, Drew. I've never heard these words before, and these feelings, I've never felt before." Tears formed. She glanced away to stare at the array of flowers in the outdoor garden, before hesitantly turning back to him.

She ducked her head in embarrassment. Her voice was soft, and Drew had to lean closer to hear her over the crowd.

"I've always compared myself to my beautiful, older sister, a clone of my mother. Any expectations of ever feeling what you are giving me, vanished long ago. From the bottom of my heart, thank you."

Drew realized his compliments were falling on foreign soil. He could see the pain in her eyes and hear the sincere gratitude flowing in her hushed voice. He paused to let the server take their order and to fill their glasses with mint iced tea before responding.

"I didn't realize you had a sister. What's her name? Where is she?"

"Her name is Riley. She's married to a diplomat. We're many years apart in age, plus opposite personalities. Riley's very close to Mother; I'm very close to Daddy, but my closest friend and supporter is Odie B, the one who raised me. She's our housekeeper and my confidante."

Drew checked his watch, shocked at how quickly the time had passed. The meal and conversation had absorbed his thoughts. But he had more planned, so he quickly paid the bill, before running to the car to get their changes of clothes. After they both changed, Hope emerged from the restroom wearing a pink sweater and matching Capri pants. Drew carried their dress clothes to the car and Hope couldn't help but admire his long legs. The denim jeans and a shirt, the color of his blue eyes, made her smile.

"How about if I take you to one of my favorite places in the Rocky Mountain Park?"

"I'd love it!"

They basked in the sunshine beating down on them as they rode up the mountain, the wind ruffling their hair. Drew took the mountain turns quickly then hearing her gasp of astonishment, he slowed when an elk, foraging in a grassy meadow, appeared.

"He looks like he's been in a fight," Drew said, pointing to his broken antlers and the dark gashes on his side. "I'll pull over so you can take a picture if you want. He's far enough away for us to be safe."

She grabbed her camera, and with Drew by her side, she aimed the lens with trembling hands. The first shots were not impressive because the majestic elk was not lifting his head. Yet, as if on cue, he spontaneously did so and turned toward Hope. Against the backdrop of an azure sky, dotted with billowy clouds, he posed for several more shots. Then he darted into a nearby wooded area.

Drew couldn't quit grinning. "Is this your first experience as a National Geographic photographer?"

"Yes! But not my last!"

"Hope, you may be published in one of those magazines one day. I'm serious."

She couldn't find the words for a dream so grand. As they continued their way up the mountain, Hope felt the air growing thinner and cooler. She quickly changed her lightweight jacket for her heavy sweater. Just at that moment, Drew pointed to an eagle soaring above them. In her mind's eye, she was recording his vast wingspread, his massive claw talons, as he searched the ground for food, no doubt. A few miles later, Drew pulled off the main road onto a gravel area.

"This is the entrance into my favorite place. We must hike a bit, but I think you'll find the scenery worth every step."

She grasped the camera lariat, as he slipped his arm around her shoulder.

"Drew, you've already exceeded my expectations with the beautiful lunch, and now this...."

"There's more to come," he said, grinning. "We'll see a profusion of wildflowers, especially Blue Columbine, Colorado's state flower. It has a beautiful bloom, and when they are in masse, as they will be, it's worth a snapshot. However, bees are attracted to its pollen, so be careful."

"You make a good guide," she teased.

"Thanks. You can donate pictures to my struggling efforts. Haven't had much business lately; in fact, you're the first." Chuckling, he took her hand. His eyes sparkled with mischief.

"Hope, do you happen to have a bologna sandwich with you? Lathered in mustard?"

"In my purse," she said, laughing.

The Other Part of Her

As they walked along, suddenly the dense forest opened its majestic doors. A profusion of color, the sights and sounds of giant trees rustling, along with lush vines filled with red, pink, blue and yellow flora, made Hope gasp. Birds filled the air with a concert of melodies as Drew gripped her hand, leading her deeper into the forest.

"Just a little farther," he said.

A roaring waterfall, streaming from the top of a cliff, sprayed them with droplets. Together, in reverence for the towering presence of God's creation, they stood frozen, until she released Drew's hand to zip up her jacket. The rapid drop in temperature had surprised her.

At that moment, Hope realized if she took out her camera to focus on shutter speeds, angles and lighting, she would miss simply standing there beside Drew, absorbing the beauty of God's magnificent formations. And to think she had only known him for two days!

Her breath caught when he wrapped his arms around her waist. Fear and reality shot through her body like a lightning bolt. This was merely a way for him to entertain himself on a Sunday afternoon, she stated silently. He'd be gone soon.

But it was a moment she wished would never end.

"This is where I come when I need to unwind," he said, leaning into her ear. "The beauty and sounds of nature refuel my mind, body, and soul." A Pygmy Owl, off in the distance, emphasized the moment.

"You're the first person with whom I've shared this sacred place."

The emotional timbre in his voice shocked her.

"Thank you, Drew. This is a dream come to life. Certainly, the most beautiful place I've ever seen," she whispered.

He placed his large hands around her narrow waist and turned her towards him. Slowly, he began wrapping his arms around her, pulling her closer. She could feel her face growing flushed as he bent his own towards her. In that moment, he met her lips in a way she would always remember. It wasn't her first kiss. But it was her first unforgettable kiss.

His tight embrace and his breath on her face were being recorded in every cell of her body and mind.

Drew couldn't help but see the emotion in Hope's eyes, as he once again pulled her to his chest.

"Hope, I would have waited to kiss you until I was more confident of your feelings, but I can't escape the ticking of the clock, the one we are racing against every day."

As he stroked her hair, she continued to lean against him, quivering.

"I know this sounds strange, but in some inexplicable way, I feel we were meant to find each other, in spite of the impending separation."

Leaning back, she stared up at him. He could see silent agreement and sadness mingling in her eyes. Silently, he answered by placing his hands on either side of her face and kissing her again.

From that point on, love traveled as fast as the storm clouds can gather. Each stolen moment brought them closer, sealing their future.

SIX

Kathryn Madison sat at her mahogany desk, while running perfectly manicured nails through her auburn hair. Her private study held shelves lined with books and original art. A large bay window provided a panoramic view of the backyard where towering evergreen trees dotted the landscape, and bright pink petunias lined the flowerbeds. "My sanctuary," she would often say, as streams of early morning light danced across the floor.

Normally, she felt comfortable and relaxed in this peaceful environment, but not today. Hope's dating history lurked at the forefront of her mind. She leaned over the desk, cupping her head in her hands.

It had always been simple. If a young man had a crush on Hope, he was gone in less time than she could hold her breath. If she approached her daughter about the subject, Hope would frown, shrug her shoulders and moan about his dullness.

Now, Drew Bartlett, the only one to reverse the pattern, was about to leave, and that concerned her.

Suddenly, she jumped up and rushed to the kitchen where Odie B stood humming in front of the kitchen window as she washed the dishes.

"Odie B, we'll be entertaining a dinner guest tomorrow night. Prepare whatever you wish for Drew Bartlett. Fried Chicken might be nice."

"Yes, Ma'am."

Odie B's voice sounded as high as a meadowlark after hearing the news. She immediately stifled a broad grin, but she wondered if Mrs. Madison noticed her large brown eyes bursting with excitement.

Mrs. Madison ran upstairs to notify Hope, where she lay across her bed talking on the phone to Sarah. Drew was made aware of the plan, later that evening, when he called.

The following evening, dusk was descending when Drew arrived. He eagerly raced up the steps leading to Hope's home. His long stride allowed him to take two large steps at a time, yet his nerves were in a battle. The anticipation of seeing Hope again, evoked a smile, but the directive from Mrs. Madison was concerning.

He paused to view the freshly landscaped lawn that showcased an array of spring flowers. Concrete urns on the front porch overflowed with color, and matching, on the balcony, were window boxes filled with the same pink and white flowers.

"Too soon to plant flowers," he mumbled to himself. But he took it into account that Mrs. Madison wasn't aware that Boulder could have a late snow, even in May. He deemed it inappropriate to educate her.

Hope answered the front door wearing a red dress. Its full skirt immediately took his eyes to her narrow waist, making him marvel at her figure. Her blond hair, swinging with each movement, hung loosely past her shoulders.

"You look beautiful," he whispered.

"Thank you. You look very handsome yourself." She observed how his pale blue shirt emphasized his eyes, the color of the Mediterranean Sea.

"Follow me." Taking him by the hand, she led him into the kitchen where she had prepared for him a unique experience.

"Drew, I'd like you to meet my *best* friend, Odie B."

"I've been looking forward to meeting you, Odie B. Hope has been telling me all about your cooking."

Drew was unaware that Hope was supplying Odie B, her best friend and confidant, with daily updates about their relationship.

"Thank you, Mr. Drew," Odie B's large brown eyes twinkled.

Her new hairstyle, brand-spanking new uniform and shoes not yet broken in, revealed her enthusiasm for meeting Hope's new friend.

"It's fried chicken night," Hope whispered to Drew, motioning for him to sit in the red leather booth, next to the bay window.

"When she cooks, it's like going to church."

Drew turned his full attention to Odie B standing in front of the stove, humming softly while she cooked. When she began belting out a song that could be heard a block away, his head jerked. He winked at Hope and grinned, then added his own deep voice to Odie B's.

Swing low, sweet chariot,
Coming for to carry me home,
If you get there before I do...
Tell all my friends I'm coming to....

She retrieved a long wooden spoon from the drawer and began to sing, *When We All Get To Heaven,* as she stirred the steaming pot of vegetables. She continued singing, while forming balls of dough into biscuits. When Drew added his booming bass voice, the festive atmosphere travelled throughout their large home.

"Amen, Odie B," he said, chuckling.

She threw her head back and laughed so hard her whole body jiggled.

"Amen! Brother Drew. Amen!"

She wiped her perspiring face with a dishtowel as Hope led Drew into the dining room.

"Odie B has been a part of our family since I was three years old. She's like an older sister, twelve years my senior, and my best friend. I don't know what I'd do without her."

"Tonight, dinner will be for the two of us, plus my mother. My father is away on business."

Drew understood why a hint of sadness shone in her eyes and squeezed her hand.

Uncertainty began slithering through his body like a snail. He'd not seen Mrs. Madison since whisking Hope away from their traditional Sunday lunch. Her obvious displeasure, a strong contrast to Hope's jubilant reaction, remained visible in his mind's eye.

Standing by Hope, he was momentarily distracted by the similar ambiance between his home and the Madison's. Serenity, elegance, and comfort blended as smoothly as the soft, sea-foam green color did on the walls and carpet. Windows, spanning one wall, brought the freshly planted flowers, along with a view of the snow-capped mountains, inside. However, the biggest surprise came when he noticed a traditional mahogany cabinet standing in the corner. The cabinet, and the dishes, were the same as his grandmother's. The soft music, flowing from the stereo, was also the same. Uncanny, he thought to himself. But it stopped there when Mrs. Madison, an immaculately groomed lady with alabaster skin and reddish-brown hair, entered.

"Hello, Drew. Please, you and Hope have a seat."

The tranquil atmosphere grew tense. Drew thought her erect posture, as stiff as the starched table linens, conveyed confidence; her no-nonsense tone exhibited control and her arched eyebrows revealed impatience, as she waited for Odie B to complete the setting of bowls and platters on the table.

Hope restrained a laugh when she recognized Odie B's unspoken message: "I'm-in-no-hurry-this-is-my-party" attitude. It was, as far as Odie B was concerned, and Mrs. Madison would have to wait, which she did while drumming her manicured fingernails on the table.

Odie B finally left the room, after exchanging a mischievous glance with Hope. Kathryn Madison asked Drew to say the blessing.

He complied, though he felt a final benediction would have been more appropriate following the revival in the kitchen. However, he quickly changed his mind when he participated in the second part of the "service," eating mashed potatoes swimming in butter, the "Lil Bit of Heaven" biscuits, fresh green beans, and garden tomatoes. Each dish accented the star of the meal: golden, fried chicken with an extra layer of crispiness.

Drew realized the kitchen had been like his childhood choir practice, a mere rehearsal before the main event, and he eagerly consumed the meal, while answering Mrs. Madison's questions about his plans after graduation.

Immediately, she realized there was more to the couple's relationship than she had realized. Her wariness increased upon contemplation of the fact that Drew, a disciplined young man, had meticulously carved out his future from a very young age. Now, with only two remaining weeks, he was pursuing Hope with the same determination he applied to his future.

Odie B felt the tension when she strolled back into the room carrying a pitcher of tea. Drew complimented her on the meal and a smile spread across her face as wide as a church door. Strutting back to the kitchen, she let her gratitude be overheard through the swinging door.

"Thank ya, Sweet Jesus. Thank ya." Hope knew her thick arms were waving high in the air while she stared toward the heavens at Jesus and Mama B, her mother.

The meal concluded as Drew pushed his empty dessert plate aside, politely folded his napkin and sipped the last of his tea; he spoke directly to Mrs. Madison.

"Eating Odie B's fried chicken is like being given a peek into Heaven. Gabriel is blowing his trumpet while angels sing the

Hallelujah chorus. Soul food is a gift she bestows on all who come to this table. My soul has been fed. Thank you, Mrs. Madison."

Hope witnessed her mother's surprise at Drew's genuine expression of appreciation. Then came another shock, one Hope didn't expect.

"Mrs. Madison, may I have a word with you in private?"

She nodded, stiffly, and as the two left the room, sounds of Hope and Odie B in the kitchen wafted through the air.

Kathryn led him to the wood-paneled den, and offered him a seat on the chocolate brown sofa, while she claimed a comfortable chair and matching ottoman. Mr. Madison's chair sat empty, next to hers.

Drew leaned forward in an open, personable manner, with his hands loosely intertwined. He took a moment to stare directly into her eyes, before speaking in a deep, steady voice.

"Mrs. Madison, may I have your permission to take Hope on an aerial sightseeing trip of Colorado?"

A gasp escaped from her mouth. For a moment, she felt blood draining from her face; her throat was parched. She knew she couldn't protect Hope forever, but the possibility of anything happening to her daughter created havoc internally.

When he witnessed her hesitation, he became concerned his request would be denied.

"I want to reassure you of my ability," he quickly added. "I know it's a huge request, but I have been involved for a year in the Navy's Flight Indoctrination Program, and I was awarded the Naval Reserve Officer Training Corps, 'Most Outstanding Student.' I've had my private pilot's license since I was sixteen and I've been flying all through college. I have built up a considerable amount of flight time and with it, experience."

She stared at him unconvinced. It had nothing to do with Drew, or very little, as she saw him as very mature and competent. He was the kind of man who would give his life for another and for his country, but the threat of something happening to Hope gripped her with panic.

Drew felt her uneasiness, as he continued speaking.

"With your permission, we will do this on the last day I'm in Boulder. It will be my departing gift to her, one I hope she will remember and cherish, as much as I."

She stared at the handsome young man and took a deep breath. Barely able to verbalize the words, she hesitantly asked,

"When do you need to know?" All color had drained from her face. "I must consult Mr. Madison."

Drew paused. Seeing her frozen face, his confidence dwindled, but he managed to stare directly into her eyes.

"I understand, Mrs. Madison. I'd need to reserve the plane, so if you were to advise me within the next three days, the flight will be promptly scheduled."

She stared at him with pain-filled eyes. "You'll have my answer as soon as Mr. Madison responds. His business takes him away frequently, so most decisions are made without conferring with him, but this one involves consequences for our daughter."

Drew rose, eager to depart. The chill flowing through him was something he had not yet experienced in life. At least, not that he could recall. And certainly not from his loving grandmother.

"Thank you, Mrs. Madison. It has been a wonderful evening, and I deeply appreciate your generous hospitality. I'll look forward to hearing from you." He turned to leave but he suddenly felt it imperative to add one last detail. "If you and Mr. Madison agree on this airborne "chariot" ride, I would like to surprise Hope and not tell her until we arrive at the airport."

He paused, looked away, then turned back to face her. His eyes were red and moist when he gently spoke.

"I wish I could introduce Hope to my mother, but I know her spirit will be with us. She, too, was a pilot, but was unable to continue flying after she learned she was pregnant with me. I always feel her with me when I'm in the air, comforting me, letting me know my destiny was charted long ago, and reminding me I was flying before I was born."

With moist eyes, he shook Mrs. Madison's hand before exiting.

Hope met him in the hall, and together they went back to where her mother sat rigid. "Mother, we're going to a movie."

"What are you going to see?" Mrs. Madison's voice sounded flat even to her own ears.

"Alfred Hitchcock's new movie, *North by Northwest*."

"I heard it was good," she said. Visible strain flowed in her voice, as well as her face.

Hope glanced up at Drew, and as the two left the room, he wrapped his arm around her shoulders.

Kathryn sat immobile, confident that life would never be the same. Hope bore all the same markings she had exhibited when dating Tennessee Madison, her husband of thirty-two-years. She wiped tears and dialed.

"Operator," Kathryn's voice was unstable as the wind. "I want to make a person-to-person call to Mr. Tennessee Madison at the Drake Hotel in Chicago."

Six minutes later, she laid her head in her hands and wept uncontrollably.

Tennessee had agreed to Drew's request, reluctantly. Partially weighing on his decision was the bond Hope shared with her grandfather, the man who had eagerly introduced his passion for aviation to all, especially to Hope.

She knew the decision had been the most difficult required of him as a father; his relationship with Hope exceeded all other relationships, except for theirs. A sense of peace began flowing through her, as she reflected upon their marriage. Together, they had survived several storms, and they were still very much in love.

"Now this," she mumbled, growing tense again.

For an hour, she sat frozen reliving the anguish she shared with Tennessee. Years had passed, but not the agony of losing their beautiful three-year-old daughter, Shelly. The recollection of symptoms, the confusion, the whirlwind of tests, somber expressions emanating from the doctors' faces, until finally, the diagnosis.

"An inoperable brain tumor. I'm sorry. There's nothing we can do."

Three weeks later, Shelly passed away.

Tonight, Kathryn, sitting in the den alone, wished for the comfort of her husband's arms. Denying Hope, the freedom she longed to enjoy, wasn't an option any longer. Then she recalled the gasp in her husband's voice when she delivered Drew's request. Together, fear rose from buried crevices, the long-remembered kind. The kind that burrows deep into bones, the kind that lurks, waiting for a trigger, the kind that sat squarely on their minds.

She remembered hearing the agony in Tennessee's voice, and his choked words,

"Yes, she can go. It's what Hope would want. It's also what her grandfather would want."

The phone went dead, and she knew Tennessee Madison had come to a painful realization: Hope's heart no longer belonged solely to him.

Drew and Hope walked to the car, after the movie, in comfortable silence. His hand gripped hers. On the drive home, silence continued. Concerned, Hope mentally questioned if she had said something to upset him. Perhaps her mother's coolness, which had been extremely obvious throughout dinner, worried him. Maybe it was due to the private exchange between Drew and her mother, she conjectured.

Hope's hands begin to tremble as the silence became awkward. The strain continued to increase, and by the time he parked in front of her home, and turned toward her, frowning, she felt nausea climbing to her throat.

He took her hand and placed it between both of his, then tilted her chin towards him. Her doubting eyes stared back at him.

"Hope, I want to steal every opportunity to be with you."

His reluctance and concern were visible, even in the dark. She held her breath, not knowing the cause, as he continued,

"I'm wondering if you ever changed your mind about going to the dance."

Hope burst out in relieved laughter. He frowned, unsure what brought on the change in her demeanor.

"Yes, Drew. I have."

"That's wonderful, but now, I need to address another point of concern," he said solemnly.

"Okay. What is it?" She heard the tension flowing in his voice.

Since their first meeting, he had struggled to wrap his head around what was happening and he had pled with God repeatedly, "Why now? Why did you bring her into my life when I'm about to leave?" No answers were revealed.

"Hope, would you mind if we didn't double date with Sarah and her date? I know that's what she wants, and possibly what you want."

Letting his words fall, he paused until the strength to expose buried vulnerabilities was found.

"I realize this may sound selfish, but there is a natural rhythm when we are together. There is no pretense, just a natural flow, one unlike any other relationship I've ever had, and I don't want to interrupt it."

He briefly shifted his gaze to turn down the radio, never letting go of her hand. Then with eyes full of intention, he continued.

"Hope, I want to spend every moment in your presence, not measuring what is said, or done. Just being together, the two of us. We have so few days remaining and on this special occasion, I would like it to be 'our night', should you agree."

He turned his head and stared out the window, before murmuring,

"After the dance, graduation is the next major event, an entirely different circumstance." He paused and looked away, then turning to her and lifting her chin with his finger, he stated firmly.

"Hope, if it means risking you thinking of me as selfish, I acquiesce. In this case, I am, but I believe we both have earned the right to make the most of our time together."

Hope took a moment to absorb his words. The tone. The expression. Gathering her thoughts close, like a cat gathering her kittens, she spoke.

"Drew, I feel the same as you, and though I enjoy the company of Sarah, I much prefer being with you, alone. I would love for the evening to be *our* night."

He pulled her next to him, kissing her in a way that spoke of dread for the impending separation. She felt his gratitude mingling with hers.

"I'll tell Ken. I can hear him repeating the same speech again, but I'll just say, 'It's too late, brother.'"

Her eyes brightened until an irresistible urge overcame her.

"May I ask you a personal question, Drew?"

"I hold nothing back from you, Hope. Of course, you can."

"Why didn't you invite Sarah to be your date for the dance, after the other girl cancelled?"

"SARAH?" He burst out laughing.

"Sarah is like a little sister to me. That's all. We tease back and forth as though we are siblings, but to tell you the truth, I never once entertained the idea of taking her. Not even if it meant going unaccompanied."

Hope felt relief traveling through her. The sound in Sarah's wistful voice when she spoke of Drew, along with her persistent enthusiasm about their double date had haunted her. Even as late as last night, Sarah seemed more enamored with the idea of Drew than with her own date.

Together and silent, the two strolled up to the front porch. He gently turned her to face him before taking both of her hands in his. Regret snaked through his body.

"I'll be going to see my grandmother tomorrow in Idaho Springs. She's back from her annual trip to New York, and she is requesting I come home," he murmured.

"When will you return?" The sadness in her eyes was evident.

"Hope, I hate leaving when so little time remains, but I should be back before you're out of church Sunday."

"I understand. I don't want any absences either, Drew, but it can't be helped."

"The thought of leaving you, Hope, is beginning to fill me with dread."

He pulled her into him, holding her firmly, before he reached down to place a lingering kiss on her lips, under the intense bright glow of the porch light.

SEVEN

The fear of losing Hope, before they had a chance to build a strong foundation, chilled Drew to the bone, as did the cold wind blowing. He zipped his jacket then turned his attention to the car radio, searching for reception while speeding around mountain curves. A vapor of his warm breath escaped into the mountain air when he joined Elvis in song. Anticipation and loneliness danced between each note.

He couldn't even remember what life was like before Hope Madison. She entered his life unexpectedly and cast an enchanted spell over him, quietly filling empty spaces he never knew existed. Now, his plan to be a Naval aviator was in question. The dream hadn't changed, but due to the presence of Hope in his life, he desperately wanted to slow the clock from advancing forward like a soldier marching to cadence.

He banged his hand on the steering wheel, shouting to the wind.

"How can I possibly leave her in a couple of weeks?"

Frustrated. Angry. Confused. His life had shredded into a thousand pieces the first time he laid eyes on her.

Now, while magenta streaks of evening filled the sky above snow-capped mountains, he turned his attention to his upcoming visit with his grandmother, visualizing her in a newly renovated kitchen. They both knew she used the project as an excuse to frequently consult with him, and though he lacked expertise, especially regarding paint and wallpaper, her enthusiasm and zeal lifted his spirits.

Drew knew little about his grandmother's background, except that Olivia Bartlett, a sophisticated and elegant lady from New York City, accustomed to a chauffeur and a well-trained domestic staff, had mingled with the upper crust of society until the age of fifty. That's when she plopped down in a small, Colorado mountain town to raise him, her six-year-old grandson.

He learned early in life she was smart, decisive, and not one to linger on copious details. Those same qualities, along with the importance of the home project, had spilled into the air during their evening phone visits.

Before he would see the finished results, now ten miles away, he imagined aromas drifting in the house and Olivia proudly displaying his favorite dessert under a glass dome, like a trophy. Music would be softly streaming from her new high-fidelity record player.

The scene made him smile, especially when he thought about her words at the conclusion of each visit.

'Drew, please take the leftovers back to school with you. I can't possibly eat all of them!'

They both knew she had prepared enough for seven, but the cherished tradition of 'love and leftovers' had prevailed through four years of college. A bittersweet ending, neared.

Tonight, the woman who lovingly raised him would provide him with assurance. That was certain. She was his solace, his succor, his anchor. In a couple of hours, she would be his guide, opening doors to the past, though she was unaware of their upcoming journey.

He slowed at the sign pointing to Idaho Springs and turned off the highway.

The town's one blinking yellow light allowed him to stare at the small white church with a welcoming red door, its steeple piercing the evening sky. Memories bounced like ping-pong balls: his faith had been nurtured within those walls and though one might think it strange, he felt sole ownership of the church. He wondered if others felt the same. "His church," draped in snow, along with the giant evergreen trees surrounding the building, appeared to be a Christmas scene, an image of comfort and peace, one he could recall when on foreign soil.

He pulled into the narrow driveway, grabbed his shaving kit and clothes then strolled up the walk. Pausing briefly, he admired the freshly painted exterior. She had consulted with him before painting their two-story home a soft yellow with pale blue shutters. When he noticed the abundance of flowers, evidence of his grandmother's eager announcement to Mother Nature, "winter has officially ended," he smiled. She did it every year, and every year she had to replace the dead blooms a few weeks later.

Olivia heard his car and was standing at the front door wearing a starched apron over her 'Sunday' dress, her arms open wide. Together they made their way into the home, following the familiar scent of a roast in the oven.

"I like how you've spruced up the house, Grandmother."

She burst with an inner glow. Pleasing him was her main desire.

"Drew, the reason I frequently consulted you was not due to my lack of decision-making skills."

He noted a rare display of emotions: the crack in her voice and tears welling up. She reached for a handkerchief and dabbed her eyes before continuing.

"I did it because of my strong desire to make it feel like your home when you return from long absences. You were my reason for the process."

He walked over and put his arms around her, holding her as he spoke.

"Grandmother, regardless of the color of the paint, which appears to be slightly lighter in color than the yellow pansies bordering the walk, this will always be my home."

Olivia smiled, though alarm bells were ringing inside of her. Drew met her with a forced smile then turned to admire the renovation. She instantly recorded a change, other than his pain-filled eyes. His jocular countenance had given into the weight of a burden buried deep within. Her heart plummeted, but she said nothing.

Drew consumed the lavish meal while she delivered updates on his friends. He listened half-heartedly, and nodded at the appropriate times, none of which went unnoticed by the woman who knew him so well. She decided to postpone delving into the problem he carried, until after dinner.

"I'm thinking about getting a new car, Drew. I've been driving the same car for five years, and I don't feel it to be trustworthy."

"Grandmother, what is it you really wish to do with a new car? The one you have, has very few miles on it. In this small town, you're perfectly safe."

"Now, don't worry yourself, Drew," patting his arm. "I might want to go somewhere. Somewhere far away and I no longer have a chauffeur. In fact, I'm pondering the idea of a cross-country trip. Don't you think that would be nice?" She noticed his determination when he locked eyes with her and leaned over the table.

"Grandmother, please don't drive across the Unites States alone. Get a luxury compartment on a train, or fly, but promise me you won't drive." His pleading tone, unusual for him, touched her heart. His eyes didn't turn away.

"Drew, you're such a spoil sport!" With eyes dancing and a sly grin, she tried to be firm. "You and Horace, my chauffeur in New York, have always thrown a monkey wrench into my plans."

"Grandmother, you pulled a fast one on him when you were on your way to Colorado from New York," Drew teased, shaking his finger at her. "I still can't believe you banished him from the driver's seat when you had never driven a car!"

"I was bored and the delicious opportunity of giving farmers and passers-by something to talk about couldn't be ignored. They're

The Other Part of Her

probably still talking about the woman in a red hat, waving from the driver's side window, in a black car the length of a Nebraska cornfield." She threw her head back and laughed, while Drew, trying to maintain his reserve, like a parent disciplining a child, only grinned. When he could no longer restrain himself, together they enjoyed the release of tension afforded to them by her long ago claim of taking a step into a man's world.

"I know you're capable of pulling a fast one on me, too, but please, I beg of you, don't. I'll be unable to help you and we both know Dad isn't available, for whatever reason, so please refrain. I'm imploring you." His voice dropped; his smile vanished.

Staring at him, she desperately wished the events that led to the changes in his father had never occurred. But sadly, she couldn't alter the past. Nor could she provide an explanation for the behavior of her son, Dr. Andrew Bartlett II.

Drew laid his knife and fork across his empty plate, shuffled in his seat, and cleared his throat.

"Can you tell me how you knew Grandfather was the one you wanted to marry?"

"I'll be happy to share that with you," Olivia said, cheerfully.

She had yearned to tell stories about his grandfather, but the desire had recently intensified. Now, she smiled at the surprise of Drew's request, and the timing.

"Did you know you're a duplicate image of him?"

Drew's eyes opened wide with surprise. "No, I didn't know that!"

"You're a carbon copy, not only in appearance, but in heart, as well."

Standing, she picked up his plate and began clearing the table.

"How about we have some lemon meringue pie while I tell you about him?" Her eyes sparkled at the sight of Drew's grin, as a tidal wave of emotions burst through her.

There were things she wouldn't reveal, not yet. *Someday,* she thought to herself. *Someday he'll know everything.* But not tonight. This evening, she would enlighten him about his heritage. It had been on her mind for two reasons: his upcoming departure and her impending birthday. Over seven decades had passed since she took her first breath in the world and tonight, she felt relief that the typical aging process had been postponed by the raising of Drew. He had kept her young; his absence would age her.

She removed the glass dome covering a warm lemon pie then reached inside the cabinet. Holding a china saucer in her hand, she turned toward him,

"Drew, do you remember when you bought these dessert dishes for me?"

"Yes, I do. I remember when and where. Birdie's Antique Store. It's forever etched in my childhood memories."

Drew finished eating two slices of pie, then filled the new automatic dishwasher, while silently reliving the time he asked Birdie to assist him. It was the summer of his tenth year.

"I'd like to buy the dessert dishes in the window for my grandmother," he said with pride. "The ones with yellow and white flowers."

He could still recall the overwhelming bolt of fear that followed, and his hands shaking when he added,

"I'm not sure I have enough money."

"Let me see." Birdie left the counter, wiggling like an eel until she reached the display window. Lifting the dish out, she carefully studied the price tag.

"Her birthday is in two days," he said.

"That's special, ain't it?" She glanced at him, as she peeled off the price tag.

"Well, look at that. They happen to be on sale," she said, slyly, "for fifty cents."

"I'll take them!" He was immediately filled with relief.

Birdie smiled and lowered her head, as she began counting the pennies and nickels he pulled from his pockets. Occasionally, her squinty eyes would peer at him over the glasses perched on the end of her nose. A purple, frayed ribbon hanging around her wrinkled neck kept them from sliding off, but he was more intrigued with the pencil positioned like a rocket behind her ear, and the bright, pink lipstick that matched the circles on her cheeks. She winked at him while popping her gum, and eventually, she handed him a sack with the wrapped dishes.

"Thank you, ma'am." He strolled to the door, very proud of his purchase and what he'd learned in those few minutes. Birdie liked chewing gum, pink, winking, and lots of heavy perfume.

She winked again as Drew headed through the door.

Drew took the percolator from the stove and poured steaming coffee into his grandmother's china cup, then in his. Olivia observed every motion. So much like his grandfather, she thought to herself. His attention-grabbing turquoise-blue eyes and side-grin, traits from her husband, always created a deep longing within her but tonight, she would allow the pain to breathe. A welcome change after years of suppression.

"So, you'd like to know how I knew your grandfather was the man for me?"

"Yes, I would." He blew on the coffee, sipping it carefully, before taking a bite of his third slice of pie.

She remained unaware of him studying her while she subconsciously rubbed the diamond wedding ring on her left hand. Her new hairstyle, a "French twist," was swept off her long neck, and in the glow of lamplight, it appeared as white as Easter lilies; a large emerald and diamond pin on her dress harmonized with her green eyes.

Slowly…words…old words…words buried for more than half a century…began to float to the top.

"When I met your grandfather, there was no shortage of available suitors in New York City, but most of the young men were too forward." A hint of irritation crept into her voice. "They insisted on holding my hand and monopolizing my evenings."

She shifted in the chair then leaning her head back, she closed her eyes, allowing the calendar to roll in reverse. A vision of Olivia, eighteen-years-old, began to emerge in her mind while expressions of joy and youthfulness crept across her face, into her voice. Drew, awed by both the visible and audible transformation, sat as still as the bronze statue on the mantel.

"The Jennings' colonial home on Michigan's Mackinac Island," she stated in a young, exuberant voice, "provided a lovely setting for my best friend, Elizabeth Jennings' elaborate birthday party. Music, from the orchestra, drifted through the air on coastal breezes while guests from around the globe arrived in horse-drawn carriages. Limestone bluffs, bordering the shimmering water, summoned guests to the expansive back lawn where hundreds of hurricane lamps twinkled in the night like lightning bugs. White-draped tables and chairs dotted the landscape; a wooden dance floor lay on a carpet of green grass. Buffet tables, filled with platters of prime rib, shrimp, scallops and lobster, were positioned around the lawn. But the crown jewels were the sweet miniature delicacies, along with the towering birthday cake. Both were positioned beneath a large floral arch, on the bluff of Lake Huron.

"A refreshing breeze blew in the evening air, as I mingled among the many New York guests who, like my family, flocked to the island for an escape from the summer humidity in New York City."

Olivia paused to take a sip of water, but her youthfulness remained, as did the sparkle in her eyes.

"I was venturing toward a group of friends when a man, whom I did not recognize, came strolling across the lawn. I slowed to admire his long gait, chestnut-colored hair, bronze face, and the most beautiful ocean-blue eyes I had ever seen. A custom-tailored white linen suit hung exquisitely on his slender, athletic body; a silk tie, the same color of his deep blue eyes, blew in the wind. Elizabeth had her arm linked in his while they walked in my direction. I could see him affectionately patting her hand, as she chatted with great animation. I remember standing motionless, unaware of anyone else, until I heard Elizabeth yelling, 'Olivia'. I didn't move as they hastily approached.

'Olivia, I want to introduce my favorite cousin to you, the man who feeds our imagination with letters about his global adventures. As you well know, he sent regrets that he wouldn't be able to attend my birthday party, but it seems he wanted to keep his attendance a secret!'

"Her gentle chiding evoked a grin on his face."

"Elizabeth returned to the guests while I stood motionless. I had not entertained the possibility of meeting Andrew Bartlett, the man with an international reputation. I stared in wonder."

Olivia opened her eyes and looked at Drew.

"Your grandfather, a prominent figure in the banking world, was well-traveled, successful, knowledgeable in the arts, plus fluent in several languages. He simply enthralled me."

She immediately returned to the story, smiling, as she leaned her head back once again.

"I pulled out my ankle-length, lace dress to curtsy, but when his eyes traveled from my shoes to my head, I flushed under his gaze. He stared at me with piercing turquoise eyes, before gently lifting my hand."

'May I?' he whispered.

"Before I could respond to his question, he brushed his lips lightly across the top of my hand."

She opened her eyes and with an expression of genuine shock, stated,

"Drew, I had never been so affected by anyone, as I was by him. Truthfully, I found it difficult to breathe, especially in my tight, corseted dress. Later, after everyone retired, I marveled in my reverie while I lay awake, near sleeping Elizabeth.

"Perhaps," I thought to myself, "my life has been groomed for such a moment as this."

"I recall him saying in a soft, but firm voice,

'My heart leaps with joy at finally meeting you. Elizabeth writes about you in each post, and I've been eager for our introduction. When the invitation came, I felt it was time I meet the one of whom she speaks of so highly. Now I deeply regret I didn't respond sooner.'

"My face grew warm with embarrassment, and I glanced down at the ground before gradually lifting my eyes upward, to meet his. Barely able to speak, I boldly confronted him.

"Why did you wait so long?"

"He revealed an unmistakable side-grin, then spoke in a hushed tone."

'I assure you, I have searched for you, but until now, you were not seen. Our time was coming, and though I wish it had begun earlier, I have no regrets about waiting to find you.'

"His words took my breath away. The remainder of the evening was spent in each other's company, unless he was pulled away to meet the many guests who eagerly anticipated meeting the renowned, Mr. Andrew Bartlett. After each encounter, he found me eagerly awaiting his return. As proper behavior permitted, we would resume

The Other Part of Her

dancing, laughing, and delighting in one another's company. By the end of the night, I knew he was the one for whom I was waiting."

Olivia opened her eyes, as if awakening from a dream. A dream she didn't want to forsake.

"You knew on your first meeting?" Drew shook his head as he recalled feeling the same about Hope.

"Yes. I knew he would be the man I would love through eternity." A warm glow radiated in her eyes.

"Throughout the summer, he returned to Mackinac Island several times, and we met again when I returned to New York City in early September. His residence, close to ours on Fifth Avenue, provided him the opportunity to court me with fervor. Thus, began a daily tradition: a handwritten note in a small ivory envelope would arrive, either by messenger or by Andrew, personally.

"Excuse me, Drew. I'll be back in a moment. I have something I wish to show you." Olivia bolted out of her chair and briskly crossed the room to where the antique secretary stood. A white silk container, the size of a medium gift box, was removed and carried to the dining table. When she lifted the lid, stacks of ivory envelopes tied with periwinkle blue ribbon, were nestled together like eggs in a nest. Drew couldn't speak when he saw his grandfather's flourishing handwriting.

"I would wait to read his thoughts until I was in the privacy of my room each evening," she explained. "There, I'd run my fingertips over the fine paper and his elegant pen strokes."

Tonight, decades later, Drew observed her returning, subconsciously, to the courtship ritual. With feathery touches, she delicately traced her name on the aged paper.

"Sometimes I would wait for an hour to open it, unwilling to rush the sight of his highly anticipated words. When I couldn't refrain any longer, I would read it.

"Why don't you open the one you're holding, Drew?" He hesitated, feeling as if he were intruding. She sensed his reluctance and tenderly patted his hand.

"Go ahead. You're a part of our love story."

Drew opened the envelope and removed the small handwritten card. She closed her eyes and drifted to the time seared in her memory.

"Read it to me," she said, softly.

Drew stared at the eloquent flair of ink flowing across the page and began reading. His voice trembled with emotion.

June 10, 1908
My Olivia,
Since our beginning, my heart and arms have been open
to you, and to you, alone. Even death will not separate us,
though I cannot bear the thought of being out of your presence,
my beloved, Mrs. Andrew Bartlett.
My heart, and I, will remain yours throughout eternity.
Andrew Josiah Bartlett

"That was the day of our wedding," she whispered.

Drew felt a renewal of strength. To her, it was the chronicle of a destined meeting. To him, it was a legacy bequeathed, one that would inspire and comfort him in the days ahead.

"Your meeting is very similar to one I had recently," Drew stated, quietly.

"Oh? I would love to hear about it." Her eyebrows raised; her eyes danced.

Nodding nervously, the impact of such a significant moment, one of a depth they had not shared, weighed on him.

"Hope Madison came into my world very unexpectedly, and within a very short time, I knew I'd have to find a place for her in my life. Not a temporary home, but a place where she would live forever.

"I know she'll inspire me to reach deeper and higher in the weeks and months ahead, but unfortunately, she's not able to start the journey with me. She'll be in college for two more years, while I fly around the world, jetting off aircraft carriers."

His fear of losing Hope surfaced; he paused to take a deep breath.

"For the life of me, I don't know how to keep her assured of my love. We've had so little time together." Tears began forming in his eyes. "I had planned on laying a firm foundation with the one I love, a foundation layered with faith and dreams, one that would withstand the harshness of absence."

His voice cracked like a frozen lake under a noonday sun, and he dropped his head. Errant tears were brushed with the back of his hand, as he swallowed the ones gathering in his throat.

"I'm confident of my feelings, and I'm somewhat confident of hers, but two years is a long time for her to wait. Especially, when we've had only a few weeks together."

His tortured expression, one she had never seen on him, startled the one who knew him well. She took a moment to measure her words carefully,

"I'm glad you found the one who will walk beside you for the rest of your life."

She leaned forward and softly rubbed his hand, tenderly, amazed that after a lifetime of losses, he had found someone who would bring meaning to his life. Yet, what would this mean for the two of them as he pursues his lifelong dream? For the moment, she is confused, but she knows she must trust God's timing.

"Drew, I can see you are convinced there is no other. Have you told her how you feel?"

"No. I think she feels the same, but I'm not sure." His voice rose barely above a whisper.

"I think you need to tell her. Every minute counts."

Drew nodded, gazing into his grandmother's face, the same face that had given him strength throughout his life. But tonight, amidst heartache and joy, he realized her sacrifice. He was all she had. He took a minute to let the impact be felt. Then he bent down beside her. Together, they wept.

Suddenly, after he noticed her raising her head to stare off in the distance, he recalled a scene that had played in his mind numerous times during his lifetime. More frequently when he was younger, but tonight he witnessed it again. His grandmother would gaze off into the distance, then her eyes, as green as a summer lawn, would cloud over and a soft smile would appear. Though he was small, maybe four-years-old, when the instance first occurred, a year or so later, he began inquiring about what she saw. She'd get flustered.

"I'm daydreaming," she'd say. He never knew what the dreams were, but she appeared lost to him. Now he understood. She was sensing the presence of her beloved husband and the grand love they shared, the kind of love that artists, musicians and writers create, the kind he desperately wanted. The kind that kept one moving forward amidst difficult circumstances.

Olivia turned to him, aware that a storm was brewing in the squint of his eyes and in his unsteady voice.

"There are many stories about military men breaking their girlfriends' hearts," his shaking voice wavering between fury and sadness. "I don't want that reputation, and I never want Hope to question my intentions. It's not who I am, but what if she thinks this is a lighthearted fling, my last attempt at love before flying to places unknown? I can't allow such thoughts to enter her mind."

Olivia, feeling helpless and broken by his anguish, removed a linen handkerchief from the sleeve on her dress, where she sometimes tucked it.

Drew began pacing around the room. This was his habit when ambiguity impeded certainty.

"How will I be able to reassure her of my devotion? Do you have any suggestions?"

"Open the valve of your heart freely," she said quietly. "Feelings build like steam and words will help ease the distance."

Olivia stared into her past, visualizing once again, the messenger arriving at her home with an ivory envelope. The power of love implemented with words!

She composed herself, though at that moment her heart lay shattered. Her halting words, in the wake of loss, were barely understood.

"A woman yearns to hear the emotional, vulnerable part of a man. Stand proudly with men like your grandfather. Let your heart shine in the distance and above all, reassure her. Let her know the oceans dividing you will be the same waters bringing you home."

Relief filled his eyes while Olivia Bartlett wiped tears from hers.

EIGHT

The next morning, Drew rushed through a quick shower then hurriedly gathered the leftovers out of the refrigerator. His grandmother always prepared enough for him to take back to the dorm, but he was a bit concerned when he observed Olivia, and a large breakfast, waiting for him. Out of courtesy, he consumed half of it while checking his watch every few minutes. He needed to get on the road.

Drew reached the Boulder city limits with restored confidence. Fresh in his mind were the notes from his grandfather. Beginning today, and during the remaining days, he would immerse Hope in loving messages with the dream that they, too, would someday occupy a box covered in fabric from her own wedding dress.

He turned a corner and suddenly realized he had driven to the Madison's home, not the dorm. He thought it discourteous to appear without calling, but here he was, staring at Hope's house, wondering if his unannounced presence would risk her displeasure. Hoping it would not, he took a deep breath and exited the car.

Hope met him at the door, surprising him with a half-smile and sad eyes. It was not the greeting he visualized. A speedy trip up the canyon ensued with only a few words spoken. Occasionally, he offered a few highlights about his trip home; Hope would nod absently.

A vacant area, by a crystal blue mountain stream and lofty evergreens, prompted him to pull over. He took her hand as they walked toward the water. They left their shoes on the bank, then carefully made their way to a fallen tree trunk that was lying in the cold stream, white with age and smooth from the river waters.

Hope's restrained detachment weighed on him. Distant and cool, she swished her bare feet among amber pebbles lying in the underwash. They stared at the small stones rising to the top like gold glitter. A clumsy stillness grew. Eventually, Drew's face was lost in confusion. Had his sudden appearance stirred contention?

"Hope, please tell me what's wrong. Have I done something to upset you?"

Quivering, she swallowed unreleased sobs. He pulled her close until she found her voice. Then she pulled away and stared at the water.

"It's nothing you've done," she said, weakly. "It's what I learned while you were away. We're going on a family trip to Europe. Not for a two-week vacation, or even a month. It will last the entire summer!" An expression of horror covered her face.

Drew immediately noticed her skin was drained of color, and her eyes were wide with fury.

She had visualized communications streaming from him. Now, she felt despair settling on shoulders that were no longer erect.

"Drew, I can't imagine anything more dismal than traipsing through museums, packing, unpacking, multiple airplanes, rigorous schedules, different cities, foreign languages, all under the supervision of my mother.

"A few hours after being given the news, I brightened at the thought of spending time with Daddy. When I told Mother as much, she gave me more grim news. 'He'll be unavailable. This is a business trip, and many foreign companies are expecting him'."

Hope moaned, unwilling to confess the root of her fear: Would her relationship with Drew end when they parted ways?

A sense of panic settled into her body. Her hands and face grew clammy with perspiration. Her nerves jittered. Even if he wrote, she thought to herself, she wouldn't be able to read them until the end of the summer.

Saddened by thoughts of loss, she leaned into his shoulder under the late afternoon sun, and memorized the warmth of his skin, plus the sound of his deep voice. A light breeze was blowing through the giant evergreens, leaving a scent of pine trailing.

Eventually, she offered another explanation for her disposition.

"The Europe trip sounds dreadful. It's certainly not the relaxing break from school I envisioned, but they have added more, as if that's not enough."

"Oh?" he asked.

"Yes. My sister, Riley, will join us. I love her, but unfortunately when she and Mother are together it becomes a three-ring circus." Her voice lowered; her puckered brow increased.

"I'm reeling from the proposed itinerary because it immediately resurrects memories of a shopping trip Mother organized for the three of us a few years back. I think we hit every fashion house in New York City. After a week, I vowed never to endure such frenetic activity again."

Tears began rolling down her face. Drew tenderly wiped them away.

"This will be more of the same, but instead of it being for seven days, Riley will be with us two weeks. Then I'll follow my mother's rigorous schedule for another six weeks. We aren't returning until August, a few weeks prior to my departure for college."

He pulled her closer, threatened by the miles and continents that would invade their lives. He, too, was worried and tried hard not to reveal the battle within. Tenderly, he brushed her forehead with a kiss and gently stroked her back.

"I apologize, Drew. I must sound like a spoiled child, but it's not the right time for such a trip. At least, not for me."

The blazing sun began its descent behind the mountains, as his mouth curved into a smile. "You better reserve quite a bit of spare time when you return."

"Why? You'll be gone." The harsh words made her nauseous. "*Gone*," so absolute, so final. A thought she couldn't bear.

"For reading my letters," he whispered. "You'll have more than you can count."

She smiled through sad eyes, as he placed a hastily written note in her lap. Her trembling fingertips swept across the gold monogram.

"What do the initials AJB stand for?"

"Andrew Josiah Bartlett. My ancestor, Josiah Bartlett was one of the patriots who signed the Declaration of Independence. My grandfather and father bear his name, as well."

"So that makes you Andrew Josiah Bartlett, the third?" she asked, smiling broadly.

"Yes, and I would like to have a fourth," he added, mischievously. She flushed, as she carefully opened the envelope.

May 5, 1959

My Dearest Hope,

You have indeed captured my heart.

Drew

Her breath caught. His reassuring surprise provided the words she desperately needed.

He gently kissed her lips, before changing the subject. "How'd you get the name, 'Hope'?"

"It's a long story, but I'll be as succinct as possible." She turned to face him, letting one leg dangle in the water. The other leg, pulled into her chest, was wrapped in her arms.

"My parents had my sister, Riley. A little over a year later Mother gave birth to another daughter named Shelly." Sadness crept into her tone. "At the age of three, Shelly suddenly became ill and died within days."

Hope stared mutely at the river before continuing.

"In the following years, after Shelly's death, Mother had two miscarriages. Consumed with grief and feelings of helplessness, Mother became despondent until one of her friends recommended adopting a child. Mother gave her physician the news. He listened, reserving his own words of advice until the end.

'Do not give up on having another child,' he encouraged. 'You are able to carry a healthy baby to full term, that we know.'

"Feelings of hope overflowed when she left his office. I was born the following year and named before I took my first breath."

Drew flashed her a grin. "Your mother has certainly been through a lot of heartache."

"Yes, but her unwavering faith has made it possible to navigate the storms."

"… and she's passed that on to you."

"Yes, I'm inspired by her calm. During times of uncertainty, I have often heard her quote an abbreviated version of her favorite Bible verse, 'For I know the plans I have for you, plans to give you hope and a future.'

Hope stared into his eyes, "I feel confident should I ever experience pain and loss, God will lead me to where I'm to be."

Drew pulled her into his chest where he held her until darkness fell around them.

The next few days were consumed with numerous challenges; however, Drew's hectic schedule didn't prevent him from pulling stolen moments to be with Hope, like a ripcord on a parachute. His desire to be with her grew with every passing moment.

On a cool, crisp morning, Drew remained quiet when he turned the Corvette toward Estes Park, and the towering mountains edged with flowing rivers. Hope huddled next to him, tense, watching him maneuver the constant changing of gears on the steep ascent. His graduation, the event he had highly anticipated for most of his life, weighed heavily on his mind. Leaving for the Navy would follow almost immediately. Two weeks remained.

Walking hand in hand around Estes Park, before settling into a corner booth at their favorite pizza parlor, each stared at the Stanley Hotel, off in the distance. Quietly, the two relived how the day, and the hotel, had been stitched into their personal history.

Drew turned to her with eyes full of emotion, as he posed a question, one he had never anticipated asking prior to their meeting at the Whitmire's home. Now, his life lay divided in two distinct categories: "Before Hope" and "After Hope."

"Would you like to attend my Commissioning Ceremony and Graduation?" His turquoise eyes sparkled. "If so, I would be honored to have you attach my shoulder boards. This act is generally performed by someone who is very significant in the officer's life, perhaps his mother, wife, or girlfriend. In my humble opinion, there's none as significant as you."

Hope fought for calmness, though an explosion of excitement ravaged her body.

"It would be my honor to attach your shoulder boards, Ensign Andrew Bartlett, and to be by your side throughout the day."

Following lunch, Drew surprised her with another question while they slowly meandered down the sidewalk.

"Would you like to learn how to drive my car?"

Her mouth flew open in surprise as she stammered with an answer.

"Y-Yes!"

A few minutes outside of town, he pulled off the road onto a gravel area and hopped out. He held the door open while Hope quickly slid behind the steering wheel, under a clear blue Colorado sky. He had begun to revel in her appetite for challenges. It had become obvious that behind a reserved exterior, she thrived in exploiting each moment until it was starved of the elements. Then she'd go to the next and live it the same way, as if she couldn't get enough vibrancy into each second.

He observed her hair blowing in the wind, the exultation on her face when she shifted gears, and eventually, the ease she felt when she mastered driving the car. Fear didn't seem to exist in her body, as she drove down the twisting mountain roads.

In a moment of spontaneity, he picked up her camera and captured her joyful expression. She pressed her foot down on the accelerator as they entered a flat, open area.

"I feel like a race car driver," she yelled.

His heart staggered at the thought of leaving her.

NINE

Hope hurriedly raced down the stairs and threw open the front door before the doorbell completed its chime.

"I'm so sorry I'm late! I can't believe it's the night of the dance." Sarah was standing on the porch with her hair in brush rollers, carrying her formal and a cosmetic bag, as she apologized profusely.

"My date for tonight called and I couldn't be rude, so we chatted awhile."

Hope chuckled, and took the dress, holding it high so it wouldn't drag the ground, while offering words of encouragement. "Don't worry, Sarah. We still have plenty of time."

"I hate blind dates," Sarah moaned. "My brother assures me he's a good guy, that we'll hit it off…but what if we don't? I sure hope he likes to dance!"

Hope, running up the stairs yelled over her shoulder,

"Sarah, when did you NOT hit it off with someone? You're Miss Congeniality."

Sarah raised her eyebrows while Hope carefully spread the royal blue dress across the bed.

"I'm glad you arrived when you did. Odie B has our dinner ready," Hope said.

"Oh, I can't wait to eat Odie B's cooking. No one compares, not even Julia Child!" Sarah stated breathlessly as she tried to keep up with Hope's long stride as they went down the stairs.

"Sarah, when did you have Julia Child's cooking?" Hope teased.

"I haven't, but my mother creates Julia's latest breads, baguettes, croissants, and her French Onion soup weekly. It's like we live in a French bakery. Tonight, she is serving Quiche Lorraine, whatever that is," Sarah groaned.

"I haven't had the heart to inform her of Odie B's culinary talents. We all know she surpasses the professionals. Even Julia!"

On cue, Odie B entered the dining room, carrying a pitcher of tea.

"You've outdone yourself, Odie B!" Sarah's enthusiasm spilled over, while Hope proudly nodded in agreement. "I can't believe the fresh flowers, formal table linens, candles, china and crystal stemware. The silver serving dishes are shining like diamonds. It must have taken you a week to prepare." Sarah jumped out of her chair and hugged Odie B.

"It's true!" Hope exclaimed with delight, "You've not omitted one detail in honor of this special evening. Thank you!"

"I'm glad you girls like it." Odie B wiped her moist eyes with the ironed handkerchief she pulled out of her apron, before hurriedly returning to the kitchen. Moments later she presented them with two plates, each filled with a roasted chicken breast, scalloped potatoes, asparagus, and a mixed green salad. Hot homemade rolls, tucked in a linen napkin, arrived in a silver bowl.

"Sarah, just wait until dessert! I saw what she was making, and it looks heavenly."

Thirty minutes later Odie B strutted in with a dessert called, "Floating Island." The girls gaped while Odie B explained the origin.

"See that white dollop in the middle," Odie B pointed to the center of the plate, "It's baked meringue and it's swimmin' around all happy-like in Crème Anglaise, a vanilla custard." Odie B held her neck up high, "I got it out of my new Betty Crocker cookbook, the one Mrs. Madison gave me for Christmas."

Hope and Sarah stared at the creation in reverent awe, while licking their lips. A few minutes later, Hope nervously checked her watch and laid her spoon across the empty plate.

"We better get upstairs. The guys will be here before we know it, and you still have my hair to do. Oh, Sarah, I hope you can manage to get my hair into a French twist. The length is there, but it's about as manageable as a busted feather pillow."

Hope's bedroom, filled with a mahogany canopy bed draped in white lace and robin-egg blue floral paper on the walls, transitioned into a beauty parlor while Sarah pulled, twisted, yanked, and sprayed Hope's long hair. Eventually, the golden hair was tamed into the confines of a proper twist, but not without Hope occasionally questioning the process. Afterwards, Sarah began quickly applying a hint of rouge to Hope's cheeks, mascara to her almond-shaped eyes, frosted pink lipstick to her full pouty lips and a touch of powder to her flawless, ivory skin.

"For the final touch," Mrs. Madison said, as she entered the room with a bottle of expensive French perfume. She eagerly squirted the fragrance behind their ears. Hope sensed her mother's excitement, as she directed them with parting words.

"Hope, don't keep the boys waiting."

The sound of the doorbell, as if on cue, rattled Hope's nerves, to the point she couldn't draw breath. Sporadic gasps of air accompanied the frightened expression on her face.

"Sarah, can you please greet the guys?"

Hope's ashen face and eyes wide with fear startled Sarah.

"Are you okay?" Sarah asked in a hush voice.

Hope nodded motioning for her to go.

"Okay, but let me know if you need me," Sarah's concern escalated. She had never seen Hope like this. Nor anyone, for that matter.

Sarah scurried down the steps and within minutes, Hope could hear her bubbly laughter, next to Drew's low-pitched voice as he greeted her parents. The sound of her mother, shrilling like a magpie, as if she were attending a once-in-a-lifetime event, came as a shock. But she couldn't hear her daddy. Where was he?

Hope had been aware of the anxiety building throughout the day, but she felt it had been successfully squashed. Until the sound of the doorbell triggered crippling insecurities.

Her heart began pounding out of her body. Her breaths were shallow and rapid. Trembling, she reached for a tissue to wipe the sweat off her face while trying not to ruin her make-up. However, the incessant questions kept coming, *"What if we can't dance well together? What if he hangs out with the guys and leaves me alone at the table? What if..."*

She began wishing she could be transformed into Riley, her gregarious sister, or glorious Sarah. Both were radiant beings treading the earth with ease.

Drew, waiting in the entry hall attired in his dress-white uniform, made light conversation with Sarah and her date while nervously checking his watch. His concern began to mount as more time lapsed.

"Is she alright, Sarah? This is unlike her." He kept his voice low.

"She's fine, Drew. Just gilding the lily." Sarah's eyes were shining.

Hope was envisioning her mother impatiently tapping her right foot, narrowing her lips with disapproval and her eyes flickering with irritation.

Drew nervously glanced at the top of the stairs, then at Hope's father, thinking him distant, almost cold. His monosyllabic answers spoke of an unwillingness to communicate. Instead, he was clenching an expensive pipe between his teeth and reaching for a silver monogrammed lighter to ignite the tobacco every few minutes. Circles of smoke and silence floated between them.

Unknown to anyone else, Mr. Madison's paternal instincts had burst into flame. The impressive young man, something he didn't expect, was a threat; stories of military men boasting about 'a girl in every port' were as prevalent as their uniforms. And the thought of Drew possibly breaking Hope's heart sent him pacing near the grand piano.

Odie B was standing in the background, near the kitchen, waiting eagerly to see Hope in her formal. When she observed Mr. Madison being as fidgety as a racehorse, pacing back and forth, and his face as red as a fire engine, concern enveloped her.

At that moment, standing at the top of the elegant staircase, under a sparkling chandelier, was Hope. She took a deep breath before gliding down the steps with grace and refinement. She heard gasps of astonishment fill the room. Her thin waistline accented by the fitted bodice, the billowing skirt, long white gloves, and pearls, along with her regal carriage gave the appearance of royalty. A soundless conversation with Drew spoke of dreams long held.

Drew moved to the bottom of the stairs. His stoic expression, one that came naturally when in uniform, remained, but like ice under a blazing sun, his reserve melted into a broad, unguarded grin, as she got closer. Gallantly seizing both of her hands in his, she quickly took the last two steps. Her face burned when his eyes glanced from the bareness of her shoulders to her slender neck. Bending closer, he whispered in her ear,

"Had you been born into nobility it would have fit you well."

In that defining moment Hope promised her heart to Andrew Bartlett III, the only one who could fulfill her every longing and every fantasy she held close.

Hope turned, and Drew briefly stared at her eyes. She found breathing difficult.

At seven o'clock, they strolled into the Trocadero with their hands entwined. The famous Guy Lombardo orchestra was playing "Blue Skies," Mr. Madison's favorite song. Instantly, Hope recalled her father singing it on long car trips, but she quickly diverted her thoughts. The cool reception he had given them when they left, still hurt. She stared at the dense crowd instead, and the beautiful decor. Along with the unique architecture, there were bold colorful flowers painted on green arches.

Drew scanned the enormous ballroom for his Navy buddies. Unsuccessful in locating them, due to the hundreds of people in the room, they began walking. As they did, Hope observed the variance in dress: Guys wore jackets and ties, in accord with the dress code, and the girls wore everything from casual skirts, bobby socks and loafers, to full-length formals. The age range varied as much as the clothing. Teenagers, plus couples with silver hair, dotted the room.

"I see them in the corner, sitting at a long table," Drew said.

Together they began zigzagging through the crowd with him still holding her hand. After reaching the guys and their dates, Drew introduced Hope. She noticed that Sarah and her date were hitting it off, as best as she could tell, and the other guys, including Ken, were in high spirits, laughing and talking about flying. Their dates were clustered in a corner, their eyes lingering on Drew. He couldn't help but notice, so he gripped Hope's hand tighter. Then he grabbed a chair at the end of the table and pulled it out for her before promptly sitting down and casually draping his arm around her. She could feel his attentiveness.

Ken sent him a non-verbal message. It was the same one he had delivered to all the Navy guys. Drew, quiet and confident, ignored him and turned to Hope.

"May I have this dance?" He was up and pulling out her chair before she could answer. When he pulled her into him, his insides wound into a tight ball. As they danced, Drew whispered in her ear,

"You're as light as air, Hope."

"Thank you. I'll tell Daddy. He's the one responsible; I've been dancing with him since I learned to walk."

"Don't sell yourself short. He may have taught you the steps, but you are a natural. I've been observing your movements since the first night we met." His words were quiet and confident.

"You have?" She blushed, but with newborn confidence, she locked eyes with him and continued the quiet conversation. "It helps to have a good leader," she said.

"Thank you. My grandmother insisted I take ballroom dancing lessons in the seventh and eighth grades. Tonight, I'm grateful." He smiled as his arm tightened around her waist.

Hope continued to lose herself in his embrace, feeling the pressure of his hand as he guided her to the music. In the middle of a turn, she noticed shadows of envy in the eyes of other women. At one point, Hope excused herself. Drew took the moment to talk to the bandleader. As he walked away, Ken grabbed him. His face was flushed, his square jaw firm. Drew braced himself for a sermon regarding Hope.

"Drew, you're like a brother to me, so I'm going to give you some advice."

Drew's arms hung stiffly by his side; his fists were clenched in a ball. His face was growing hot, as he stared directly into Ken's face. He was furious that his best friend would lecture him, especially on this night.

"Drew, if you don't marry that girl, as soon as you get out of pilot training, I will." Before Drew could absorb the fact that Ken was teasing, he delivered another message.

"She is the most beautiful girl here. I've always thought of her as my other 'sister' however, tonight that all changed. Hope is gorgeous and it's easy to see you two have something special. I don't know what it is, but don't let her get away!"

Ken slapped him on the back and returned to the table. Drew was still standing in the same place when Hope returned. He took her by the hand, guiding her back out on the dance floor, as he waved across the room. At that moment the band began playing his request, "Sing, Sing, Sing."

"What kind of Swing dance do you prefer, m' lady?" He made a grand gesture of bowing while extending his hand.

"My favorite is the Lindy Hop!" With an exaggerated flourish, she held her head high, as she placed her gloved hand in his.

"Then let's show them how it's done."

"How what's done?"

"THIS!"

He twirled her into a spin, and she instinctively fell into step. Without a word, Hope anticipated every move, lift, spin, twist, swing, kick, and flip. Drew felt she resembled a beautiful doll, bendable and light on her feet. The crowd on the dance floor quickly thinned, but Drew caught the sight, out of the corner of his eye, of people lining the edge of the dance floor, clapping. He and Hope were the only two left dancing. Afterwards, the band and the crowd gave them a standing ovation. Ken shook his head in disbelief.

An elderly couple strolled toward them, holding hands. She wore a white corsage, he, a boutonniere.

"Hello, are you celebrating a special occasion?" Drew asked. She reminded him of his grandmother.

"Yes, we are." The lady, with a twinkle in her eye smiled, as her husband boasted proudly.

"It's our forty-first wedding anniversary."

"Congratulations," Hope and Drew said in unison.

"Thank you. We're the Barkers," he boomed, while extending his hand to Drew.

When Drew introduced Hope as his girlfriend, the slightly stooped gentleman's eyes shone with eagerness.

"Girlfriend, uh? Good job, Son. We've been coming here since we met in 1918 at the USO. I had just come back from the war and the Trocadero was brand new. It's our tradition to return each year on our anniversary."

"That's wonderful!" Hope said.

"How long have you two young kids been dancing together?"

"This is our first time." Drew, standing tall and proud, squeezed Hope's hand.

Mr. Barker rocked back on his heels, until he found his voice.

"First time? That's hard to believe, but you two have what we call 'the magic.' Not many people have it, not like you two do, but we hope you are dancing together for another fifty years, at least."

"Thank you, sir. I plan on dancing with her that long, and even longer." Drew winked at Hope before changing the subject.

"Mr. Barker, I heard you mention the USO. Which branch of service?"

"Army Air Corps. Pilot."

"Wow! You guys have always been my heroes, along with the inspiration for my goal to serve as a pilot. I'm confident there's nothing in comparison to being in air combat with flimsy planes, no protective covering, and seeing the enemy's eyes when they aim their guns at you. Grateful you made it home, sir."

"Thanks. When I returned, she was selling "Forget-Me-Not" flowers at the USO. Four weeks later we eloped."

"Four weeks?" Drew and Hope turned toward each other. Both realized it to be the length of time they had known each other.

"Yes. It was love at first sight. We wouldn't have waited, but her daddy said she couldn't marry until she was eighteen. Four weeks later, on her birthday, we were standing in front of the Justice of the Peace. Been together ever since." Mr. Barker's reached around his wife's back, pulling her into him.

"We love our men in uniform, don't we?" Mrs. Barker said, as she leaned over and patted Hope's hand.

"Yes, we certainly do," Hope replied.

Mr. Barker then turned to Drew with concern in his eyes.

"I sure hope President Eisenhower will be able to give you the support you're going to need. Unfortunately, it's his last year in office, and it looks like most of you young boys will be going to Vietnam, after pilot training."

"Thank you, sir. I feel confident we will have the support of the President, as well as the people in this great nation, the United States of America."

TEN

The following afternoon Drew raced to Hope's home and minutes later they were on top of Flagstaff Mountain discussing their future careers: his as a Navy fighter pilot, hers as a photographer.

"When I'm old, I want to share a love that speaks to the next generation and beyond. A love story on film," she stated, quietly. He was feeling confident that he'd be the one to give life to her dreams.

A refreshing breeze broke the still air as Hope snapped several pictures of the valley below, until a sudden shift in the wind took their attention. Drew quickly realized the towering cumulonimbus clouds were ready to bring thunder, lightning, hard wind and rain.

He grabbed Hope's hand and began to look for shelter. As the rain began to pour, he observed what appeared to be a cave beneath giant boulders.

"Hold on to me," he bellowed. "We're going over there."

Thunderclouds pounded the sky like roaring, vicious lions while heavy raindrops, the size of small stones, pelted their bodies. When they reached the cave, he immediately wrapped his arms around her trembling body, comforting her with words of assurance, hiding his fear and knowledge that lightning frequently kills people in higher elevations.

She remained calm, shaken, but calm.

"You're a true adventurer, Hope," he said admiringly.

Still holding the one he never wanted to release from his grasp, he gently removed wet strands of hair away from her face.

"These types of storms don't usually last long," he assured her.

She found comfort in his soothing voice and lean, athletic body. Eventually, he released her to make a place for them to sit. He was able to find some suitable dry brush.

"Now we can sit down."

Startled by his voice, she jumped and kept standing.

"What's wrong, Hope?"

"Nothing. I was just lost in thought, and the echo startled me." Her words, flowing like a stream of rich molasses, were hiding the fact she never wanted to leave his presence, a new feeling for her.

"What were you thinking?"

When she saw his teasing eyes and side-grin, she ducked her head in embarrassment, her face and neck turning red, of course. He nodded, grinning.

She felt her heart pounding when he sat down on the damp ground and reached up for her hand. Gently lowering her next to him, Hope curled her shivering body next to his, as ear-splitting claps of thunder shook the earth.

While they waited for the rain to stop, he shared how he once waited out spring storms in mountain caves when he was young.

"Were you afraid?"

"Yes. I never knew what monsters might be lurking, but when I shared the experience with my grandmother, it was always with an attitude of bravado."

They both chuckled, but suddenly a bolt of lightning flashed near the cave entrance. Drew tightened his hold on her.

"Tell me about your life, Drew," she whispered.

He took a deep breath. Like sand being poured in careful measure, the pain had crawled down to the depths of his soul, and it had nowhere else to go. There it had stayed.

"When I was six years old, my mother died." Hope felt the deep ache in his heart, as he began to talk.

"We were standing on a street corner when a car jumped the curb. She saved my life by pushing me out of the way, but the car hit her, and she died a short time later in the hospital." He paused, pulling her closer.

"I have no memory of this, but it is what I was told."

"I'm so sorry." She placed his large hand in hers and waited for more.

"After the accident, my father, a doctor, immersed himself into his medical practice during the day, and a bottle of Scotch at night." A familiar knot formed in his stomach. "I was too young to understand his withdrawal, but I rarely saw him after the accident."

"Who took care of you?"

"My grandmother came from New York. I can still remember the exact moment she pulled into our driveway. I dashed out the door into her arms.

"A year later my father remarried, and my grandmother moved to a home of her own, three blocks away."

"Why would she leave?"

"The new wife relished the role of being married to a highly respected physician in the community, but not the role of stepmother." Hurt still lingered in his eyes.

"Drew, that's horrible!"

He nodded.

"A week after my grandmother moved from our home, I packed a suitcase with games, books, one pair of pajamas, and my stuffed bear, then I walked to her house. I remember standing on tiptoe, as I stretched my arm to reach the doorbell. When she answered, I marched in, plopped down on her sofa, and crossed my arms. In a firm, six-year-old voice, I announced that I had come to live with her. She immediately raced to the phone and called my dad. After a brief conversation, he agreed it would be best for me to remain with her, since she had been the one immersing me with parental care. I recall hearing her trembling voice, as she thanked him profusely.

Then I watched as she wiped her eyes with the handkerchief she kept in her sleeve.

"Did you ever have a chance to see your dad?"

Drew sat motionless, staring at shallow pools of water forming in the cave.

"Dad took me on a few camping and fishing trips. These times are seared into my brain, due to the rarity of having his attention. But growing up in a small town where my grandmother filled the roles of mother and father, I felt different, unlike others who had parents and siblings. Everything changed after Mother's death." He closed his eyes, blinking the unshed tears away.

"Embedded in my memory, is the vision of my grandmother sitting in the bleachers, cheering me on loudly and tirelessly. Sports were my passion. I was hers."

Taking a deep breath, he leaned his head against the wall. Hope sat silent, absorbing the devastation in his voice. After a while, she inquired further.

"Did you have a girlfriend in high school?"

"No," he chuckled. "Girls were a mystery to me, but I would take a date to the important events. When I got to college, my football team pulled me through."

"Your football team?" Speechless, she stared at him.

"Yes, all I had to do was tell the squad I needed a date, and they would volunteer their sisters, friends, and ex-girlfriends. They set me up all four years." Their laughter ricocheted against the damp walls of the cave.

In a serious tone, he added, "I did date one girl my junior year in college, but I broke it off when I realized she wasn't the one for me." Hope gave him an inquiring glance, but when he didn't volunteer details, she remained quiet.

The Other Part of Her

Drew gazed out the cave opening while trying to swallow the tears clinging to his throat. The wind was blowing giant evergreen trees sideways, as heavy rain fell in solid sheets. After a lengthy pause, measured words came slowly, filled with raw emotion.

"My father never came to any of my football games, even though I was the quarterback and team captain. My grandmother would propose an excuse for his behavior, which was always the same. 'He was on duty at the hospital', she'd say. I'm not sure that was true, at least, not all the time."

He swiped the ground with his hand in disgust.

"When the pain became so deep because of his shunning me, I talked about quitting football, but my grandmother insisted I continue.

His head began to throb when agonizing, long suppressed feelings began to force their way into his mind. Memories of the rejection, the embarrassment, and the loneliness made him shudder. He took a deep breath.

"Due to my grandmother's encouragement, I was successful in football, academics, and Boy Scouts, which led to my being given a full Naval ROTC scholarship to the University of Colorado, and a place on their football team."

He took a deep breath. "All I've accomplished, I owe to God and to my grandmother." The tremor in his voice crackled; tears welled.

Hope was stunned by Drew's proficiency at covering a lifetime of holes and empty spaces with a list of achievements. Each were accomplished with humility and faith.

"I really admire you," she whispered.

Shaking his head, he paused to gather his thoughts - the ones he wanted her to always remember.

"Hope, do you know how you've transformed my life in the short time we've been together?"

The question hung in the air.

"When I look into your eyes, I feel an immediate desire to know more about you, to share life with you. I've fallen in love with you, Hope."

Tenderly, he placed his hands around her face and kissed her. Without words, he penned a book. After a deep breath, and with a raspy voice, Drew shared what he knew to be certain, beyond any doubt.

"I cannot visualize my life without you, not for a day. You have come to me unexpectedly, like a dream, and changed my world. My life will never be the same. You are what I've longed for, and never knew existed. My dream of becoming a pilot is soon to be realized. But I secretly harbor a larger dream: to be a husband and a father. I want to give my children what I missed, and to build a life with the woman I love."

Hope's luminous smile revealed understanding. He paused to soak up the fragrance of her before continuing.

"Hope, do you know how much it would mean to have you waiting for me and how it would impact my performance as a pilot? My resolve to survive conflicts around the globe would be strengthened by thoughts of you, of us, and our future together. Don't get me wrong. This isn't just about me. I want you to live your life in full measure while I'm away…" He fought for composure.

"But it will be your face bringing me home. Whether it is in the darkest hours of war, or in the dazzling light of victory, you'll be my compass."

Gazing at him through a veil of tears, Hope breathed in slowly and swallowed hard. She knew he was the man she had prayed for, the one she would marry; however, the thought of being transparent about her feelings was as alien as the surface of the moon.

The Other Part of Her

Desperately, she tried to summon the courage to be vulnerable and truthful, to respond to his outpouring of words. Finally, she did what she had never done before, as she nervously stared into his eyes.

"Drew, I want you to know with complete assurance in both my mind and heart, I'll wait for you. This brief time together, I am realizing has been part of God's overall plan." She glanced downward, rubbing his hand gently before continuing. "And I also believe we've been given a glimpse of what can be ours in the future. Until then, we will have memories to warm us and dreams to fuel us."

A bright future emerged within the dim, shadowy cave. They felt every dream of theirs was possible. Shoving painful thoughts of a long separation into the background, they could only pray there would be a map that would lead them back to each other.

ELEVEN

Drew stood on the front porch anxiously ringing the Madison's doorbell. He held a cream-colored envelope behind his back. Hope threw open the door, surprised by his unexpected arrival, but any concerns quickly vanished when she saw the grin spreading across his face.

"I wanted you to have this prior to the graduation ceremony." He placed the envelope in her hands.

"Thank you, Drew." She quickly glanced behind her before responding. "I am looking forward to the day with great anticipation." Her luminous smile created a wave of emotions in him.

Leaning forward, quietly speaking, he said, "I never dreamed of the possibility that you would be with me on my graduation day." He stopped and shook his head. "It means everything to me, Hope. Everything!"

The sincerity in his voice captured her attention, as she responded, "It will be an honor for me to be there, Drew." Reaching for his hand, she warmly squeezed it.

Drew galloped back down the steps, as his voice trailed in the wind, "See you in a couple of hours."

Hope dashed up the stairs, her heart racing with renewed confidence. Andrew Bartlett had been the answer to a lifetime of voids and longings. He had pursued her with intent, even to the end of his time there in Colorado.

Laying the envelope on her dresser, she began her rituals: a warm bath, rolling her hair in brush curlers, laying out the dress that had arrived from Neiman's, her panty girdle which snapped to sheer stockings and the dreaded addition of her new merry widow bra. All the while, the envelope lay still, like a buried treasure.

The delay in opening letters, she recalled, began with her daddy's frequent trips overseas. Before opening his correspondence, she would lay it on her dresser, where Drew's note now lay, and there she would study the foreign stamp, the postmark, the gliding penmanship. Then, after her daily tasks and dawdling were completed, she would open it and revel in her daddy's words, colorful descriptions, and loving closures. She knew she would do the same anticipatory ritual with Drew's letters.

After applying make up the way Sarah taught her, including the pink frosted lipstick to her full lips, Hope smoothed the fitted, white linen dress over her shapely figure. She then stepped into sandal-strap high heels and fastened the clasp prior to taking a few steps. They slithered off her heels, so she changed the clasp and tested again, until she was certain of the fit. Then she ran a brush through her pageboy hairstyle, letting it flow softly past her shoulders.

Only then did she, with trembling fingers, reach for the note and slowly slip one finger under the seal, taking care not to rip the envelope. Her heart pounded against the constraints of the merry widow corset, the dreaded device Miss Bain sent to flatten her bust; Hope's breathing quickened when Drew's unique penmanship, direct and straight, was now recognizable to her.

My Dearest Hope,
Today, the past, the present and the future come together
with you, my grandmother, and I sharing this pivotal moment.
The future, with two incredible women by my side, is bound with
a golden thread into my heart forever. With great eagerness, I
await the day when the golden thread is not just in my heart, but
only a heartbeat away.
My love,
Drew

Hope read it several times, smiling wider with each reading. She placed it in the drawer where his notes were gathering. Then she quickly grabbed her purse, pausing to sift through the contents for lipstick and the car keys, before posing for a few photos for her mother.

"When does Drew leave?" Her dad, standing out of camera range, startled Hope with the question. To her ears, the inquiry carried more than curiosity; it seemed to be edged with a twinge of resentment. Immediately Hope became as pale as a pearl and her transparent eyes lost their glow.

It appeared at that moment that Kathryn was flashing a silent scolding to her husband, a very rare occurrence. Tennessee ducked his head and turned his attention to filling his pipe.

"Drew leaves in two days," Hope whispered.

She tried to shove her daddy's question to the far corners of her mind, while she navigated the car in the direction of the university, and then to the designated rendezvous point. When she caught sight of Drew, towering over the parked cars, excitement pulsated through her body. He quickly ushered his grandmother over to Hope's car and made the introductions, before sliding in behind the wheel.

Hope noticed his tongue and nerves seemed to be faltering, but his eyes never did.

"Thank you again, Hope, for the use of your car today." Drew glanced at her with a grin that spread into his crinkling eyes.

"I appreciate your solving the dilemma when I realized my two-seater wouldn't accommodate the three of us."

"Of course. It's my pleasure, Drew."

Olivia, sitting in the back seat, her eyes brimming with delight, reached up and patted Hope's bare shoulder. Her affirming touch sparked a strong connection between the two women. Both loved

Drew unconditionally and instantly, Hope felt herself a part of their small family circle.

Minutes later, Hope and Olivia were seated, staring at the Ensign candidates standing in formation. The cloudless, sunny morning and light breeze allowed for comfort as the Commanding Officer administered the Oath of Office to the group. Then the name, Andrew Bartlett III was announced, and the two ladies walked forward, arm in arm.

Hope held Olivia's hand as they approached the lectern. Drew had asked her to join his grandmother in doing the honors.

"Attaching the insignia for Ensign Andrew Bartlett will be his grandmother, Olivia Bartlett, plus Miss Hope Madison," stated the Commanding Officer.

Today, the two most important women in his life were now standing on either side of him, each snapping a shoulder board onto his uniform. Hope couldn't help but observe his slight smile. He saluted, did an about face, and Ensign Andrew Bartlett, an officer in the United States Navy, returned to formation.

That afternoon, Hope and Olivia were seated side-by-side in the Folsom Field stadium when Drew, and a group of eighty-seven new officers in their dress-white uniforms, entered to the rendering of "Pomp and Circumstance" by the Colorado University band and orchestra. A large group of graduates were clad in traditional academic robes.

Olivia reached over and gripped Hope's hand when they heard, "Ensign Andrew Bartlett III" announced. Drew, looking taller in the white uniform, covered the ground between his seat and the stage in a few steps. Olivia abruptly felt an immense longing for her husband, and absent son, Drew's father. Each was a legacy for the name, Andrew Josiah Bartlett.

For all intents and purposes, she had lost both men.

The Other Part of Her

This pivotal ceremony impacted each one there. For Hope, it meant counting the days until she would receive her diploma. It also meant Drew would be asking for her hand in marriage, the moment she had only dreamed of in her young life.

"I've made dinner reservations for us at the Flagstaff House," Drew stated, as they walked to the car.

"Oh, wonderful, Drew," Olivia enthused. "I have such fond memories of dining there with you during your freshman year. I still recall the breathtaking views and the elegance. Their attention to detail is reminiscent of the era your grandfather and I shared."

"Yes, it continues to grow in renown and the unique setting, nestled on the mountainside, makes it a dining event like none other." Drew paused and reached for Hope's hand. "Their presentations, along with their impeccable service, make for the kind of evening that I wish to share with the two most important people in my life."

The evening passed swiftly as waiters tended to every detail. He toasted Hope, and his grandmother, with glasses of champagne while devouring appetizers, and eventually filet mignon. At the beginning of the third hour, as the sky transitioned to shades of red and ginger and the sun began descending behind the mountain, the waiter delivered a trio of desserts: Crème Brulee, Triple Chocolate, and Tiramisu. Afterwards, they sipped dark-roasted coffee from china cups.

"Grandmother, why don't you tell Hope about the time you learned to drive?"

Drew's smile was infectious, and Olivia couldn't deny him the pleasure. It had been his favorite bedtime story when he was a child.

"Hope, I was living in New York City when my son called me with the news that Drew's mother had tragically died. I was heartbroken, but I set the heartache aside when the urgency to get to my five-year-old grandson became clear. However, I agonized over the logistics, moving from New York to Colorado, until Horace, my chauffeur, volunteered to do the driving. Horace had been my driver for years, as was typical in New York since women were not yet driving, but this would be our first cross-country trip. To tell you the truth, I think he wanted to drive my black Cadillac La Salle automobile as long as he could. What a wonderful luxury automobile it was!

"A week later, on a humid summer day in 1942, both of us were huffing and puffing as Horace loaded the car with two large pieces of luggage, along with hatboxes from Saks Fifth Avenue." Olivia grinned while whispering to Hope, "I would have brought more, but the large car lacked luggage space. Can you believe that?" They both laughed, fully grasping the dilemma. "For days we traveled through cities and cornfields and more cities. That gave me plenty of time to execute a plan." Her emerald eyes twinkled with mischief.

"I thought Nebraska, with the vast farmlands and wide-open spaces, would be the perfect training ground for learning to drive. There was no congestion on the roads, except a tractor every now and then." She took a sip of coffee, smiling the entire time.

"When we stopped for gas, near the capitol of Nebraska, a young service station attendant rushed out with his mouth hanging open like a broken zipper. The surprise of a rare automobile traveling in the plains of Nebraska caused him to stutter as he asked how he could help. Horace instructed him and with great pride, the boy began filling the car with gas, checking the tires, and cleaning the windows. Horace was pacing back and forth in front of the station, smoking one of his hand-rolled cigarettes.

"I exited the car and proceeded to stroll around." Her eyes grew brighter. "I can still remember thinking it's 'now or never.' Then I realized I had lost some of my courage, now that we were closer to the time I was to execute."

Olivia squirmed in her chair until she was sitting as straight as an arrow. "I wasn't content to think about the 'never' part. After all, the future had changed for both of us, and my new life required adjustments. As I walked around, I reminded myself of the modifications I executed after I lost my husband. That gave me the strength to proceed."

"How old were you when you came to Colorado, Grandmother?"

"I had just celebrated my fiftieth birthday, prior to making that cross-country trip."

Solemnly, Olivia relived in her mind the life-changing events, as her eyes grew dim.

"I had not yet comprehended the magnitude of raising a child again, or functioning without the aid of a staff, but I knew one thing: I had to be independent." She pounded her fist on the table. "I would have no chauffeur, nor would there be a staff to run our home, and I knew the learning curve would be extensive, but it was time for me to take charge in every area of my life. Thus, I began by literally taking the wheel." Her green eyes were sparkling.

"How did you do it without any prior driving experience, Mrs. Bartlett?"

"Oh, Hope, please call me Olivia." She patted Hope's hand.

"When Horace returned to the car, I barked instructions for him to get in the passenger seat. He stared at me and frowned, but he knew that once a decision is made, my mind does not waver.

"My hands trembled as I gripped the steering wheel, and for a moment, my heart was pounding so loudly I imagined him hearing it. But I continued in my stern, no-monkey-business tone.

'Horace, the open roads and miles of farmlands in Nebraska present a golden opportunity for me to master what few women know in New York City, that is, how to drive an automobile.'

"Horace got in and begrudgingly instructed me on the basics of driving. It took several attempts for me to synchronize the clutch with my left foot and the accelerator with my right. Startling jumps and neck-jerking stops were repeated time and time again. She giggled, remembering Horace swearing under his breath.

"Finally, holding my head triumphantly, with one hand gripping the steering wheel, I waved to other travelers on the road, and the farmers, who paused to gape at an automobile as long as a row of corn. Heads would swivel when they realized it was being driven by a woman, so I would wave even more. One farmer got so distracted he drove his truck into the ditch!"

Drew almost choked on his coffee as he and Hope dissolved into laughter. Olivia was radiant, as though she had just circled the globe with Colonel Charles Lindbergh.

A soft blanket of warmth hovered over the table for the next few minutes. Olivia's retelling of her driving experience brought them together in a way neither Hope, nor Drew, could have ever imagined. After a pause, Drew raised his half-full champagne glass.

"I'd like to make a toast." His somber expression hinted of the weightiness. The two women grabbed their glasses.

"Grandmother, the events today are the result of your selfless, unsung deeds. Because you believed in me, I learned to dream. Because you loved me, I have a future.

"Here's to my mother who gave me life, then lost hers so I might live." He brushed away the tears spilling down his cheeks.

"Hope, here's to you too! You are the answer to my prayers, my dreams, my hopes, my future. You have brought me immeasurable joy since our first meeting and I cherish each memory, confident there are many more to come."

TWELVE

The following morning, she flew out of bed, fearing she had overslept, until she realized it was still dark, and dawn was yet to break. This was to be her last day with Drew before he left for his Navy assignment.

How they would spend the day was a closely guarded secret by Drew; yet he had promised her it would be an adventure.

Fiercely, ignoring the harshness of reality, she began making decisions on what to wear, wading through several options she selected the night before.

Suddenly, out of the quiet, a weatherman began bellowing from her clock radio.

"Our high today will be fifty-seven, with winds out of the north. The current temperature is a cool thirty-nine degrees at 4:16 AM, Rocky Mountain time."

Hope had to decide what she should wear with the weather being cold. She chose her blue-and-white plaid skirt and white turtleneck sweater. New leather loafers were pulled out of their box and socks out of the drawer. Then grabbing her favorite small white purse, she took out a pair of small gold earrings to complete her ensemble.

A last glance in the mirror, after applying a little rouge to give her ivory skin a hint of color, provided her with the needed assurance that she was ready for whatever the day would hold. She grabbed a white leather jacket and bounced down the steps to the kitchen. Surprised by the lights and drifting smells, she waltzed in, radiant.

"Good morning, Mother."

"Morning."

She found her mother's greeting rather somber, as if she wanted to shut down any communication, but before Hope could inquire, the doorbell rang.

"I'll get it," Hope said.

To her surprise, her mother accompanied her. Here they were, the two of them standing side-by-side when Hope threw open the front door. Drew, standing there grinning, immediately noticed the scowl on Mrs. Madison's face. But she quickly spun around and scurried back to the kitchen.

"Hi, Drew," said a jubilant Hope. Her mother returned, carrying a white bakery box.

"Here's something for you two to nibble on, since it will be a while before you eat lunch."

"Thank you, Mrs. Madison. That's very kind of you." He took the box from her hands.

In shock, Hope asked her mother, "Do you know where we are going?"

Kathryn nodded, while quickly lowering her head to hide errant tears escaping from her tired, green eyes. Desperate to hide her overwhelming fears, the ones that had her pacing the floor throughout the night, and at times, thinking it was more than she could bear, she, with great determination, had dressed to make her daughter's favorite breakfast.

Assessing the situation, Drew quickly ushered Hope out the door. She felt the warmth of being shielded from her mother's harsh reaction, and her heart began a buoyant, happy dance.

Drew smothered a smile as he reached under the car seat for the well-kept secret. He felt confident it was going to be an experience she'd enjoy! After placing an envelope in her lap, she gently pulled out a card bearing his initials.

Hope,
This adventure will not only be a first for us, but I also intend it to be symbolic. I know we are meant to fly together, literally and throughout life. That's why you will be sitting next to me in the cockpit today.
With love forever,
Drew

Hope's fervent laughter quickly dispelled his concerns regarding Mrs. Madison.

"Did my mother really give you permission?"

"Yes, after checking with your father."

"Now, I understand her reluctance this morning," she whispered, while opening the bakery box. The scent of cinnamon filled the car.

"What's in there? It smells delicious."

"My favorite breakfast, homemade cinnamon rolls." Her voice wavered. "Mother only bakes them on my birthday and holidays. For them to be ready this early in the morning, I doubt she ever went to bed."

Hope's pensive response wasn't lost on Drew and for an instant they didn't speak, until she couldn't contain her enthusiasm any longer.

"I can't wait to see where we're going."

He breathed a sigh of relief at her zest and swift recovery.

The moon was still visible when Drew took her hand and briskly strode toward the red and white Piper Cherokee. But her long stride could not measure up to his. She tried to quicken her pace, but Drew had already transitioned to being the pilot, and didn't notice.

He glanced at the horizon. His goal was to be in the air at the break of dawn. He was determined for Hope to witness the breathtaking sight of a Colorado sunrise from the sky, so he quickly began inspecting the plane, rapidly touching each item while steadily commenting about the importance of each one.

His final concerns about Mrs. Madison escaped into the morning air while Hope eagerly stood next to him, staring at the tiny glimmering lights off in the distance. A whiff of pine, floating in the cool air, reminded her of Christmas. In some ways it was.

Drew stole a quick glimpse of the faint morning light on the horizon, as he began checking the cylinder wiring and the oil level. He moved to the left wing and with a fuel tube in hand, he drained a bit of fuel from the wing tank, checking for any water in the fuel. They continued around the aircraft as Drew made sure the control locks were removed, and that there was no damage to the aircraft skin and navigation lights. He inspected the landing gear and tire inflation last.

Satisfied the exterior was in flying condition, Drew, with a flourish, took her hand.

"Your chariot awaits, m' lady."

He opened the aircraft door and gently lifted her into the seat, as if she were a porcelain doll. He then slid into the pilot seat and picked up the clipboard, rapidly glancing at the controls before putting on his headset.

"Flying requires checklists. It matters not whether a pilot is highly familiar with an aircraft and has many hours of flying. There's always a chance that something could be overlooked if committed to memory only."

Hope heard him rattling off technical jargon: "Undercarriage. Landing gear. Mixture. Prop." Overwhelmed by the numerous tasks, she sat quietly, observing him as he then started the engine. His brow knit together as he listened to the spinning propeller while noting the oil pressure and temperature. The loud noise made it difficult to understand his words, but she did hear him say, "It's a good day for flying," and she smiled.

He handed her a stick of gum and told her to chew, that it would help with the ear pressure during altitude changes. She unwrapped it and stuck it in her mouth and began chewing until her jaws hurt.

"Put on your headset; we're about ready," he instructed.

The engine moaned, as Drew performed another check prior to calling the tower; then slowly, he began taxiing toward the active runway. Hope recorded the view with her camera: the time between night and day when the soft light gradually increases; she then observed his hands in constant motion and aimed the camera at him, determined to have a memory of his long, muscular legs in khaki slacks, and the black shirt, a match for his dark hair. Drew concealed his approving smile.

"Okay, here we go. Just got a green light from the tower. Ready to imitate the birds?"

She heard the excitement in his voice, as he taxied into place on the runway and made a last check of settings and pressure before running the throttle up to proper RPM. When he released the brakes, Hope immediately placed the camera on the floor, and braced herself against the seat, continuously chewing her gum.

The engine moaned, then became louder when he began the takeoff run. Together, they were racing down the runway, faster and faster. The ground rushed toward them… her heart was pounding in her throat, her stomach somersaulting,

Abruptly, the glorious morning sun, closer and larger than Hope had ever witnessed, began its ascent directly in front of them. Gasping at the fiery-orange ball, appearing to scale the backside of the mountains like a goat, quickly reached up into the heavens, brushing the sky with vivid streaks of red, coral, and pink. Drew smiled.

"We're looking for about eighty knots on the takeoff roll, which should happen about 700 feet down the runway. And...there it is. Rotating."

Her heart was pounding. He was taking her to places she had never been. Places filled with excitement and adventure, places where boundaries are tested and redefined. Where thrills come faster than breaths.

Suddenly, he pulled the nose of the aircraft upward. Her stomach was leaping and rolling as they were climbing, then climbing higher, like trapeze artists trusting one another, as they rose. Tops of massive evergreen trees, first appearing close enough for them to touch, now swayed below them; rows of houses were emerging like a Monopoly game, miniature and colorful.

They were soaring together. Now she was craning her neck, looking in all different directions. There were peaks of purple snow-capped mountains, rolling hills, and deep valleys below while a crimson sunrise began majestically painting the sky. Green farmlands, each patterned into various sizes, colors, and shapes resembled a jigsaw puzzle.

Every concern vanished. Her mother's behavior, her dad's attitude toward Drew, plus the danger, fears, and anxieties about the man she loved, the man sitting beside her, were all blown away in the wind. Giddy with a lightness she had not known, she trusted Andrew Bartlett completely. Certain he'd protect her heart, the man who managed to break every barrier buried deep within her, would, in the same chivalrous manner as today, be there through the tomorrows. No longer would she fear chasing her dreams, nor be consumed with insecurities. She would trust God's plan for her life and like the drifting clouds above, she would just be.

"Views should be pretty spectacular today." His positive words, along with the lilt in his tone, relieved any lingering fears she might have suppressed. He seemed more relaxed as he leaned back into the seat, after reaching the proper altitude. Keeping his eyes on the sky, he leaned into her.

"Ever been kissed in a plane?"

"Not by a pilot." Mischief was obvious in her smiling eyes.

He quickly leaned closer, and she willingly met his lips.

"Now you have," he said with his unmistakable side-grin.

The hero of her fairy tale was sitting beside her, the only one who could lift her from the ordinary to the extraordinary with a simple glance, touch, kiss, or a note beautifully crafted. Drew Bartlett, the one who flew toward his dreams with passion and determination, had reduced his contemporaries to mere mortals.

Drew kept a scan of the skies going, giving position reports to Denver, at each planned point along the route while pointing out scenery along the way. He gestured to the Garden of the Gods, just as the sunrise cast a red-orange glow on the rocks and their sandstone formations.

Travelling on south, Drew pointed out the Air Force Academy with its famed chapel, then he banked the plane and pointed out the Broadmoor Hotel.

"My daddy plays in golf tournaments at the Broadmoor." She craned her neck for a better view of the building draped in flags, and the azure-blue water meandering through the manicured grounds. "It's one of my parents' favorite destinations. They go there often, to 'recharge their batteries'. Especially after he's been abroad."

Drew stowed her comments into a mental folder marked "Destinations" which already contained a few surprises for Hope once they were married.

Flying on southward, they saw the Pueblo airport to the east; then Drew altered course slightly to the west, keeping a sharp eye out for traffic around the Alamosa airport area. Turning further right, Drew put the nose on course for Durango and pointed out the Sangre de Cristo range.

"It's some pretty high terrain in there, and winters usually are not kind."

It wasn't long until Drew pointed out the Durango-Silverton railroad, and as they neared the airport, he asked,

"Would you read off the landing checklist item by item?"

Then, with complete concentration, he set the mixture to full rich, set the propeller pitch and throttle, and adjusted airspeed for the approach.

Hope observed his concentration to be like steel, his neck rigid, and posture taut. Tension was heard in the clip of his words and the silent pauses as he glanced around the sky like a bird choosing its prey. A safe landing was foremost on his mind, and hers.

They both exhaled a sigh of relief as he taxied to the general aviation hangar and shut down at the fueling pits. When they exited the plane, Drew took her hand and announced, "We're having lunch today in Durango, Colorado."

Hope, feeling like a princess who had been swept away from the castle, couldn't contain her happiness when she caught a glimpse of Drew's sparkling eyes. Then the attendant appeared, and Drew introduced himself.

"We need fuel and a pay phone, and we need to pick up a rental car that I reserved. We'll be back in a couple of hours."

"Okay." The guy pointed them toward the direction of car rentals, the same area where the pay phone was located, while he began to refuel the plane.

"Hope, I promised your mother we would give her a 'safe arrival call', so let's do that before getting the car."

The Other Part of Her

She nodded, and as he pulled the coins out of his pocket, she felt Drew's sincere intent to protect her and her family. Hope nervously dialed, remembering how frosty her mother had been hours earlier.

"Mother, we just landed in Durango and the flight was wonderful." Hope could hear the relief in her mother's choked voice. "Yes, I'll call when we land in Boulder."

There was a pause on both ends. "Mother, thank you for this trip and for staying up all night to make the cinnamon rolls. Today is an incredible dream." Her mother mumbled "good-bye" and hung up.

Drew drove to a nearby restaurant on the border of the Las Animas River, where a host guided them to a patio table with a reserved sign. Hope couldn't help but absorb the many details Drew had personally handled.

A picturesque view of the mountains and swift currents in the swollen river, as melting snow made its way down the terrain, created an idyllic photo opportunity. She grabbed her camera, firing off several shots, until the waiter appeared with enchiladas, heaping servings of hot sauce, chips, and frijoles. Occasionally, a breeze would douse them with fine sprays of river water and a hummingbird, with colorful iridescent wings, would flutter amongst the blossoms on a nearby hanging basket. A woodpecker could be heard off in the distance.

The completion of their meal, a unique praline ice cream dessert, alerted Hope to remove a gift from her purse; a small card was tucked under a gold ribbon. Surprised, Drew first read the note.

Dearest Drew,
I have created a permanent home for you in my heart, a
place where our wait is not measured by the length of time,
but by the reason.
I will love you for as long as I have breath,
Hope

Unable to speak, he opened the gift, a photo album of their journey. She had documented every event since their first meeting.

"The blank pages are for pictures from the history-making flight today. I'll mail them as soon as they're developed." Her voice was so low he could barely hear her over the roaring rapids, but he noticed her eyes filling with tears when she added, "It won't be until we return from Europe."

Absorbed in her emotions, he almost forgot the remembrance hidden in his windbreaker. He reached for the monogrammed card and placed it in front of her, along with a small gift box wrapped in silver paper.

Shock danced across her face when she read his poignant words.

Dearest Hope,

My heart will always be with you, and yours with me.
Anywhere I go, My Love, you go. From now through
eternity.

I love you.
Drew

Hope knew Drew held her life in his hands, both in the air and on earth. And he had, since their first meeting. She swiped away trailing tears and opened the box.

Nestled between layers of black velvet lay a heart-shaped, gold locket. Drew encouraged her to turn it over. In flourishing script, were the words: *"Two Joined Souls, One Heart."*

She breathed in slowly and opened the locket.

"There's a place here for two small photographs," he said.

Trying to fasten it around her neck, and failing, she revealed her quivering hands to Drew. Pleased by her reaction, he got up from his chair, and expertly closed the necklace around her long neck.

"Drew, when you visualize us in the days ahead, make this lovely keepsake a part of the image. It will forever remain where you have placed it."

Out of the reverie, he heard his grandmother's words.

'She will bring purpose to your life, a reason for every task'.

"Hope….," his dry, raspy voice broke when over-powering emotions curled up his throat. He drank the last of his iced tea then placed her delicate hand between his. She waited pensively, as he held her eyes. In a clear, low tone he spoke.

"Hope, I want you by me for the rest of my life, but until that is possible, I'll be intent on creating a future for both of us. I know you're the one God chose for me, but I feel guilty that I can't continue with our journey now." Sadness streamed from his eyes.

"Drew, wherever you are, I am with you. Your journey is my journey. There won't be anyone, but you, until my last whispered breath on earth. I know this because I've prayed, since I was a little girl, for God to give me complete assurance regarding the man I will marry. He has done that."

Drew, surprised by these words from his wise and beautiful soul mate, shook his head.

Thirty minutes later, while they stood in the flight planning room, Drew turned to her with worried eyes, "We may have a bit bumpier ride on the return flight. They're predicting high winds and mountain waves around Castle Rock. Best we don't delay too long. We might be able to beat it."

Drew did a quick walk around the plane, verifying that the fueling doors were secure, and visually checking all the usual points while Hope strapped herself into the seat. The airport employee manned the fire bottle as Drew started the engine. Drew eyed the bright sky and rising terrain to the north and west, wondering if they could indeed, beat the arrival of the high winds as they began the taxi.

Takeoff was smooth, and they settled in for the scenic four-hour flight back to Boulder. They flew past Alamosa and again marveled at the beautiful scenery. Turning north, Drew kept an eye on the mountains to the west. All seemed clear as they passed to the west of Pueblo. As they were approaching Colorado Springs, Drew pointed out some strangely shaped clouds over the mountains ahead.

"See those clouds that look like lenses up there? They indicate winds coming across the mountains. Make sure everything is stowed away and check to see that your seatbelt is low and tight across your lap. We're probably going to have some turbulence."

It started with a few rises and falls, but nothing out of the ordinary. Approaching Castle Rock and the Palmer Divide, though, it got increasingly rough, tossing the little plane to the point where Drew began gripping the yoke tightly.

"We shouldn't be in it too long. I can see the hills in the north haven't formed any of the same clouds." Drew anxiously stared ahead; his brow ruffled.

As he said that, the plane was hit with a large downdraft, followed immediately by the right wing dropping, and a sudden rise of one hundred feet. Out of the corners of his eyes, he saw Hope turn as white as a swan's neck. Her hands were trembling, and she gasped when she spoke.

"Have you ever flown in weather like this?"

His breath was short, his eyes darting, "Yes, I've ridden the turbulence in a number of training flights."

All conversation stopped when the plane continued to dip like a kite dancing in a hurricane. Drew quickly began experimenting with different altitudes, trying to find smoother air, though each remained ineffective against the unpredictable winds. He made the decision to alert Denver.

"Denver Radio, Cherokee November 3692, 120 knots, 11,000 feet, LARK at 42, Boulder. Reporting extreme turbulence in vicinity Castle Rock and Perry Park."

Hope stared at his rigid shoulders. Then at his hands. They were white from gripping the yoke. She knew she'd always remember how he looked as he courageously protected her and the sound of calm in his voice when he assured her. Denver acknowledged the report and said that other aircraft had reported the turbulence had subsided somewhat as they proceeded north.

After spending forty minutes on what felt like a roller coaster, Hope reached for the paper bag. As she did, the ride suddenly became as smooth as glass, so she placed the bag back in the holder.

Drew reported their position and destination and kept a sharp eye out for traffic to the various regional airports. Finally, he was able to contact Boulder Municipal Airport and enter the pattern. Hope turned to him, thinking about how, through the storm, he had remained focused, though concerned about her. She knew beyond any doubt that he would always protect her, if he could.

She felt unsteady as she stepped out of the plane. The queasiness disappeared as they strolled hand in hand to a small office tucked away in one corner of the airport. Drew completed the required paperwork and shared highlights of their Durango trip with student pilots in the room, who listened attentively, in obvious admiration of Drew.

Hope had learned, both from friends and strangers, that Drew was known for being an excellent pilot, an outstanding leader, and a skilled quarterback. Hope now understood, on a deeper level, his excellence appeared in all types of situations. Drew Bartlett had proven himself to be as proficient in the air, as he was on the football field.

At that moment, she realized the stormy winds had blown any speck of doubt into oblivion. She straightened her shoulders, gripping his hand with confidence, as they strolled toward the parking lot.

Drew turned the car away from the airport and began winding through residential areas. The hour of saying goodbye, the time they both dreaded, had arrived. She felt lightheaded, her hands clammy. His angst screamed soundlessly in the evening air. His head pounded; his pulse raced. They had just been through a harrowing experience, one that brought them even closer, and now they were being separated.

He slowly turned onto an unmarked, narrow road then drove around winding curves to the top of Lookout Mountain where they laid their heads back in the open convertible and gazed at the star-filled sky. Both were subdued. Drew pointed to the constellations, calling them by name; she heard nothing but his soothing, deep voice and shuddered with fear of how long it might be before she would hear it again. Just as she summoned the courage to ask, he pointed to the sky, filled with excitement.

"Look, a shooting star! An omen of promise." He quickly took her face in his hands, staring into her eyes.

"All the stars in the universe don't hold a candle to how much I love you. There's no place I'd rather be than right beside you, Hope Madison." Her breath suspended at the sound of her name flowing from his deep, gravelly voice; it would be almost a year before she'd hear it again.

He wrapped her in his arms and with broken hearts, at the thought of being apart, they clung to one another. Yet, Drew knew he should remind her that there would come the day when they would no longer be apart.

He turned the last corner, reluctantly, before parking in front of her home. Tears welled in his throat as he reached for an envelope hidden under the seat. Slowly, he handed it to her; countless questions swam in her eyes. She had grown quiet again.

He answered with a kiss she would remember in the harshness of his absence, before slowly getting out of the car.

Sluggish steps. Faltering words.

Under the porch light, he memorized her features, lightly trailing his finger over her face. Unable to leave, he held her in calm desperation, staring into the eyes he'd never forget.

"Hope, we don't know what God has in mind, but as far as my heart is concerned, there'll never be a goodbye."

Their final kiss was not tender and sweet. It was a kiss filled with despair, grief, and the impending agony of separation. Eventually, Hope turned the doorknob and went inside, crying inconsolably as she rushed by her parents in the living room. Racing up the stairs, she threw herself on her bed and opened his letter.

My Dearest Hope,

And that is appropriate on several levels. Not only are you my "dearest Hope" but you are my dearest hope for the future.

Know that whatever may intervene in the next few years for each of us, you will be held in my heart, mind, and complete being. We are meant to be, and you may hold that in your heart forever, for that is how long I will love you.

Hope, I will remember all the times we've been together, beginning with your smile lighting the dark when we met. Your sapphire eyes warmly greeted me with tenderness and gentleness, taking me to a place I've never been. There was an igniting within my soul that was beyond your physical beauty, and though

I did not understand it at the time, I have come to realize I have been waiting for you all my life.

The glow of your presence and the look in your eyes, all gave the pain I desperately tried to bury, a magical and wonderful release.

Ensuing days with you brought comfort and contentment. An unbridled ease flowed in our conversations, as if we had been together since childhood.

I am in a classic conflict, torn between leaving you and aspiring to the dream of something I was destined to do. I am so eternally thankful for the time we've shared but filled with regret that we were not granted the luxury of more, especially after finding the one I've longed for, and never knew until now.

Hope, my heart will remain full of the memories we created together: Dancing to the Guy Lombardo band, (I never knew I would be grateful for the dance lessons my grandmother insisted I take when I was twelve!) Thankfully, my first waltz was with you, and I pray my last one will be, as well. Your being at my graduation and commissioning ceremony, pinning on my Ensign's shoulder board, will remain one of my favorite memories of all time. I am confident that these, among others, will keep me company, as will your letters. In the light of your radiance being a world away, I will depend on our correspondence to lift the burdensome weight of distance.

My dream of returning to you will remain at the forefront of my days and nights, for it is one that is etched upon my being.

I will hold you in my heart, and trust that you will keep me with you as much as I feel your presence every day, whether we are physically in the same location, or not.
I love you, my darling Hope,
Drew

Hope buried her face into the pillow sobbing as anxiety tightened its grip. The stark terror of his absence ravaged her heart, causing her to tremble uncontrollably. He had loved her beyond reason, with unimaginable depth, the only person to ever do so. Now when she needed him the most, she curled up in a ball, shaking with the inconsolable fear she'd never see him again. She loved him so completely and sincerely, but in despair, she realized she had no talent for partings.

Hope pleaded with God to give her the strength to walk into the future without the one she loved beside her, and to give her the assurance of Drew's return.

The following day Drew made a last-minute decision. After packing the car with his dorm belongings and telling the Whitmires goodbye, he drove to the Madison home for one more glimpse of her. Mrs. Madison greeted him at the door and politely explained, in her typical reserved manner, that Hope was out shopping for their trip to Europe.

"But I'm glad you stopped by Drew. I have something for you."

She excused herself for a moment and returned with an envelope. His name was scrawled across the front.

"I'm glad I can give it to you in person, instead of waiting to learn of your new address."

"Thank you, Mrs. Madison. I'm sure you'll tell Hope I stopped by."

"I will. Good luck to you, Drew."

"Thank you."

He got into his car, tossed the envelope aside after noting Mr. Madison's name in the top left corner, deciding to read the 'God-Speed, Good Luck' message later.

THIRTEEN

Drew arrived at his home in Idaho Springs with feelings of ambivalence and apprehension trailing through his body; he mentally listed all he needed to do before leaving in three days. But Hope was uppermost in his mind.

On the morning of his departure, he lingered with his grandmother over a second cup of coffee.

"Drew, I know this is very difficult for you. I've seen the faraway look in your eyes, the struggle when we talk about Hope." She reached over and gently patted his hand.

"Let me assure you, I saw her eyes, heard her words, and there is no doubt in my mind that she has given her heart to you, for now and forever."

The emotions gathering in his throat rendered him wordless.

"My dear grandson, you have a different part to play in life now, a duty to fulfill. You must give yourself permission, without any remorse or guilt, to perform in service to your country with the same excellence and dedication you've exhibited in all your endeavors." Her eyes brightened, as she stood up, and pushed the chair out from behind her.

"Drew, do you recall my telling you stories about Horace and me joining the local people in small, rural towns when we made the journey from New York to Colorado in 1942? You were only six years old when I would tell you how we, along with the crowds, would gather on the street corners, to wave miniature American flags as the young boys, sons, brothers, husbands, and friends boarded smoking locomotives. Those brave young men had volunteered to risk their lives in World War II."

"Yes, I do remember. It was my favorite bedtime story, and you let me wave the same flag you had waved in each town. I remember marching around the room, shaking it high in the air, and asking if you would wave one for me someday."

Olivia walked over to where she kept her husband's treasured notes. Opening a small drawer, she pulled out the same flag he had waved in his early years and turned to him, waving it in the air.

"This is my part to play now, Drew. And I will. Just as you will perform to the same excellent standards you developed early in life. I know from experience God's grace will cover you and Hope, during the long absences, just as He has never relinquished His hold on my hand.

"You may not feel that all the time, and that's okay. I haven't always felt God was with me, but I've come to realize He will never loosen His hold on us-not on me, not on you, and not on Hope."

With tears streaming down his face, Drew jumped out of his chair and embraced the woman who had devoted her life to him.

"Thank you, Grandmother. You've always provided me with the encouragement I needed, and at just the right time in my life."

She held her tears as Drew hugged her goodbye for the final time. One last glance and after one more wave of the flag, he pulled out of the driveway. That's when he noticed, out of the corner of his eye, Mr. Madison's unopened letter stuck between the seats. Not wanting to waste any more time before hitting the road, he vowed to read it when he stopped for the night.

Three hundred and twenty miles into the cross-country journey, he was hit with reality. He had made a crucial mistake, and there was no one to blame but himself. He began banging his fist on the steering wheel and gritting his teeth.

"How could I have done this? How could I have forgotten to give Hope my military address? How can I go the entire summer

The Other Part of Her

without hearing from her? How will she handle not being able to mail the letters she had promised?"

"Granted, she'll be able to send letters at the end of the summer," he mumbled to the empty car, "but what about until then? When she's across the world, touring Europe?"

He knew correspondence would keep them close in heart and in spirit. His heart sank at the memory of her radiant face when she spoke so optimistically about sharing the trip with him through frequent letters. His assurance of sharing every step of his new life with her, and the future they'd build together, had made her giddy.

Now, out of all the countless details he had attended, he had forgotten the most important one. Beads of sweat were breaking out on his forehead while disgust slowly crawled up his throat.

"I need to hear from her as much as she needs to hear from me! Why?" He banged his fist again. "How could I have made such a critical error?"

Frustration continued to blow in the wind, along with his words. His fists were sore from the pounding. Angrily, he turned the radio off, even though singing made the miles disappear. Not this time. He couldn't relinquish the critical error, nor could he forgive himself for the oversight. Hopefully, she would, he prayed.

Four hundred miles later, blinking lights on a motel caught his attention, and the attached restaurant guaranteed him a late meal. He pulled off the highway, got a room, and threw his duffel bag on the bed before sitting down in an almost-empty restaurant. A plate of dry meatloaf, instant mashed potatoes, corn, and a salad satisfied his hunger pangs; a slice of coconut pie met his sweet cravings. He washed it all down with several glasses of iced tea while chatting with the waitress. He then paid his bill and went to his room. After a fast shower, he sprawled across the bed, exhausted. A short time later, he opened his eyes and squinted at the penetrating light invading his room through ill-fitting curtains. He hurriedly checked his watch and realized he hadn't moved for seven hours.

He hastily threw on clothes, put his bag in the car, and headed back to the same restaurant, with Mr. Madison's letter in hand. A redheaded waitress greeted him, poured black coffee into his cup, and smiled while chomping on gum, as she took his order.

"I'll have orange juice, two fried eggs with bacon, biscuits and gravy," he said, grinning.

"It'll be right out." She winked and walked away.

He blew on the steaming beverage while leisurely opening the envelope. Dappled sunlight, entering through the window, spilled onto the table like a white lace cloth.

Dear Drew,

I know you and Hope have hit it off in rather dramatic fashion, and that your feelings are obviously genuine. Over the years, I've learned that Hope is and has always been, an "all-in" type of person. She attacks any task with fervor, and that has been her tendency in matters of personal interaction, as well.

What I am going to say, you may not understand now, but in time, I hope you realize where I am coming from, as Hope's father. My concerns reflect nothing on you, Drew, as I admire all that you represent and are. In fact, if timing were different, and you and Hope continued along the same path, I would feel nothing but pride and gratitude to have such a fine man beside her. Your college years are exemplary! I admire you for your many accomplishments on the football field, and in the classroom. Hope has told me you have been a perpetual Dean's list kind of man. To add service to the country on top of that is truly admirable, and you have my deepest respect.

What I am addressing is the timing of the situation, nothing more, nothing less. Hope is two years your junior and, though she is more mature than many her age, she needs to have time to grow further, to enjoy the college experience, to continue steps toward independence, and to graduate, a young woman ready to fulfill her dreams. The age of twenty, I am sure you will agree, is a bit early to make lifetime decisions, especially for Hope who has lived a very sheltered life. You may not be thinking along that line with her, especially so early in your relationship, but I remember when I was your age, twenty-two, the desire to find a wife was making an impression on me. And Hope has looked forward to the same all her life.

My other great concern is the distance, potential heartbreak, limited visits, and Hope foregoing her continued college experience, emotionally or altogether, while she pines for someone far away. Hope does not give 50% she gives 1,000. That is the way she came into this world, and in this case, it may be a disservice to her. I know that Navy life will bring you into contact with numerous women, and though I sense you as being a sincere, direct, "know what you want" kind of guy, the possibility does exist of a breakup, perhaps during her Junior or Senior year. That part of her life would be by-passed due to her heart being somewhere else. We would be heartbroken since she wouldn't be able to go back and repeat those years. On that note, I ask that you not have any contact with Hope going forward, until she graduates from college. If you both connect following that time, you have our fullest blessings on pursuing her with all vigor.

If you love her, as I suspect you do, you will honor her. I just ask that she be given more time, without enduring a heavy, lonely heart during what should be some of her happiest years. Thank you for respecting my wishes.
Tennessee Madison

Stunned and sick at his stomach, Drew threw a wad of bills on the table for the untouched meal and stumbled to the car. In disbelief, he laid his head on the steering wheel. Perspiration poured from his forehead; a vise gripped his stomach. He quickly jumped out, jogged down a path covered with dead grass, to the back of the motel, just as he was overcome with dry heaves.

Drew resumed his journey in a state of shock. Confused and disoriented, he missed exits on three occasions due to his concern for Hope. How would she cope when there were no letters from him? With gritted teeth and pulsating temples, he vowed to write Mr. Madison before reporting for duty.

The next day, in the wee morning hours, he sat in a Florida diner drinking black coffee. He felt completely alone though truck drivers and waitresses surrounded him as he penned these words:

Mr. Madison,

I will honor your request with this exception: that you let me know how Hope is doing, and what her state of mind is. I don't expect regular correspondence, but please ease my mind as to her welfare from time to time. I think your restrictions will be very confusing, hurtful, and sad for her. I NEVER want her to experience the kind of pain I've lived with since reading your letter. To be quite honest, I question your demands.

I love your daughter, and I believe she loves me. Without a doubt this isolation is going to be the hardest thing I've taken on, especially with no action on my part. And I can't help but think it will be the same for her.

For the last several years, I've been busy applying myself to academics, athletics, and learning my Naval Officer's craft. To leave Hope, to not have any communication with the only girl I have ever loved, is beyond any grief I've had to endure.

You say you think Hope needs to mature a bit on her own and have her own college experiences. That sounds fair, but I need you to know that Hope is my life, and after she graduates from college, I will be asking you for her hand in marriage. Please keep that in mind.
Drew

Drew purchased a two-year calendar from a corner drugstore and did the math. In 1961, roughly twenty-four-months, or seven-hundred-fifteen-days, he'd reunite with Hope at her graduation. He took a deep breath and circled the approximate date on his new calendar, then drove through the gates at the Naval Air Station in Pensacola, Florida. Mr. Madison's updates, plus his own faith, would be keys to his survival.

FOURTEEN

Hope bit her lip as the plane moved her farther away from Drew. Hiding her tears and sagging spirits, she listened as Riley, sitting next to her, lamented about leaving her husband. At that moment, Riley's dark, glossy curls bobbed up and down, as she reached into her bag for her new embossed stationery and pen. It would be the third letter she had written to her husband in the last five hours. Hope cringed.

Hope determined it would be a tedious two weeks, as she abruptly jerked a magazine from the stewardess strolling the aisle. Burying her face into the pages didn't deter Riley from rambling on about her life as a wife of a US diplomat, the parties, the social life, her husband's future career prospects, how many children they would have and what they would be named. Irritated, Hope read every word of the first magazine and found some more to read in the back of the seat in front of her, even ones that didn't interest her. Eventually, Hope directed her attention to the European brochures her mother had accumulated.

Tingling with excitement for the first time since she had learned of the trip, Hope devoured details regarding Italy, France, Switzerland, London, Germany, and Spain. She knew Riley and her mother had no interest in seeing historical landmarks, ancient castles, world-class museums, and the cathedrals she'd only seen in pictures. But she did, and hopefully, she could free herself from the restraints of her mother's goal: to visit all the major fashion houses including those of Coco Chanel, House of Dior, Yves St. Laurent, and Givenchy.

Hope realized Paris was the global center of fashion, but she wanted to absorb the local culture of each country. Fluent in French and Spanish, and comfortable with navigating the Italian language, she began scouring the brochures for local points of interest and famous restaurants, especially those in France. Their specialty dishes included Coq au Vin, Beef Bourguignon, Chocolate Soufflés, and French Apple Tarts. The photos and descriptions would be shared with Odie B, giving her more opportunities to experiment. Especially on her favorite guest, Drew Bartlett.

Hope paused briefly, to swirl the name "Mrs. Hope Bartlett," on her notepad. For a moment, her mind was bubbling like a bottle of champagne, exploding at the thought of the new title! Then she returned to the brochures.

Town squares with flowing fountains in Italy, and the night life in Spain appealed to her curiosity, even further reducing her interest in going from one designer house to another.

In the middle of the night, somewhere over the Atlantic Ocean, the thought of shopping with her mother and sister, along with the loss of communication with Drew, sent her mind spiraling downward. She prayed for a change of heart, as she desperately wanted the trip to be an adventure, not a duty. She needed her connection with Drew to remain throughout the long absence.

London was the first stop on the family's whirlwind summer tour. Fortunately, Riley and her mother expressed their desire to see Buckingham Palace on their first day there. Hope had her camera ready early. She was chatting with the hotel doorman when they arrived.

She was still heartsick from the realization Drew would not receive any letters until she got home. Once she received his, she would be able to send her letters. However, the fact that he wouldn't have any correspondence until then weighed heavily on her mind. She agonized over the same question daily, *"Why didn't I ask for his military address before our last parting?"* She knew the absence would be as disappointing to him, as it was to her. But tonight, as she did every night, she wrote him a long letter before stowing it in her luggage.

Day one melted into day two, day three, day four as planes, trains, taxis, and chauffeurs whisked them from one country to another. Her father made an occasional appearance, disappointing Hope with the rarity of his presence. Riley eagerly departed at the end of two weeks, after purchasing additional luggage for her new wardrobe.

Hope strolled through the markets, continuing to take every opportunity to talk with local people and to capture them in pictures. Unbeknownst to her, she caught the attention of everyone from the hotel staff to bistro servers, shop owners to salesclerks. Each one was eager to assist her.

Her mother insisted they visit additional couture fashion houses, much to Hope's chagrin. The joy and excitement she felt with the people on the street and in small shops couldn't be duplicated in the fashion world. However, no one could ignore how the designers immediately brightened when Hope entered their showroom. Her height, slender figure, and unforgettable eyes against her porcelain skin, had them clamoring for her attention.

One designer described Hope as the epitome of elegance, a natural, a world-class model. Visualizing her on runways, wearing his creations, he pleaded with her mother not to return to the United States. A lively discussion ensued, as the famous designer continued to praise her style and God-given attributes. All perfect for a high fashion model, he exclaimed with great eagerness. In that moment, Hope discovered a new appreciation for her appearance, her birthright, and her future.

She knew the effusive designer remained unaware that perhaps he had changed the trajectory of her life. He had gifted her with praise and admiration for the traits she had long despised. Now, gratitude and self-confidence swept over her like rushing waves.

That night, as Hope eagerly explained the events to Drew in a long letter from her hotel suite in the heart of Rome, Mr. Madison returned from a lengthy business meeting. Discovering everyone in bed, except Hope, he invited her to join him for a late-night dinner. Hope jumped at the chance. She had only seen him in passing, either on planes or taxis, but minutes later they were strolling toward an Italian cafe tucked away in the corner of an alley, near the Trevi Fountain.

The owner warmly greeted Mr. Madison as an old friend and within minutes, Mr. Madison's food and wine preferences were delivered to their table without his request. Hope beamed with pride, seeing the respect her father garnered everywhere, as she eagerly relayed her experience with the world-renowned designer who was urging her to stay in Italy.

Mr. Madison's eyes were wide with shock and his face drained of color when he hesitantly inquired about her interest in modeling.

"Oh, Daddy, I could never be so far away from Drew. We'll get married as soon as I graduate. For now, I need to be as near to him as possible. Perhaps, Drew and I can honeymoon in Paris, my favorite city."

Mr. Madison ducked his head and remained silent. Hope found his response rather disappointing. She knew Drew would have responded enthusiastically and offered his full support. Without Drew there, she was engulfed with a deep longing and the time until they could be together again weighed heavily on her.

Days later, Hope's initialed and glinting suitcases were filled with the latest designs from the famed Parisian fashion houses. But more than the stunning wardrobe, Hope wore her newly discovered confidence as well as she did the custom-made suits, coats, hats, and dresses.

The trip had swelled into a life-changing experience. Previously, there had been a certain feeling of protection in being the plain one. Expectations didn't exist, especially any regarding her ability to be dazzling. But the entire experience had changed that perception. It had taken her from familiar boundaries to the foreign. She had eagerly acquired a passion for adventures, different customs and cultures. These traits would serve her well when she and Drew married. Most importantly, she hadn't experienced one anxiety attack during the entire ten weeks.

Her stomach was dancing in anticipation on the return flight home. Only a few hours remained until she could read Drew's letters. It brought a smile to her lips when she reached for her new Chanel purse, the one her father insisted on buying for her.

FIFTEEN

Hope, hastily getting out of the limousine in front of their home, ran straight to where Odie B had been instructed to place the mail. That's where Hope now stood, in her mother's office, frowning. A stack of bills, letters, invitations, church bulletins, advertisements and flyers did not reveal any correspondence from Drew. She repeated the search, and this time she checked inside every new magazine.

Her face was pale; her hands were trembling. She then raced up the stairs to her bedroom, stumbling on the last step. She caught herself and smiled at the realization: Odie B must have placed Drew's letters in her bedroom, safeguarding them until her return. Hastily, Hope opened each drawer in her desk, dresser, chest, and nightstand. No letters.

With her heart pounding so loudly she could hear it, Hope frantically ran back down the steps to Odie B's small bedroom, off the kitchen, but there was no sign of her anywhere. She ran back to the study where her mother was arranging multiple stacks of mail.

"Mother, do you know where Odie B is?"

Mrs. Madison immediately glanced up, shocked by Hope's shortness of breath and the quiver in her voice. She was even more shocked at the sight of Hope's face. She was as white as salt.

"She's visiting her family in Texas, but she'll be back tomorrow. Why? What has upset you?"

Hope was on the verge of a full-blown anxiety attack, and her mother immediately turned away, pretending to sort the mail.

"Drew promised to write and there's not one postcard or letter from him…." Hope felt her knees buckle as reality rang in her ears.

Like a dream, he had disappeared.

The next day, with tears in her eyes, Odie B validated Hope's biggest fear. There were no letters from Drew.

Hope rushed to the phone to contact Sarah for answers, then remembered the Whitmire family was on vacation. With no other option, Hope desperately dialed "Information, 113," knowing there'd be a charge on her phone bill for the service. Strangely, it was a luxury that would upset her mother. She didn't care.

The fatigued lady on the other end of the line gave her Drew's home phone number in Idaho Springs. Hope began nervously jotting the number down. Then she started to dial, but she was shivering so hard she had to start over twice. Finally, she heard the ringing of Olivia Bartlett's phone and the echo of her own rapid gasping. Each empty ring delivered a silent message, something must have happened to Drew.

Like the cold breath of death, there was no answer. But she'd hear from him, now that he knew she was home. He had her itinerary.

Each day began with Hope eagerly trekking to the mailbox.

One week. Twelve days. Three weeks.

Harsh reality began slowly seeping through Hope's veins. Drew had given her wings to touch the sun then he took it away. All of it.

By the beginning of her last week home, her spirited gait had slowed to a crawl, her head hung bent, and her shoulders drooped like wet tree branches. How would she survive?

The pain during the darkness of night accompanied the shadows of day. No reasoning could be made regarding the lack of explanation for Drew's location, along with the absence of the letters he had promised.

Still echoing in her head, were the words, 'It is my mission to take care of you.'

On the final day of summer break, Hope limply trudged down the walk to the mailbox for the last time. Quaking like an aspen leaf when she reached into the mailbox, she began to examine each piece of mail carefully, hoping to find a letter that would provide the answer she needed. But Drew, the one who had carried her to a place she had never been, had vanished.

Now permanent tears, like silent raindrops, were falling to the ground. She buried her head in her hands and trudged back up the walk.

Odie B witnessed Hope's agonizing amble toward the house from the kitchen window. She immediately threw down her dishtowel and dashed to the door. Hope stumbled inside shuddering as Odie B's arms wrapped around her. Together, they cried and grieved. Later, when Odie B was alone with Mrs. Madison in the kitchen, she voiced her concerns.

"Hope wears grief like a winter coat turned inside out. To the world, her life appears silky-smooth, just like the satin lining, but the irritating wool of reality, next to her skin, robs her of any peace."

Odie B then placed two eggs by the electric mixer, turned on the oven, got out a pan and while reaching into the pantry for a can of cocoa, she commented,

"For the life of me, I can't figure out what happened to that boy. He was so crazy about Hope." Mrs. Madison continued to stare at her social calendar.

"What do you think could have possibly happened to him, Mrs. Madison?"

Kathryn quickly exited without commenting.

Forty minutes later, Odie B was carrying a plate of warm brownies up the stairs, to Hope's room. Before reaching her door, she could hear Hope burying sobs into her pillow.

Odie B set the tray of brownies on the dresser, then she gently sat down by Hope. While the uncontrollable stream of tears continued, Odie B began to softly sing a hymn.

Suddenly, Hope jumped up and began to search for a box of stationary.

"I'm writing one last letter to Drew," she choked.

"Good," Odie B stated softly. "God knows your pain and He'll answer your cries. Maybe not today, but in time He will. You can be sure of that!"

Hope calmed herself long enough to eat one of Odie B's brownies and in a breaking voice, she asked for the truth.

"Do you think Drew ever loved me, Odie B?"

"Oh yes! And he still does! This whole thing sticks in my throat like hair in a biscuit. For now, you just tell Drew everything on your heart; then you go back to school and hold your head high."

She was shaking her finger while continuing to speak softly. "With God as my witnesses, Hope Madison, that boy loved you! We may not know what happened to him, not yet anyway, but the story isn't over, Baby Girl!"

Hope spent the remainder of the night glancing at the clock on her bedside table. A pale blue dress, the same one she wore to the Whitmire's dinner party on the night she met Drew, lay stretched across the chair; a strand of pearls for her long neck and new stockings lay beside a pair of high heels. White gloves lay to the side of her purse.

The next day, Hope was confused and wounded, as she boarded a plane bound for Fort Worth. Unable to give voice to the tragedy of losing Drew, she remained silent. She could not bear to authenticate his absence, something she had yet to fully comprehend.

"This can't be happening," she would mumble to herself over and over.

The Other Part of Her

At unexpected times, the truth would slowly ebb its way through her body and mind, revealing to her it *is* happening. That's where the pain lived. Where love doesn't vanish like a bird taking flight when dreams disappear. If only it would.

The absence of Drew was shaking her faith, but she knew she must continue to trust God to bring him back to her.

SIXTEEN

November 1959. America is thriving under the presidency of Dwight Eisenhower. Talk of war in Vietnam has escalated, but it hasn't posed a dangerous threat. Not yet anyway. Businesses are booming. Elvis has young girls fainting in the aisles of concert venues. Routines of upper-class women, such as Kathryn Madison, evolve around collecting silver serving pieces, popular china patterns, entertaining lavishly at home, volunteering at hospitals, and following the latest trends in fashion. If they are lucky, the women play bridge and attend monthly garden club meetings and if they are extremely fortunate, they join the country club, and travel.

But some things remained the same. Andrew Bartlett III is still indelibly stitched into the fabric of Hope's heart, even though the burden of his absence continues. Silently, she holds on to him, and to the dreams, even during the lonely nights when sorrow ebbs its way through her body.

Another hidden truth lay buried in the depths of her soul. A truth she couldn't admit to herself. A truth so painful she'd not speak it aloud. A truth she tried to run from or hide so deeply it wouldn't emerge. But she knew if she were given the choice of loving him again, even with the same outcome, she would.

The weight was melting off Hope's slender body like a snowflake on hot pavement. Hollow eyes stared back at her from the mirror. Her grades dropped from the exhaustion of coping with the loss and confusion.

As autumn bowed its red and gold leaves, Hope dashed out of class on a crisp, cool afternoon with a smile stretching as wide as the Trinity River. She jumped into her new convertible, a surprise gift from her parents, and headed toward Meacham Airport in Fort

Worth. Fresh feelings of independence surged, as she quickly parked the car in the sparsely filled lot and confidently strolled toward the main building.

A tall young man, with sandy blonde hair and friendly eyes, greeted her when she entered through the glass door. Hope bristled at the flirtatious gleam in his green eyes and hurriedly covered the distance to his desk in three long steps. In a business-like tone, she began clipping her words.

"Do you have someone who can take me on a short flight over the city?" She didn't even recognize the abrupt tone flowing from her, but determination was emerging between each word.

"When would you like to go?" His eyes flickered with amusement at her curtness.

"Now," she replied, standing rigid with her fists balled in a knot.

He fought for composure when he met her fiery blue eyes.

"I do have someone available. Come with me." He turned to face his snickering co-worker whose mouth was hanging open.

"Ralph, I need you to cover the phones for a bit." Then he remembered his manners and stuck out his hand.

"My name is Patrick Dyer. Let's get your paperwork filled out."

Ignoring his hand, she nodded and introduced herself.

The introduction was not necessary. Patrick recognized her the minute she entered the building. He had helped her, and other returning co-eds, move into a sorority house at the beginning of the semester. He also recognized her from a class they shared. Now, he had more questions about the beautiful girl. Why did she always keep to herself? Why did she avoid making eye contact by keeping her head lowered in her books? On one occasion, when Hope took note of him looking at her, why had she hurriedly escaped like a scared deer running into the woods?

Now, standing near the airplane, she felt excitement shooting through her like the Fourth of July fireworks. In a matter of minutes, she'd be flying again. She knew, without a doubt, Drew would be beside her.

Patrick smiled when he positioned portable steps by the aircraft door.

Confused, she stared at him. "Where's the pilot?"

Patrick's laugh, genuine and deep, irritated her.

"He's standing before you."

Then, once again, he held his hand out to assist her up the steps.

She looked at his welcoming face, and then down at his hand. With her lips pursed, she reluctantly placed her hand in his grip and climbed into the cockpit.

He saw pain and questions in the eyes staring back at him.

Hope was finding that life requires adjustments, but that didn't relieve her suffering. Nor the fact that Patrick's relaxed and congenial manner was a strong contrast to Drew's intent focus.

Immediately, she silently questioned Patrick's competence and her decision to fly in a private plane with someone other than Drew. But he'd be there in spirit, protecting her, and she'd finally feel close to him. Anxiety was rushing through her with a vengeance. Her palms were now wet, and beads of perspiration were zipping across her forehead faster than a speeding freight train.

Patrick, unaware of her trepidation, began chatting about what they would see. His casual manner jolted her, then suddenly, she was staring at the runway that stretched in front of them.

Her mind was doing cartwheels. Fear, doubt, and heartache were bubbling as she recalled the moment when she and Drew were doing the same. Now she felt like a traitor to the one man she had promised her heart. How could she replace treasured memories with this stranger? Why would she even try?

Patrick appeared relaxed as he waited for permission from the control tower. At once, approval was granted, and they were racing down the runway, faster and faster. Finally, lift off and they began climbing toward the billowy clouds, rimmed with gold by the lowering of the sun. He checked his watch. An hour would be ample time to give her a view of the city before evening crept into darkness.

Tense, then giddy, Hope marveled that she was once again flying. And for reasons, unclear to her in that moment, she trusted this man, who was clearly different from Drew. Then she abruptly felt light-headed as a maze of questions began doing flip-flops in her mind. How could it be that this man was sitting where Drew should be? Why had she trusted a stranger with her life? What had she done? Was she so desperate she'd risk her own life with a smiling, happy-go-lucky stranger?

His self-assuredness flowed through the headset as he announced well-known landmarks in Fort Worth: the ambling Trinity River, the zoo she'd been visiting since she was a toddler, the famous stockyards, the "Big Apple", a barbecue restaurant she and her family frequented every Friday night in her youth, the coliseum where she attended the rodeo each year, sitting in front row seats her father secured every season. Sprawling grounds looked different from the air, as did the Woolworth building standing tall in the heart of downtown.

"Hope, where did you live growing up?"

"Fort Worth. In an area called Oakhurst, within walking distance of Oakhurst Elementary."

Minutes later they were flying over her childhood home and school. Happiness and joy exuded from her voice, as Hope began describing her childhood years. The change in her demeanor startled him.

Soon, the gathering shadows of evening appeared, and they were once again on the ground. An hour in the sky, seeing the brilliant streaks of crimson and purple, filled her with a rush of emotions. The whole flight had been more emotional than she had expected. At times, she was euphoric and at other moments, she felt saddened beyond words.

So much she had lost. And the reality had just begun. Memories of a day with Drew, and flying with him, erupted. It was the same day he had walked out of her life.

She and Patrick strolled in silence toward the terminal. He could see the change in her demeanor, her tone and pain-filled eyes. He knew she had been juggling an onslaught of emotions the entire time.

Suddenly, she burst out with the announcement that she would return soon, and he smiled to himself.

Patrick wanted to see her again, but not just in this setting. However, he knew it was too soon to approach her about a date. This seemed a good time to explain the rules for choosing a pilot.

"When you return, we have several flight instructors; however, if it meets with your approval, I'd like to do the honors. He felt his face warming under her stare, certain he was now as bright as the crimson sun.

"Thank you. I'll be sure to request you, Patrick." She stared at him through guarded eyes, while chewing on her bottom lip. "Can you keep it a secret?"

"What? The flight? A secret from whom? The names of passengers are logged into a record book."

"I understand, but this is very personal. No one is aware of my desire to soar amongst the clouds."

She hesitated for a moment, responding as one would who had been living emotionally enclosed by four walls. "I wish to keep it private for reasons I'll not disclose."

Wounded eyes stared back at him, and he immediately felt the opportunity of seeing her again vanish. But he decided to pursue her.

"I'll agree to your terms, Hope, if you'll go dancing with me Friday night. A bunch of us go country-western dancing every weekend." A bashful grin crept across his face.

"I'm sorry. It's Thanksgiving weekend so I must decline your offer," she said, as she turned to leave.

"How about the following Friday night?"

She turned toward him. His appealing smile and down-to-earth friendly persona created a swirl of confusion. The unresolved ending with Drew, the one who was to be her dance partner for life, left her questioning the appropriateness of a date with another. Then a silent whisper abruptly reminded her of Drew's inexplicable disappearance.

"By the way, pardon my manners, I forgot to pay you. How much do I owe for the aerial view?"

He considered her appetite for flying and assumed she was from a "well-to-do" family. The flight had not been cheap, but she didn't blink an eye at the cost, and now she was providing him with a generous tip. He placed it back in her hand before she turned to walk away.

"I can't accept the tip, Hope. If anything, I should be tipping you! Your enthusiasm and emotions were certainly not the typical reactions we normally see when we take people for a flight over the city. I could tell how much it meant to you. That was reward enough."

It was true. The flight had been more emotional than she expected. In fact, she felt like she did in high school when riding the roller coaster at the Texas State Fair. Only this time, she was vacillating between euphoric highs and swamp-deep lows. So much had been lost, all the dreams she had carried throughout her life, and

The Other Part of Her

the reality had just been exposed in a sky ablaze with the fire of the setting sun.

Patrick observed her from the back, strolling across the long shadows on the ground. He knew she was intentionally skating by the question.

"Do we have a deal, Hope?"

She turned back around, placing her hand over her eyes, shielding them from the sun.

"You drive a hard bargain Mr. Dyer, but if all I have to do is go dancing in exchange for you being my pilot, I accept." Amusement flickered in his eyes, though she appeared to have just signed a funeral contract.

Hope hopped in her car and drove one block before tears began blurring her vision. It had been more emotional that she expected. One minute she was euphoric and the next saddened beyond words. So much she had lost. And the reality had just been exposed. She pulled the car over and parked. There, in her ache, in her brokenness, she angrily cried out,

"It should have been Drew in the pilot seat! Why, God? Why wasn't it Drew? Why the confusion? The lost dreams?"

When the first sprinkling of stars appeared, she still didn't move. Words choked in her throat. The night grew dark. Finally, she turned the key in the ignition.

In the weeks ahead, Patrick did not go away. He persisted on Friday night dates and church on Sundays. When their junior year neared the end, Patrick didn't debate on how he'd spend the summer. In order, to be near Hope, he would continue as her flight instructor. He would also continue breaking down the walls that stood between them. The clock was racing. Only one more year until they would graduate, and he'd leave for the Air Force.

Hope had begun to eagerly test the advice she had been given by the famous designers abroad. She first secured the assistance of her mother, who was a friend of Stanley Marcus, the owner of Neiman Marcus, the popular department store in Dallas. The dream of becoming a high-fashion model took hold on a warm day in June, at the close of her junior year. In one more year, she could pursue modeling full-time.

Her friendship with Patrick continued, but her summer schedule became extremely intense, more than she would have ever dreamed. Fashion shows in New York, Los Angeles, and Dallas consumed her time. Top designers were impressed with her style, beauty, and work ethic; each promised career opportunities after she graduated. Until then, they would keep her busy.

When the ache for Drew grew unbearable, as it sometimes would, she would hire Patrick to take her flying. But as the days and weeks marched on, even the pain of Drew dulled.

Hope never mentioned Patrick to her parents, even though they now lived ten minutes away. Their sudden return to Texas had not been what Hope desired. It took her farther away from Colorado, and from Drew, however her father unexpectedly retired a few months after their trip to Europe. Hope kept her distance while carving out her own career. She made personal decisions with the confidence that had been planted in her by some of the most elite designers in the world.

At times, in the darkness of night, she was reminded of how much had changed since she granted that all-important favor to Sarah Whitmire. Now, she barely recognized her former self in the mirror.

Through the weeks and months of her senior year, Patrick's light-hearted manner remained enjoyable, and eventually, she became aware of how he was respected by both his peers and the faculty. She also became aware that she was the envy of many girls who had tried to date him, but to no avail.

In the cool, crisp autumn days of their last year, they were known as the "perfect couple." He would accompany her to sorority parties, and she would do the same for his fraternity events. Time together, otherwise, was limited to study dates and church on Sunday.

Winds of change ushered in the Christmas holidays. That's when Patrick noticed a difference in Hope's demeanor, an edge he couldn't identify. A palpable strain would greet him, along with forced smiles and awkward silences. If he inquired, as he often would, she would flee into her shell.

Finally, her fears erupted like a bubbling volcano, as they were ordering graduation announcements. A teasing remark by Patrick, about getting married the week of graduation, the same week he was to leave for the Air Force, covered her like molten lava. She could not bear a repeat of another disappearance.

Pilot. Military. Never Again.

She abruptly wrapped herself in laments without offering an explanation.

Patrick's easy-going smile became forced and strained, matching hers, as doubts about their future intensified. He was convinced it would bring a permanent parting, a thought he couldn't bear. But as hard as he tried, he couldn't reach her.

Hope would avoid the topic of the future like one would avoid long stares at the sun. To him, she was the sun.

On a cold day in 1961, Patrick took a bold risk.

SEVENTEEN

May 1961 - Aboard USS Ranger in the China Sea.
Drew sat in one of the heavy steel reclining ready-room chairs, sketching as others dozed, drank coffee, and played Acey Deucy at the corner game table. Drawing was his form of relaxation.

"What're you doing, Picasso?" asked the skipper.

Drew wasn't sure he was talking to him, until he saw the skipper leaning over his shoulder.

"Oh, just sketching our Crossing the Line Initiation a few weeks ago, when we crossed the equator," Drew said.

"Mind if I take a look?"

"Not at all, skipper." Drew handed him the book and stood up. The skipper quickly glanced at the drawings.

"Hmmm, who's the girl?" he asked.

"My girlfriend, sir," Drew said.

"She's good looking." The skipper gave the sketchbook to him, then added, "You should submit cartoons for the back of the wing airplane! Up for that, Picasso?"

"Yes sir, I could do that," Drew said with enthusiasm.

"Outstanding. I especially like the Peanuts bunch."

"I'll see what I can come up with," Drew said, as the skipper left the room.

Several guys teasingly chimed in, "Hey, Picaaa-sso," when the skipper was out of hearing distance.

So, it seemed that Drew had received his call sign from the skipper. "Picasso" would be his name aboard ship, and especially when airborne, where true names were rarely used. They shortened it to "'Casso".

"Hey, Casso," Java yelled. "Why don't you give the pre-qualifying speech from a Flight Instructor?"

"Oh, the 'encouragement' speech to the students prior to their first carrier landings?"

"Yeah. That one."

Drew, in a booming voice, shouted the words in rapid-fire succession:

"Gentlemen, the price you pay for the benefit of my vast knowledge and experience, and the small compensation for my standing on a hot runway in summer, a cold runway in winter, and on the back end of the boat in all kinds of weather, keeping you from busting your butt on the ramp, is that you run this risk: Should you pass the 180-degree position on your approach without either your gear, flaps or tail hook in the proper position, gentlemen; I drink Scotch!"

Laughter and comments erupted.

"Sounds like a great way to replenish the liquor cabinet."

"No wonder Landing Signaling Officers have a full liquor cabinet since screw-ups are possible on every approach!"

About that time, the yeoman walked in with a stack of mail and proceeded to call out names. Mail was such a crucial, uplifting part of deployment.

"Bartlett."

Taking the letter, Drew was immediately filled with relief and excitement when he saw "Tennessee Madison" in the upper left-hand corner. He had complied with Mr. Madison's request to not contact Hope until she graduated from college, and he eagerly grasped the reward in his hand. The letter would provide him with pertinent information regarding Hope's graduation.

His departure from the ship, and four-week leave, were strategically planned to coordinate with her graduation. But, in order to have the luxury of spending time together afterwards, he made the decision to arrive three days prior to the graduation ceremony, knowing she would need time to absorb the shock of her father's demand to not communicate. Then they would spend the remaining weeks together.

Specific dates of when their reunion would take place lay in his hand. His heart raced as he quickly sprinted toward his stateroom and opened it.

Dear Drew,

I regret that I must write to you of this most unexpected circumstance, particularly given your very honorable and strict adherence to my request to cut contact with Hope.

A week or so ago, Hope called Mrs. Madison and announced that she was getting married in three days. It came as a complete surprise to us, as we had no idea that she had gotten serious with anyone.

I know this will come as much a shock to you as to us. I have no idea if you still were planning to contact Hope after she graduates, but I suspect you were, given your annual Christmas letters and the depth of feelings for Hope you seem to have. I am so sorry that this seems to have backfired regarding my intent of furthering Hope's development. I don't know how to make it any better for you.

I wish you well in your career and will pray for your safety over there. I know it's a tough situation, and that you're standing in harm's way every day. I've always liked and respected you and regret that life has thrown us an unexpected curve ball.

Most Sincerely,
Tennessee Madison

Drew threw Mr. Madison's letter on the desk. His head sagged into his hands. He sat there for some time, contemplating all the ramifications of Hope's sudden marriage. His heart was heavy, and he wasn't quite sure how to handle his feelings, or how to reply to the letter. He swung into his bunk, stared at her picture mounted on the underside of the upper bunk, and the calendar that marked off the days until her graduation and his leave.

Between gritted teeth, he agonized aloud.

"Twenty days until she gets her diploma. Only nineteen days until I'm to be in the states, supposedly in her presence, after two years of waiting. Why did I agree to his request? Sure, there *was* a slight age gap between Hope and me. But no contact with Hope? I let the love of my life slip away. No! It can't be!"

He pounded the pillow with his fist. His temples throbbed as seething anger mounted. His mind was filled with frustration, despair, denial, and confusion. Then anger, at himself, at Hope's parents, at the entire situation.

He couldn't muster any anger toward Hope. After all, because of her dad's request, he was sure she felt abandoned. Then the depression hit when he realized he'd never find that kind of love again. Drew agonized. "Why, why, why?" He shook his head, wishing he could cry, but years of suppressed tears remained in him. He couldn't even breathe.

He thought of searching out his air-wing buddy, "Java" Coffey. The two of them had become good friends while sharing a lot of triumphs and tribulations with one another. Drew especially appreciated Java's keen instincts in different situations, and when he sensed something wasn't right with Drew, he'd encourage him to let it out.

Java was pouring himself a cup of coffee when Drew mumbled to him, "Meet me on the flight deck, so we can speak privately." When Drew relayed the contents of Mr. Madison's letter, Java's predictable reaction matched his own.

"What??? Who did she marry? How did that all come about without any warning?" Drew grimaced, shaking his head, pained by the thought.

"I don't know. I should not have kept the promise of no contact for those two years."

"Mr. Madison has no concept of how you really feel about Hope, does he?"

"No, and I don't have any effective recourse, now! If her dad had let me know things had gotten serious with another guy, I could have reached out to Hope. Perhaps, I could have gotten her to postpone a decision like that. Now it's too late!"

"A response will require some thought," Java said. "Hang in there, buddy. We'll come up with something. I suggest you don't send a reply right away. Wait a bit, and let it simmer."

"Okay." Drew realized it wasn't a crisis that would be solved by an immediate reply. Reluctantly, he resigned himself to not answering in the short-term.

He had squadron paperwork to tackle and angrily threw himself into getting the job done. At each pause, the bleak prospect of life without Hope flooded back into his consciousness, and he was beginning to get really irritated with it.

That evening, Java came up with a reasonable solution: Drew should write a very difficult but needed letter.

"Casso, you must write the Missing In Action/Killed In Action letter to Hope."

"Yeah, I think you're right." He had written ones to his grandmother and to his father before deployment.

"In case anything happens to me," Drew said, "she'll have the truth because I will reveal her father's wishes from his own hand. I have Mr. Madison's correspondence in a drawer under my bunk, so I'll write a letter to her and include, with his letters, my response to his request for no contact with Hope until her college graduation. Would you make sure she gets it, Java?"

"You got it. At least, if anything does happen, she'll know why the enforced separation," Java said.

Drew nodded. "Yes, this brings me some relief to know the letters will be delivered to Hope. I desperately want her to know the truth."

"It will be done, Casso."

They ended their discussion with Java patting him on the back.

"Thanks, Java, for listening, Drew mumbled. It helped a lot to be able to talk about it."

"No problem. You'd do the same."

"Yes, but I hope I never have to."

"So do I, Casso. So do I."

Drew returned to his room for the second phase of closure: he pulled his trunk out from under the bed, opened it, and gathered up all the unsent heartfelt, loving messages he had written Hope over the years, the ones he planned to present to her when he returned to the states. He stuffed them in his laundry bag and quickly made his way to the hangar deck, and out onto the fantail. He hesitated briefly, then quickly opened the bag and deposited four years of his personal Navy history, and the desires of his heart, into the foamy wake.

Returning to his stateroom desk, Drew stared at Hope's picture, the one he'd carried since deployment began. He also looked at the sketches he had drawn of her, and their times together. He glanced back at Mr. Madison's letter and felt a despair he'd never known. He wanted to reply, but any response, at this time, would contain resentment and bitterness.

I'll let this process for a while, Drew thought, and maybe I can provide a civil reply later.

The Other Part of Her

His reverie was interrupted by a pounding knock at his door. He opened the door to the commanding officer's yeoman.

"I don't think your phone is working, sir. The skipper wants to see you in the ready room right away!"

Drew thanked him, saying he'd be there immediately. He closed the door and reached over to put the phone back on the hook. He had not wanted any interruption while contemplating the letter. Drew quickly pulled on his olive drab flight suit and boots and hurried to the ready room. Mentally setting aside the "situation," he shifted into Naval aviator mode.

"Ah, Casso, there you are!" greeted the Commanding Officer.

"Yessir, Skipper, sorry you had to send a messenger," Drew stated, somberly.

"Forget it. We've got a hot one cooking, and I want you on division lead. Air Intelligence has the particulars. You'd better get used to the pace, 'cause the air group commanders want you in any hot area strikes. Says you have a cool head and a steady hand. Get Rodeo and head up there!"

"Yes sir, Skipper." He saluted, while attempting to push down the shock of Mr. Madison's letter.

"Rodeo", a cowboy from Wyoming, had been crewed with Drew for a little over a month. During their short time together, he had proven to be a highly competent Bombardier/Navigator with a flair for keeping the A-6 Diane computer in working order, even when it got into one of its "electronic snits." Drew was glad to have him as his B/N.

The two of them arrived at the air intelligence hatch at nearly the same moment. They were buzzed in and greeted by the squadron air intelligence officer who had been working with the others in command. They assessed the target of their mission.

The photos showed heavy defenses, with Surface to Air (SAM) Missile sites and Anti-Aircraft Artillery (AAA) in profusion. The Alpha strike would involve over thirty aircraft, including A-6s, A-4s, and F-4 Phantom fighter cover. Any strike that size would need thorough and intensive preparation. Drew threw himself into the process.

As division lead, Drew's strike element consisted of four A-6 aircraft. He met with other strike element leads in the A-4 division, and determined attack headings, as well as escape routes. The Phantom F-4 leads discussed an air cover plan. Their job was directed to any airborne threat, for example, any enemy MIGs that might show up.

The planning and discussions lasted through the evening, then the aircrews retired for a few hours of attempted sleep prior to the dawn launch.

Drew's alarm clock went off at 3:45 A.M., but he had been awake most of the night. He figured he got maybe two hours of real sleep. He pulled on his flight suit and boots and headed to the ready-room for the final weather and aircraft maintenance brief. He was filled with tension, and a heightened sensory perception, as he briefed the eight guys in the A-6 Division.

"The weather doesn't look good. There's a broken, scattered 2,000-foot ceiling, with rain showers, which makes our mission that much more treacherous," Drew announced. Their expressions were focused, and tense as Drew continued.

"Air intelligence told us it is a heavily defended area, but that doesn't begin to cover it. It is generally a hot locale with everything from small arms, Anti-Artillery Aircraft, and SAMs to airborne MIGs. In addition, we all know that there were two A-4's shot down in the area last week. Lt. Paul 'Cat' Pershing didn't make it, and there was one confirmed capture, Lt. Jerry 'JJ' Johnson. Mutual support is essential. Keep checking your buddies' six."

Drew wiggled into his harness and survival vest, grabbing his helmet before he and Rodeo headed up to the flight deck, where the A-6, with the name "Andrew Bartlett" painted on the side, was waiting. Wing pilots didn't always get the aircraft with their name painted on it for every mission, but Drew felt it was good luck when he did have "his" aircraft assigned. In the darkness of pre-dawn, Drew spoke briefly with the plane captain, Bob Stewart, as they went through the pre-flight check.

"She's ready to go, Lieutenant. I checked everything myself. All panels closed, and cockpit set up. I started the alignment with the electronic guys."

"Thanks, Bob. I know it's ready to go, if you say so." Drew quickly finished his walk-around, as Rodeo began entering coordinates into the navigation computer.

Around the flight deck, all the thirty-plus flight crews and their plane captains were similarly engaged. The launch and taxi-director personnel, called yellow shirts, were on station, checking chocks, tie-downs, start carts, all the catapults and associated equipment. The tension surrounding a major launch was palpable.

Bob climbed up the ladder, assisted Drew with his parachute harness hookup, and pulled the first safety pin on the ejection seat.

"One." Bob said, as he placed the first safety pin between his fingers. Drew nodded.

"Two." Second safety pin between his fingers.

Drew observed each step. Bob held up both hands showing Drew all seven pins between his fingers, before stuffing them in the boarding ladder compartment and stowing the ladder. Drew would be ready to eject, if necessary.

Another yellow shirt assisted Rodeo. Shortly thereafter, Bob signaled all clear for engine start. Drew gave a "thumbs up", commenced the start sequence, and brought the engines online one at a time. With everything showing optimum, Drew signaled to disconnect the start cart and electrical umbilical. They were ready for launch.

Drew looked around the deck and saw his three wingmen were similarly ready. The dawn sky was beginning to brighten.

The plane captain signaled for chocks to be pulled. Bob emerged from under the aircraft, showed Drew the tie-down chains, and saluted him smartly. The plane director signaled engine turn, and forward taxi. Drew taxied the Intruder into the queue for catapult launch. As the ship steadied up, the roar of the first two F-4s on the bow catapults indicated the launch had begun.

It appeared Drew and Rodeo would be number four off the starboard bow cat as they put their oxygen masks on. They moved forward with each successive launch, and then were positioned directly behind the blast deflector as number three aircraft ran up to full power for its launch. The catapult fired, and the deflector retracted into the deck. Drew immediately taxied forward into launch position, easing the plane into the holdback link. As Drew felt the plane "squat" a bit, he went immediately to full power, checking that his instruments indicated optimum conditions.

He heard Rodeo say, "Ready to go."

Drew placed his head against the headrest and saluted the cat officer. About two seconds later, the cat fired, and Drew and Rodeo felt the exhilaration of a good shot. Another two seconds, and the aircraft was flying at 160 knots off the deck. Drew immediately retracted the gear as he rotated nose up and made a clearing turn to the right. He proceeded to his designated rendezvous coordinates with the other three A-6s.

Rodeo reported a good system; Drew climbed to rendezvous altitude. On station, he commenced an orbit and was pleased to see the first of his wingmen, Ozzie, already in sight. He had apparently been launched immediately after Drew's shot. Ozzie slipped into position to Drew's right and awaited the second section to find and join them. Two minutes later they appeared inside the rendezvous circle, joined as a section. Obviously, their cat shots had been closely spaced, as well; they joined smoothly. Drew felt a quick rush of pride.

"I'm darn glad to have a competent bunch of squadron mates out here," he said. All crews signaled "good to go," and Drew led them to the next rendezvous point, where they would join with the whole squadron of planes.

Drew caught a flash of sun off an aircraft wing, spotted three divisions of A-4s, and looking higher, saw two of the F-4 escorts covering from above. Check-in commenced on the tactical channel, and it was only about seven minutes after check-in that the entire strike group was assembled. Drew called for the gaggle to come to initial heading, and Rodeo switched the computer to the next waypoint, the coast about twelve miles southeast of the target. They heard a bit of fighter and E-2 radar plane chatter, but so far, no air opposition.

The group took tactical formation, weaving slowly to confuse any radar tracking. The threat indicator gave out random chirps here and there.

About twenty minutes later, Rodeo said, "I have our coast-in point on radar. Looking good!"

Drew started the checklist and called for bomb stations to be selected. They'd drop the whole load in one run.

Drew noted they were over land, and announced, "Feet Dry", then reached over and switched the master armament switch on. It was as if that action turned on the threat indicator, as well. They suddenly heard and saw indications of Anti-Artillery Aircraft gun-laying radars. He checked the other elements of the strike and nodded in satisfaction that the entire group was flying like a woodcock, changing altitude, and heading about every seven seconds, making it difficult for the radars to predict the aircraft tracks. Drew saw landmarks and got confirmation from the other A-6s that they were armed and ready. Initial point, where the various elements would split to line up their bomb runs, lay eight miles ahead and would be covered in a little over a minute.

At that moment, SAM alerts started on the indicator, and in their headphones. They heard a low warble, indicating they were being painted by radar. As Drew checked the bearing to port for any sight of the SAM, the warning warble went to high frequency, indicating a SAM launch. At about the same time, Ozzie reported a high warble with a launch from the starboard side, as well. Drew called for evasive maneuvers and saw the telephone pole-size missile pass an A-7 in a hard turn. The missile couldn't hack the turn, and upon passing the little plane, exploded in mid-air. The A-7 immediately dove back to attack heading, continuing toward the target. Drew checked for any further launches, and after seeing none, banked back to attack heading. He confirmed his wingmen and other strike elements around him. His division remained intact.

Drew wondered why only two SAM launches, unless... Yes! His attention was drawn to an air-to-air missile trail above, and he saw a Phantom take out a MIG-17. The enemy wasn't firing more SAMs, because their aircraft were in the area. He immediately called for attack split, and the division fanned out for their individual bomb runs. Drew rolled hard right, then back left and down into his weapons delivery dive.

Rodeo began calling altitudes from 17,000 feet,

The Other Part of Her

"Rolling In. 16, 15, 14, 13, 12..." Rodeo declared.

Drew scanned airspeed and dive angle, setting his bombsight on the pre-briefed target section. About that time, passing 12,000 feet, tracers started zipping through the air, as the Anti-Aircraft Artillery sites around the target opened up.

"9, 8, 7." Rodeo and Drew both knew they were at bomb release altitude.

Drew pressed his thumb on the top of the stick releasing 12,000 pounds of bombs at a slight angle to the target. The drop took one and a half seconds.

"One, Bombs Away. One's Off," Drew proclaimed to the division, as he pulled up, and broke left to the briefed exit corridor.

"Two, Bombs Away. Two's Off," Ozzie announced.

"Tracers to the....." shouted Rodeo, "We've been hit! Tracers to the right! We've been hit!"

Drew broke left hard, keeping track of his wingmen, enemy aircraft, and the instrument readings, as he talked on the radio and to Rodeo on the intercom.

"Splash One MIG!!" the fighters reported.

Drew checked above, left, and right, and saw Ozzie and the other section closing on him. He heard a Mayday call, and was shocked to see an A-7, from another division, explode below and to the left of him, the result of a SAM hit.

Drew commenced zigzagging as they climbed out. There were calls of "Good chute," referring to the A-7 pilot, and Drew hoped they'd get him out. It was very thick enemy territory in which to evade capture.

Several minutes later, Drew checked for the rest of the strike. Several elements were in sight, as he headed for the carrier's position. Ozzie pulled up alongside and checked Drew's aircraft.

"Casso", Ozzie's voice full of concern, "you've got some holes in your vertical stabilizer." Drew nervously checked all instruments.

"Fluctuating hydraulic pressure," Drew stated.

"Okay, now let me check you over, Ozzie."

Drew passed the lead to Ozzie, and eased back and down, checking his aircraft for any damage.

"You're okay, Ozzie. You've got all your arming wires. I assume I do, too."

"That's a roger, Casso."

The second division reported, with all arming wires present, indicating the bombs armed upon release from the aircraft.

Drew led his division into the break-in order. His apprehension over the hydraulic pressure was confirmed when his landing gear failed to lock down. He waved off the landing and announced the malfunctioning gear to the ship's tower. The other three A-6s landed with no difficulties.

Drew turned downwind under the direction of Carrier Air Traffic Control Center, as the squadron rep in operations read through the gear emergency procedures. Drew felt his nerves of steel kick in, as he listened and rotated the landing gear handle ninety-degrees, then pulled sharply when he added "Gs" to the aircraft. A bottle of compressed nitrogen was released into the hydraulic system, and the sharp pull-up snapped the gear into locked position. A couple of tense seconds followed before Drew got three green lights on the gear indicator. They both exhaled sighs of relief when the wheels were locked down. He notified the tower and flew one of the smoothest approaches of his career.

As he taxied out of the wires, and followed the yellow shirts to his parking spot, he wondered about the A-7 pilot, and if rescue attempts were underway yet. Probably so, he thought to himself. Hot area... they'll want to get him out quickly.

The Other Part of Her

Rodeo shut down the system, and Drew secured both engines, opening the canopy as he did so. Bob was already up on the side of the aircraft, with the seat pins in hand. He assisted Drew with helmet bag and seat buckles, saying,

"Uh, lieutenant, did you know you..."

"Yup. Got some holes, I hear."

Drew exited, and immediately went to the tail to assess what might have hit him. There were six holes, and they appeared to be from a twenty-three millimeter.

"Guess one of the four-barrel ZSU-23 guns got lucky on my pullout from the target. Sorry to get your aircraft messed up, Bob!"

"No problem, sir! We'll get 'er fixed up. Welcome back aboard!"

Drew and Rodeo headed to debrief, both curious about the effectiveness of the strike. They probably wouldn't know for several hours.

They threw off their flight gear and grabbed a cup of the stuff that passed for Navy coffee. They concluded it tasted pretty good, as they proceeded toward maintenance to log their gripes. Maintenance would investigate the needed repairs. Drew reflected on the fact that this would be the first time he logged "bullet holes in vertical stab." He wondered if it would be the last.

He and Rodeo then reported to air intelligence for debrief and were relieved to hear the downed pilot had been plucked out of the rice paddies by the Air Force search and rescue team. Each element covered their portion of the attack, and the air intelligence took notes. Drew and Rodeo, with the other three aircrews, went back to the ready-room. The Skipper had been at the brief. He strode into the room twenty minutes later.

"Good job, Casso. Understand you got shot up a bit?"

"Yes sir. Looks like twenty-three-millimeter holes in the vertical stab."

"Glad to have you back."

"Thanks, Skipper. The tower deserves a nod for their help. Sure hope we don't have to go through that again."

"I'll pass that on to them. Anyway, this thing is going to be active, and I want you to be prepared," the skipper announced.

EIGHTEEN

1970
Fort Worth, Texas

Hope basked in the early morning calm as a fiery orange sun illuminated the wall portraits of her nine-year-old son, Lee. Each whispering image, a reflection of her heart, bore her signature.

Leisure was a luxury, a frivolous indulgence, but with Lee at summer camp for two weeks, she felt a strong desire to drift through memories of when her passion for photography launched a career laced with several challenges: the balance of motherhood, entrepreneurship, and widowhood. Suddenly, the memory of her husband, Patrick, being killed in Vietnam burst into her consciousness. She quickly replaced the horror with visions of loved ones. This morning her mind drifted to one person in particular, Drew Bartlett.

Hope agonized over his continual presence in her dreams; his memory was impossible to escape. Almost nightly, as of late, she could see him standing before her, dressed in his Navy uniform, holding an envelope. The sight would fill her with unrestrained joy. Immediately she would reach out to him before reality would cloak her with feelings of inconceivable loss.

A common routine would follow. She'd throw back the silk bedding, sit straight up on her bed, as she was doing now, and thrust her arms out to the side, drawing invisible circles to release knotted tension. She would pray for inner strength with each motion. Afterwards, she would rub her hand across the tear-soaked pillow, a mute witness to her buried pain, and wonder how long she could maintain the veneer of being happy. Anguish bulged beneath the surface, ready to explode.

She glared at the calendar on the bedside table, while raking her disheveled hair with her fingers. She would return to Colorado in one day.

"Why didn't I decline Annie Ruth's invitation to photograph her daughter's wedding in Estes Park?" Frustration could be heard in the empty room.

It was the same question she had been asking herself for three months. There was no plausible answer, and the need to transition from photographer-to-archaeologist was imminent. Visual reminders of Drew, and their relationship, had been hidden from sight since the moment she realized he was never coming back. Now their love story awaited confrontation. And the mask of pretension she'd been wearing for eleven years needed discarding. Hiding the unanswered questions, the eternal desire for his return, the sadness she had laboriously suppressed, along with the inability to explain his absence was no longer an option.

Hurriedly, she grabbed a rubber band from the nightstand and pulled her shoulder-length hair into a ponytail, before retrieving her tennis shoes from under the bed and slipping on a pair of blue shorts and a faded navy shirt. Afterwards, she glanced into the mirror at a thin, stressed, anxious woman who had lived multiple lives. She was only thirty-one, but her eyes and smile had dimmed. Restless grief lay buried in her bones. Even her mother had begun asking questions.

Hope immediately went to the phone. The morning calls with her mother were enjoyable, but today was different. She was in no shape for cheerful chatter. Nor her mother dropping by.

"Hi Mom, I just wanted to let you know that I'll be occupied this morning with preparations for the trip. Let's talk this evening. 'Bye."

She exhaled a sigh of relief. Her mother's answering machine had absorbed her message, freeing her of an interrogation. Now she could begin the steps of closure.

Hope gathered her beloved dog, Zoey, into her arms before opening the bedroom door. Together, they headed toward the back door where the Pomeranian eagerly pranced outside for her morning routine: chasing squirrels and barking at the birds.

Hope headed to the kitchen where numbly, she placed a slice of bread in the toaster, and absently hit the button on the coffee maker. Instantly, the sound and aroma of fresh coffee filled the room. Taking a cup out of the cabinet, she leaned up against the counter. An eerie, unfamiliar stillness filled the air, underscoring Lee's absence.

Memories of when she purchased the home, situated near her alma mater, Texas Christian University, erupted. At the time, a year had passed since she learned of Patrick's death and the home represented a fresh beginning. She had tackled the remodeling with zeal. Six weeks later, the home gleamed: antique roses twirled around pillars on the front porch greeting guests. Red geraniums tumbled from window boxes. Polished hardwood floors glowed throughout; walls burst alive with color, and new kitchen appliances begged for use. It was her haven.

Hope absently blew on a steaming cup of coffee while running her hand across the antique French dining table. Friends and family had shared lavish stories when gathered around the keepsake. Creations of appetizing delicacies, along with other welcoming signs of hospitality, were in every fiber of her home.

Zoey interrupted the quiet with her soft bark and generous brown eyes pleading for a bite of toast. Hope consented to her wordless request, but when a glance out the window revealed the sun ascending higher into the sky, she resigned herself to the task ahead.

"Zoey, the weatherman said Fort Worth is to reach 101 degrees today. That means it will be so hot we can fry an egg in the attic." Her voice sounded as depleted as her spirits.

She placed the partially consumed cup of coffee in the sink while praying for strength to make the overwhelming journey into her past. Slowly, she wrapped her hand around the garage doorknob and turned the handle. Her breathing became rapid and shallow.

Once inside the garage, she retrieved a ladder and placed it under a section of rope hanging precariously from the garage ceiling. Hesitantly, she pulled on the cord. A folding staircase began to slowly descend. Hinges whined. Her throat constricted. She paused to take several deep breaths. With quivering knees, leaden feet, and wet palms, she began the climb. Each step brought her closer to the secrets she had attempted to bury.

When she reached the dark opening, she gingerly placed her feet on the timbered rafters and stared at the lone light bulb suspended from the ceiling. Perplexed at the distance and unstable flooring, she reminded herself that with one successful pull on the chain, she'd have light.

Stretching forward, she nervously tugged on the links. Instantly, a dim glow spread across the area and moths began fluttering around the bulb, interrupting the ghostly silence.

Her heart picked up its pace, leaving her slightly breathless, as she placed her grandmother's stool near a large antique trunk and sat down. Emotions swelled within her body when she began nervously wrestling with the trunk's rusty lock. After several attempts, abruptly, a loud click echoed. She paused to take several deep breaths before wiping the perspiration from her forehead. Finally, she summoned the courage to raise the lid. A minefield of memories was instantly visible: Lee's baby clothes, a lock of his hair, and a photograph of her father.

Grief swept over her when she recalled giving birth to Lee three days after her husband's death, nine months after their marriage. Before that, Drew's painful disappearance, then the unexpected passing of her father a few years later. Each left a cavernous well of sorrow, but it was Drew who shattered her life. He was the only man she had loved with every fiber of her being.

She combed through the trunk with her hand. The green scrapbook, with "Hope Madison" stamped in gold, lay on the bottom. When she felt the thick cover, a gasp spontaneously emerged. She lifted it carefully from the buried yesterdays, as deep sadness seeped through her fingertips. She gently held the leather album close to her chest, perspiration and tears mingled.

 She opened, with great reluctance, the vault on all the memories she had yet to release. Each one felt as recent as yesterday.

The first few pages revealed menus from Colorado restaurants, along with movie tickets, matchbooks, and a multitude of photos. All these things were prior to Drew Bartlett. Then she turned the page. There lay Drew's graduation program and the photographs that told their story. She stared at the image of Drew standing proud and erect in his formal white uniform, his dark hair covered by the Navy cap. She, in a white linen suit and pearls, had her arm casually looped through his. The two were radiant. The inscription read: *"Drew's Graduation from University of Colorado. May 1959"*.

The following page revealed another milestone: a picture of Hope and Drew standing in the foyer of her home. Evening gloves traveled from her fingertips to the middle of her upper arm, her hand was resting comfortably in the crook of his elbow. The white strapless dress, with layers of billowing organza, blended in striking combination with his dress-white uniform. She read the inscription: *Our First Formal Date. May 22, 1959. Destination: Elitch Garden's Trocadero Ballroom in Denver. We danced to the Guy Lombardo*

Orchestra. Her hands quivered at the sight of joy on both of their faces.

When she moved to the next page, Drew's bold handwriting on yellow-tinged envelopes startled her. Tenderly, she lifted out each monogrammed note and lightly touched his gold initials before reading.

Hope,

You lift my heart and spirit as no other. I didn't know this feeling existed to this extent, anywhere in the world, much less in my world. It seems like I've known you for years, even though you are only now being fully revealed to me.

My Dearest Hope,

I'm sure we've been given an incredibly precious gift; we were meant to be together. It is my regret that we were not placed in each other's lives earlier, though I shall not question God's timing. You are here now, and that is enough.

I love you, Hope, and wish it were the weekend already! I know, I know...don't wish my life away. I'm NOT...for that which I wish for IS life! You are a part of me so very quickly and yet...I think it really wasn't that quickly. I was just unaware of what God had placed in my heart before first laying eyes on you. You are with me, and I am with you.

My Dearest Hope,

Happiness greets me at the beginning and closing of each day. I yearn for the time when I can greet you at such times, and all times in between.

Suffering filtered through her body when the sensation of being wrapped in his arms surfaced. She ached to feel his cocoon of protection, to hear his voice, to feel the warmth of his hand. Finally, she turned the page. There lay the envelope that had been a part of her recent dreams, the one he had given to her the night before he left.

She held it next to her chest, letting her fingers feel the aged paper before opening. Trembling like leaves in a windstorm, she began carefully pulling the letter from the envelope. Tears veiled her eyes.

June 4, 1959

My Dearest Hope,

And that is appropriate on several levels. Not only are you my "dearest Hope," but you are my dearest hope for the future.

Know that whatever may intervene in the next few years for each of us, you will be held in my heart, mind and complete being. We are meant to be, and you may hold that in your heart forever, for it is how long I will love you.

Hope, know I will remember all the times we've been together, beginning with your smile lighting the dark when we met. Your sapphire-blue eyes greeted me with tenderness and gentleness, taking me to a place I've never been. There was an igniting within my soul, and though I did not understand it at the time, I have come to realize from the moment we met, I have been waiting for you all my life.

The glow of your presence: your hair kissed by the light, the sweater framing your face, and the look in your eyes all gave the pain I desperately tried to bury, a magical and wonderful release. You've brought me joy, peacefulness, and a sense of wholeness I've not experienced since losing my mother.

Ensuing days with you brought comfort, as we wandered in the Colorado Rockies. A disclosed ease flowed in our conversations, as if we had been together since childhood. Now,

I'm in classic conflict, torn between leaving you and aspiring to my dream of serving my country. Though I am eternally thankful for the time we've shared, deep regrets for not being granted more time threaten to overwhelm me tonight. Especially since I have found the one person I have longed for, and never knew until now.

Hope, please know that my heart will remain full of the memories we created together: Dancing to the Guy Lombardo band, waltzing around the ballroom, (I never knew I would be grateful for the dance lessons my grandmother insisted upon my taking when I was twelve. Thankfully, my first waltz was with you, and I pray my last will be, as well).

Your being at my graduation and commissioning ceremony, pinning on my Ensign's shoulder boards will remain one of my favorite memories of all time. It was at that moment, when the transition of our past and future merged, I felt life being breathed into all our dreams.

I am confident that these, among others, will keep me company, as will your letters. In the light of your radiance being a world away, I will depend on our correspondence to lift the burdensome weight of distance.

My dream of returning to you will remain at the forefront of my days and nights, for it has been etched upon my being. I will hold you in my heart and trust you will keep me with you as much as I feel your presence every day, whether we are physically in the same location, or not.
I love you, my darling Hope!

Hope postured into the fetal position, quavering with deep sorrow, as she pored over the profound loss. Wails of grief echoed in the hollow, dust-filled archives before she could eventually find her voice. Then, in agony, she screamed.

"What happened, Drew? Why did you disappear without a word? Where did you go?" She felt her heart breaking like shattered glass.

Drew Bartlett, the one who had showered her with adoration and love, had created an immense wound, one that had never healed. While unimaginable grief and raw agony persisted throughout her trembling body, choking sobs escaped into the silent abyss.

After what seemed to be hours, the flood of torrential tears broke when a narrow shaft of light shone through a small opening in the roof. A tranquil presence enveloped her. The scrapbook eventually rested in the trunk once again before she began descending the steps.

Zoey, waiting patiently at the bottom of the attic ladder for Hope, eagerly swept the garage floor with her tail. Hope scooped the dog into her arms, and the two retreated to the patio where sounds of babbling water in a small fountain, songbirds, and mild breezes filled the air. Hope gently relayed her experience to her beloved four-legged friend while stroking the dog's thick amber coat.

"Healing has begun," she said in a trembling voice. "The archeology dig today was in hopes of finding the man I love."

Wiping a stream of tears, she stammered in a barely audible voice.

"I found him. Felt him. Touched him. And I let him go."

For the first time since 1959, Hope Madison was at peace. And ready for Colorado.

NINETEEN

After closing the door on the past, Hope felt excitement and confidence rushing through her while sitting in the Dallas-Fort Worth airport, smoothing the skirt of her emerald dress. She was now prepared to return to the past, regardless of all the unresolved questions.

Abruptly, a man's voice belted through the air.

"Flight 464, for Denver, is now boarding."

Hope grabbed her camera bag and proceeded to the gate.

A well-dressed man with silver hair smiled when she passed his chair. She responded with a broad grin in return; thoughts of her father bubbled to the surface. Whether memories of her dad were evoked by the man's gentle glance, a father proudly admiring his daughter, or if more had been caught in the brief exchange, she determined the silent encounter favorable.

As he continued to follow her with his eyes, he found something unidentifiable about the young lady that touched him. Suddenly, she stopped, frozen in position like a statue. The color drained from her flushed cheeks.

The silver-haired stranger quickly turned to see what provoked the change. He noticed two men in their early twenties walking ahead of her, each wearing shirts emblazoned with anti-war slogans on the front, and a burning American flag on the back. Her rigid stance propelled him forward. Concerned, he asked,

"Are you okay? Is there anything I can do?"

She shook her head, unable to speak.

He quickly lifted the camera bag from her shoulder before guiding her to a seat. He glanced at the two war protesters then turned his full attention to her.

"Can you tell if they are boarding your plane?" he asked.

She shrugged her shoulders; her waxen face framed wide, unblinking eyes.

"Let me walk you over to the agent," he said. "We'll make sure you aren't seated near them, if they are on your flight."

She recalled how difficult it was to observe war demonstrators burning the American flag while Walter Cronkite narrated the CBS Nightly News. But seeing the protesters up close created waves of nausea. Had the Vietnam War claimed both men she had loved?

The courteous man handed her ticket to the American Airlines agent and quietly explained the situation. The airline employee listened while observing Hope's ashen skin and trembling body. His kind eyes and gentle voice brought a sense of assurance when he spoke.

"I will personally take you aboard the plane to ensure they are not seated anywhere near you," he stated firmly.

She nodded.

He motioned for a fellow employee to cover for him while he escorted her down the gateway. The helpful stranger went to the window to watch. After a brief time, the agent returned, strolled over to the man and with a solemn tone he relayed the events.

"She's sitting next to an older lady in the middle of the plane. The men are seated in the back. The restroom facilities are near them, so I whispered instructions in her ear:

'If you need to use the restroom, go to the one in first class.' I also alerted the stewardesses."

"Did she respond?"

"Slightly. Her eyes remained blank, as if in shock, but she nodded which made me think she understood." The employee looked down, shaking his head.

"Do you know what happened to her," he asked.

The Other Part of Her

The stranger responded in a low voice,

"I don't. I can only surmise from her reaction that someone dear to her had been killed in the war. One minute she was glowing; then the two men stepped in front of her, and she appeared to be traumatized. It was as if she catapulted to another place."

The stranger's concern was evident in his whisper, "I'm sorry I couldn't be on her plane."

Hope turned to stare out the window at the luggage handlers loading the last bags onto the plane, while the ground crew waved their bright orange batons. Gradually, the plane pulled away from the gate. She took a deep breath and mentally willed the lady next to her to be quiet. She then opened a book to emphasize her desire for solitude. Occasionally, she would turn the pages. When her seatmate appeared restless and on the verge of unleashing an endless amount of chatter, Hope would lean back, close her eyes and let her mind slowly drift to years earlier.

The dilemma of being a young widow had frequently aroused people's curiosity. She would address their inquiries, but her pain didn't go away when they did. Efforts to be polite while keeping her spirits up continued to be a futile struggle, until she consulted with her pastor.

"You have every right to reserve disclosure," he assured. "You can choose the people with whom you wish to share, and you have gracious permission to limit your responses with others. Above all, you need to nourish the healing of your wounds in a climate of protection."

She needed specificity and he graciously offered her a tactful response:

"I'm too emotionally raw to talk about it. The pain is still very much with me."

His words poured over her like warm honey.

Thoughts returned to the other compassionate man: the gray-haired stranger in the airport. Silent words of thanksgiving flowed to the nameless individual. He, too, had comforted her when grief had spread over her entire body.

"Would you like anything to drink?" asked the flight attendant.

"Coca-Cola, please."

Hope unfolded the tray table, took the drink, and stared out the window. She consciously changed her mental direction to when she learned Odie B had elected to stay in Boulder, instead of returning to Texas with Hope's parents. Odie B's decision was the right one, but Hope had missed her best friend and confidant.

Lengthy letters had been exchanged over the years, and on two occasions Odie B had traveled to be by her side. The first was after Patrick died; then a few years later when her father, Tennessee, suddenly passed away.

Hope smiled to herself as anticipation of another visit neared. Especially, since heartache wouldn't surround them like rats in a deserted attic.

Her mind began drifting to the time when Odie B became a part of their family.

It was two weeks after Fort Worth's devastating flood. Hope was eight years old, in her room playing, when she heard her mother shouting from the kitchen.

"Hope, someone's ringing the doorbell. Would you get it?"

"Okay, Mama."

Hope raced to the door with her long curls flying.

"Mama, it's Odie B!!"

She threw her little arms around Odie B's large girth and squeezed.

"Odie B, I'm so glad you're back! I've missed you."

Odie B responded with a sad smile.

"I'll go get Mama. I don't think she heard me." She scampered away, leaving Odie B in the living room alone.

The twenty-year-old maid nervously yanked on her skirt while holding back an unrelenting army of tears. A few errant ones rolled down her face when Mrs. Madison rushed into the room, wiping her hands on the starched apron tied around her trim waist. Beneath the apron, a sage floral dress complimented her auburn hair and green eyes.

"Odie B, it's so nice to see you. Please, have a seat." Mrs. Madison gestured toward a velvet sofa. Hope curled up beside Odie B while her mother sat opposite them.

Mrs. Madison, confused by Odie B's unexpected appearance, and particularly, the absence of Mama B, pelted her with questions.

"I tried to call your mother when she didn't show up for work, but I couldn't reach her. With so many phone lines down, due to the terrible flood, I felt yours must have been affected. It wasn't like her not to show up or call. How is she? Where is she? Everyone is talking about the flood being the largest disaster in Fort Worth history."

Odie B stared at the floral rug while nervously wrapping a worn handkerchief around her finger. She remained silent, biting on her lower lip while wiping tears. Hope studied how the straw hat, perched on top of her black frizzy hair, managed to stay on, while Odie B nervously blotted perspiration on her neck.

Mrs. Madison noticed her distress and offered to get her a glass of iced tea.

"No, thank you, Ma'am."

"Well, tell me about you and your Mama. Hope has been lost without you to talk to, especially since her sister, Riley, is busy getting ready to leave for college."

Odie B looked up at Mrs. Madison and choked out words amidst sobs.

"Mama B passed in the flood. When the levee broke, the water swept us away."

Mrs. Madison gasped, and Hope ran to the kitchen to get Odie B a glass of sweet tea. When she returned, Odie B was trying to explain what happened.

"Streets turned into rivers, and houses floated by with dogs and cats on the rooftop; I even saw a horse on top of one. Some people came in a boat and got me, but when they found Mama B, the Good Lord had already taken her to the Promised Land."

"Oh, Odie B, I had no idea! I never even thought of that possibility. I'm so, so sorry!" Mrs. Madison, shocked and distressed, spoke softly.

Hope placed Odie B's large hand between her tiny hands and clasped it tightly.

"What can we do? Do you have any other family?" asked Mrs. Madison.

"No Ma'am."

Mrs. Madison silently gathered her thoughts.

"Odie B, would you like to work for us?"

"Yes Ma'am, I would," she whispered.

Mrs. Madison continued with questions.

"Where are you living?"

"I'm at my church, on a cot in the basement with the others who lost their homes."

"Well, Odie B, let me do some checking and if I can find a friend who has extra space, would you be willing to work for two families?"

"Yes Ma'am."

"Okay, let me check. How can I reach you?"

"I'm at the Baptist Church on Riverside."

Mrs. Madison stood up, left the room briefly, and returned with a twenty-dollar bill. She placed it in Odie B's hand.

"I will help you all I can. This is all I have in my purse today, but I will tell Mr. Madison, and he will help you until you get back on your feet."

"Thank you, Ma'am."

"Your mama was a wonderful lady, Odie B." Kathryn Madison's rare display of emotion was caught in her throat. She took a minute to compose herself.

"We'll figure something out. Don't you worry."

"Thank you, Ma'am."

As Mrs. Madison rushed from the room, filled with determination to find a solution, Hope threw her tiny arms around Odie B's neck. Together, they cried on that warm spring afternoon.

A common sight followed in the days ahead - Hope sitting on a kitchen stool visiting with Odie B.

"Did you want Mama B to have more babies?"

"When I was a little girl, I did; Mama had two babies before I was born. They were stillbirths."

Hope had no idea what that meant, but she knew it wasn't good from Odie B's contorted face. Hope bowed her head respectfully and nodded. She also made a mental note to ask her mother for an explanation.

"Do you have a daddy?"

"No, he's gone. Never seen him."

"Do you have a grandmother?"

"No, just Mama B."

Hope promptly jumped down off the stool and placed her hands firmly on her waist, like she had seen her mother do. Her voice was stern.

"Odie B, we're your family now!"

A broad smile crept across Odie B's face until her gold tooth sparkled in the window light and salty tears formed in her large brown eyes. Hesitantly, she replied.

"I'd like that. Yes, I would."

At that precise moment, they became family, and, in Hope's eight-year-old mind, the solidifying bond entitled her "sister" to hear her every thought. The twelve-year age difference never intruded.

Odie B quickly learned Hope Madison could talk the horns off a goat!

Hope was jolted to the present by an announcement.

"The captain has turned on the seat belt sign. Please, put your seats in upright position and lock your tray tables. Stow all personal belongings under the seat in front of you. Prepare for landing."

Hope peered out the window, craning her neck to see the majestic mountains dressed in small patches of snow and the swirls of crimson and persimmon aimlessly floating in the sky. She gasped aloud when emerald, green meadows, sprawling farmland, and rushing rivers came closer and closer. Her heart was pounding so loudly she wondered if the lady sitting next to her could hear it. So much had changed in her life, but her love for Colorado remained.

She hurriedly exited the Stapleton International Airport in a pre-arranged rental car, rolling the windows down as she did, and for the next two hours she would absorb the unique smells of pine and cedar in the darkening sky.

The Stanley Hotel, her destination, filled her with dread and an onslaught of heartbreaking memories. She agonized over each: having brunch with Drew at the Stanley, traipsing through the forest to reach the magnificent waterfall, their first kiss.

Annie Ruth was pacing across the marble floor in the lobby when Hope entered. Together, they deposited her luggage and photography equipment, then the two ladies strolled, arm-in-arm, to a popular steak restaurant. Gasps of astonishment punctuated their conversation throughout dinner. Even as close as they were, Hope had not shared Drew's existence, even though Annie Ruth had spent much of her time arranging dates for Hope. All to no avail.

Their conversation sped through topics as fast as a speeding train until both finished their steaks, and the cheesecake had no remaining crumbs.

"Let's meet at eight o'clock tomorrow morning for breakfast in the hotel dining room," Annie Ruth suggested, as they ambled back to the hotel.

"Sounds wonderful!" The obvious lilt in Hope's voice surprised and warmed her friend. She'd not seen it in the years they had known each other, which in truth, hadn't been that many. But it had been long enough to see Lee grow from a toddler to a nine-year-old. And to see Hope alone night after night.

They strolled back to the hotel under a full moon with Annie Ruth profusely chatting. Hope found herself silently battling an onslaught of emotions. In particular, the day she and Drew dined at the hotel, where she was now staying, and the trip up to the forest where they shared their first kiss.

Hope cringed in fear that the weekend might be a replay of their time together, as she put on her pajamas and fell into luxurious linens that dressed the four-poster bed. Thankfully, exhaustion consumed her.

TWENTY

Aboard the USS Ranger, China Sea

A military trunk, filled with paraphernalia of a Naval officer, sits in the middle of the stateroom, waiting to be closed. Drew hesitates. Wavering on the act is unusual after years in the military, and after living the dream for which he had longed. Now, at the age of thirty-three, he knows he's a different man from the one who began the journey. Years ago, he had answers. Today, he has questions. Profound love does that to a person. So does war.

Heavy footsteps halt in front of his door, then a loud knock.

He opens the door, reluctantly. There, in full red-headed glory, stands "Java," the guy known for being spring-loaded to party position.

"Hey, you want to…" Java stops, but his Kentucky drawl stretches across the room like a kite blowing in the wind.

"What happened?" he asks. Shock is heard in his voice.

Drew glares at him. Java pushes him aside and closes the door. Drew could smell his cologne, something new and musky. His wife must have sent it to him. "It's her thing," he had said long ago.

"What's bothering you, Drew? Where's your upbeat attitude and trademark cocky grin? You look like you have something bothering you. You BETTER get it off your chest or you're going to blow a hole right through this ship." Anger flashes in Java's eyes, his fist knots into a ball, and suddenly the atmosphere is as tense as the Combat Information Center during an air strike.

Naval Commanders, of which Drew is one, are tight-lipped. He understands Java's motivation and appreciates his intention but denies his observations. Until he gets a glimpse of himself in the mirror. Frowns crease his forehead, and a splinter of gray pokes through his dark hair like a crescent moon on a dark night. But he refuses to acknowledge the alterations. Instead, he gives him the Commander glare, and voice.

"Talk about what?" Drew bellows.

"Don't play games with me!" Java's ruddy complexion is now deep red. "I've always been able to tell when something is on your mind, even during our first deployment together."

Drew remains mute while Java stares at him with worried eyes. They each grab a door handle to steady themselves, as waves gently roll the 60,000-ton aircraft carrier. Silence hangs suspended. Finally, Java delivers the message that aviators fear.

"Pent-up pressure will threaten to impair your performance, Drew, as well as your ability to function. Furthermore, if the hierarchy were to get wind of your current stress level, flying restrictions and medical evaluations would ensue."

Java begins to pace back and forth.

"We're talking about your career here, Drew. Everything is on the line. You're a distinguished aviator, one of the best in the Navy. All this speaks of a brilliant career, but you look like you're about to crash and burn. Let it out! What happened?"

Java shakes his head in frustration, then pauses in front of the trunk and points to a small photo resting on top.

"Does the change in you have anything to do with her?"

Drew bites his lip. Java repeats the question, louder, as he leans up against the wall with arms crossed and eyebrows raised.

"I'm about to return to the place where it all began..." Drew's voice fractures. He reaches for a chair, sits down, and stares at the floor while he clears his throat.

"Eleven years have passed since she transformed my world in a millisecond. When the dream disappeared, I held on to a speck of hope with a death grip like my whole life depended upon it. I still do today." Drew sat in agony, barely able to form the words.

They stared at each other in uncomfortable silence.

"Are you telling me that returning to Colorado, where you two met, is doing this to you?"

Drew nodded, unable to make eye contact, as he stumbled through an explanation.

"I know it sounds crazy. It does to my own ears, but every sight and sound will remind me of her, of what we had. And lost," he said.

Java's eyes opened wide when Drew began to reveal what he'd never verbalized or accepted.

"The worst part will be coming face-to-face with stark reality and continuing to live a life empty of her," his voice cracked.

"She had *that* much impact on you…?" Disbelief echoes in Java's voice.

"Yeah, even though she…" Drew catches himself from recounting the story, the same one Java already knows. Instead, he reaches into the trunk for a manila envelope with "PERSONAL AND CONFIDENTIAL" boldly stamped across the front. Beads of sweat form on his forehead when he hands it to Java.

"What's this?"

"It's all there. Everything."

"What do you mean it's…?" Java quickly clamps his mouth shut when memories surface.

Drew ducks his head, as the sound of the envelope being tightly gripped merges with the sound of engines. A moment later the door closes.

Drew stands and quickly places a duplicate envelope inside of his briefcase, as an act of precaution.

****

When the pilot came on the speaker, Drew checked his watch. Ten-fifteen. Almost twenty hours had passed since the plane left the runway in Asia. Fatigue crawled in every cell of his body, but the colorful glow of Denver's lights, off in the distance, evoked recollections of the brilliant stones in his grandmother's jewelry box.

Darkness prevented him from seeing the rivers, but he knew the sight from memory, where they were, their speed, the location of the bends, as well as the mountainous terrain nearby. He visualized lush greenery and summer flowers peeking through rocks, as the flashing runway beacon welcomed him home.

Emotions raced through his battle-weary body while he retrieved his luggage and secured a car from the rental agency. He adjusted the seat to fit his lanky frame before turning the automobile toward his hometown, Idaho Springs.

Drew drove the dark, winding mountain roads, restless from ghosts and wired from caffeine. The teasing moon played hide-and-seek behind towering evergreen trees; a breeze blew through the open windows.

A recent letter from his father's lawyer lay heavily on his mind.

"Dr. Bartlett's Will has been updated and he has appointed you as the Executor. You'll be in control of his financial and physical issues."

The lawyer added a personal note:

Drew,

I have good and bad news. Your father's wife divorced him after years of draining his finances. I'm sorry to say he's almost bankrupt. The good news is, your father has quit drinking, but health issues require him to have assistance. His caregiver, Fiona Hills, hired by your grandmother three years ago, has been serving him on a part-time basis. Since the recent death of

your grandmother, Ms. Hills now tends to him daily. I'm sorry I don't have better news.
John M. Rutledge, Attorney at Law

Drew knew the homecoming would be difficult, but his father needed him. Nothing else mattered. "Too late for a father-son relationship," he grumbled.

Regret mingled with the scent of pine in the night air, as memories of Hope began gasping after years of suffocation. He didn't suppress them, nor did he choose their direction of travel like he had throughout the years. The truth was, a day never ended when he didn't think of her, especially when he stood on the bow of the ship, staring at the stars. Every detail of their time together remained etched in his mind like an engraved memorial honoring the past. His heart remained the same.

Drew took the Idaho Springs exit, turned at the corner drugstore, and drove two more blocks. A porch light guided him to the third house, his dad's home. He took a deep breath, drove in the driveway, and wearily removed his luggage. He retrieved the key from under the doormat and stepped inside.

His father's snoring resembled the rising and falling of ocean waves. Drew turned the TV off, though he wished to watch, and perhaps he'd chuckle while Johnny Carson performed his opening monologue.

Instead, he gently shook his father.

"I'm home, Dad."

His father snorted, then lazily opened his eyes. His unshaven face, stale breath, and soiled clothes alarmed Drew.

"Glad you made it home," he muttered.

"Thanks, Dad. I am, too."

In some odd way, he knew his dad meant it and so did he.

Drew assisted with his dad's bedtime rituals before going to his childhood bedroom, a place he hadn't seen since the age of five. As quick as an eyelid's blink, grief consumed him.

A month had passed since his grandmother died peacefully in her sleep. Memories of her waiting at the door, fueling him with love and leftovers, consumed him.

Intense pain for the whole situation burst like rockets into one wide blaze: his absent dad, the loss of his mother and grandmother, along with Hope and the shock of her marriage.

Grabbing his duffel bag, he noticed a small photo of Hope spill onto the floor. Quiet cries of agony followed.

When the anguish dissolved, he reached for the alarm clock, staring numbly at the dial while calculating events for the following day: breakfast with his dad, a phone call to his auto mechanic, a trip to the florist, then to the cemetery.

He set the alarm for six-thirty, which would allow him ample time to accomplish the list and be in Boulder by mid-morning.

Drew felt optimistic when he awoke. Thoughts of a new future, one free of the past, began when he and his dad enjoyed a pleasant visit over breakfast. After a shower, he slipped on his dress-white uniform, made a few phone calls, then drove to the cemetery where he placed roses on the graves of his mother and grandmother.

All tasks had been promptly executed prior to his driving to Boulder. Drew was happy he could attend Ken Whitmire's Change-of-Command ceremony at the University. Drew congratulated him on his promotion to Captain and his appointment as Commanding Officer of the unit. They briefly shared a couple of laughs and stories, then Ken urged Drew to hang around a bit.

"Let's continue our relentless treasure trove of sea stories over a burger at the Sink.

Drew checked his watch.

Ken observed the reluctance in his eyes but continued just the same.

"It's just across the street, so if you don't have some place you have to be or some hot chick waiting, we can be twenty-one again and re-live our triumphs, on the football field and off."

They both chuckled, knowing there were plenty of mishaps they would ignore while exaggerating their wins. All held a small degree of truth.

"I'd like that, but I have an appointment in a few minutes, and I can't be late," Drew replied.

Ken gave him a questioning glance but didn't pursue the matter.

"Okay. It really meant a lot to have you here." Ken shook Drew's hand while thanking him for coming.

"I wouldn't have missed it, Brother. Not on your life."

Drew's grin was forced, and they both knew it. Being back in Boulder had triggered unexpected emotions, and he felt more would come in the hours ahead. He tried to conceal the avalanche, but Ken was thinking about Drew while wandering slowly back to the ROTC building.

It wasn't their conversation, Ken decided, but the change in Drew's demeanor at the end, as if he were hiding something. He wondered if it had anything to do with Hope, and quickly dismissed the idea, since years had passed from when they last saw each other. Nothing could survive that long, he determined.

Drew removed his gold lace-encrusted cap, placing it carefully on the back seat; then he reached into his pocket for a handkerchief to wipe the driver's seat. His white uniform, a magnet for residue, required precautions. When he felt confident the seat held no threat, he slid in behind the steering wheel, lifted his aviator sunglasses off the visor, changed the radio station, and shifted into reverse.

The realization that he had forgotten to make a follow-up phone call to his mechanic, prior to leaving Ken's office, made him uneasy. The mechanic had picked up his Corvette that morning, but Drew needed to address problems, if there were any. A lump formed in his throat when he remembered how his grandmother would always have the car waiting for him when he came home on leave, complete with a tune-up and a fresh coat of wax.

He drove through the campus where little had changed since he was a student. Off in the distance, the last remaining snowfall clung to Longs Peak, the mountain he had often climbed. The cerulean-blue sky and cool air were a welcome diversion from the scorching heat of Asia.

He continued to cruise down Broadway, through several neighborhoods, before he found himself directly in front of Hope's former home. He pulled over, aware the Madisons had moved back to Texas shortly after returning from Europe. For some strange reason, he resented the current owners.

Memories gradually emerged, but the front door, a silent memorial of lingering goodnight kisses, made him ache.

He recalled the time Hope had appeared at the top of their elegant staircase, dressed in a white formal. The scene grew fresh in his mind. Her tiara glistened under the chandelier light, as she moved with grace and refinement down the steps. He met her piercing, blue eyes with a stoic expression, one that came naturally when he wore his Navy uniform. But like ice under a blazing sun, his reserve melted into a broad, unguarded smile when he slipped a corsage of pink rosebuds over her wrist. Her face burned when she observed his eyes traveling to the bareness of her shoulder and slender neck. His insides wound into a tight ball from the touch of her.

Sounds from the Guy Lombardo Band were playing in his head, and a mental movie of that night, their first formal dance together, came into sight. In his opinion, it was poetry in motion. His buddies referred to them as "Fred Astaire and Ginger Rogers," the most popular dance team in Hollywood.

Sad and angry that life had taken something so beautiful away, Drew's well-controlled emotions began to unravel like a skein of yarn. With her, he had found an escape, and the realization of the depth and passion with which he had loved her, reminded him that he still did.

He glanced in the rearview mirror. Despair trailed in his eyes; his tanned skin appeared pale and drawn.

Haunted by the memories, attempting to compose his thoughts, but a moment later he found himself comparing Hope with all the ladies he'd met through the years. There had been plenty around the world, but attractive appearances didn't connect him unless certain characteristics were present. He knew the list and quickly ran through it:

"Inborn Intellect": a heightened intuition and sensitivity to others, similar to an animal's awareness. Natural instincts were her birthright.

"God Listener": one who would allow the quiet crucible of personal sufferings forge her faith in God. Inner peace, immeasurable hope, and abundant gratitude would flow from her as easily as water from a faucet.

"Lover of Life": one with an insatiable zest for living. Adversity and positivity would mingle with success, defeat, and courage in her light spirit. A crown of faith, joy, and generosity would be her finest accessories.

Only one person possessed all three attributes. Hope Madison.

Now, a cloud of intense yearning, greater than any during their years of separation, fell over him.

He took a deep breath and checked his watch. The moment had arrived for him to drive to Odie B's. The possibility of her regaling him with stories about Hope, along with tales of her husband, plunged him further into despair.

Nine years had passed since Mr. Madison informed him of her marriage.

Angrily turning the key in the ignition, he headed the car toward Pine Street. A taste of bitterness crawled up his throat. Love had been struck down, not by a sword, but by Mr. Madison's mighty pen.

At that moment, the guilt he had suppressed for years surfaced. Mr. Madison wasn't the only one to blame. He, too, had failed to live by the profound lesson from a former instructor, a Navy Seal: *Never leave anyone behind.*

The one he loved above all others, had been left. Not purposefully, but in retrospect, he had left her behind. And he had never forgiven himself for failing to reassure her that he would be waiting for as long as it took.

TWENTY-ONE

Odie B peeked out from behind her living room curtains, clapping her hands in delight as Drew unfolded his long legs and reached for a bouquet of red roses. Unable to contain her excitement any longer, she ran out the door yelling,

"Well, butter my butt and call me a biscuit!"

"Hi, Odie B. It's good to see you!"

"It's good to see you, too, Mr. Drew. You sure look mighty fine in that uniform. Yes sir, you're a sight for sore eyes, all right." She gave him several hearty pats on the back.

"It's a pleasure to see you and your new place. Thank you for inviting me." He handed her the roses and together, they walked up to the porch.

"Oh, Mr. Drew, no one's ever given me roses before!" Her smile made the bright sun appear faint.

"I'm glad to be the first. Your yard sure looks pretty, Odie B. Everything is in bloom."

"Thank you, but it's so dry, the trees are bribing the dogs!"

Drew followed her into the house, chuckling.

"I will get us a glass of iced tea, Mr. Drew, then we can visit."

Odie B shuffled off to the kitchen before he could respond. Then she yelled back, "Make yourself at home."

"Thank you, I will."

Drew noted her comfortable arrangement: a recliner by the window with a small table standing next to it, where her reading glasses and Bible rested. Her polished dinette table stood near the kitchen with its leaves folded down. A framed picture of the "Last Supper" hung above.

Odie B entered, proudly carrying the bouquet of roses. She quickly moved the bowl of plastic fruit from the center of the dining table and placed the vase in its place, beaming as she did. She then stepped back, putting her hands on her hips while she admired the bouquet. She then hurriedly fixed two glasses of sweet tea. While handing one to Drew, she directed him to sit on the sofa, opposite her recliner.

"Just put your drink on the end table."

Drew set the drink down on a coaster. "I really like your house, Odie B. You've done a nice job; it's very comfortable."

"Thank you, Mr. Drew. I'm a very proud homeowner, and it's all because of Mr. Madison. God Bless Him."

"How is he, and Mrs. Madison?"

Her eyes opened wide, and she shook her head back and forth while staring at the floor, "Oh, Lawdy boy, we have some catching up to do. When was the last time you heard from the Madisons?"

"Nine years ago," he said. "That's when I got a brief message from Mr. Madison telling me Hope was married." The words clung to his tongue like a bad taste.

"I think you need to know some things. Do you want me to tell you?"

Before he could answer, she continued,

"When I contacted you a few months ago, I asked if you were married, or had a girlfriend. You said, 'no' to both. Is that still true?" she asked.

"Yes, that's still true. How did you find me?"

"I saw an envelope addressed to you laying on Mr. Madison's desk. I thought I might need it someday, so I quickly copied down your address, then I saved it for a long time. I'll give more details, but first, do you still have feelings for Miss Hope?"

"I'm afraid I do, even though I shouldn't with her being married."

He was trying to process the speed at which Odie B unveiled the subject of Hope. Bracing for updates about her happy life, he felt his stomach lurch.

"Mr. Drew, her husband was killed in Vietnam a few months after they married."

"WHAT?" he exclaimed.

"Yes, and Miss Hope was pregnant."

"Oh no." He threw his hands over his face, as he tried to grasp the words.

"Let me go back to when you and Miss Hope were together. I'll just hit the high spots because I must get to my church so I can help the Bee Blossoms in a little while. We're a quilting bee."

"Sure, that's fine."

"The first thing I want to know is why didn't you write Miss Hope?" Her frown and tone were grim.

Drew stared into her eyes, as he recounted the events.

"Mr. Madison wrote me a letter before I left Boulder."

"Now this is news I haven't heard before!"

"Yes. Mrs. Madison handed the letter to me when I stopped by their house to see Hope one final time before I left for the Navy. I wanted to surprise her, even though we had said goodbye the night before, but she wasn't home. Mrs. Madison greeted me, spoke briefly then handed me a letter Hope knew nothing about. Mr. Madison had asked her to mail it, but since I showed up unexpectedly, she handed it to me, instead.

"In it, Mr. Madison demanded that I have no contact with Hope until she graduated from college. He felt she needed to mature. He added that she was 'all or nothing' and he didn't want her to ruin the college experience pining away for someone so far away; someone who may or may not be that interested in her."

Odie B's mouth, void of sound, gaped open.

"I can tell you nothing has ever hit me so hard, but I agreed to his demand with one stipulation: that he would let me know how she was doing from time to time. The next correspondence from him, other than his annual updates in a Christmas note, was a few weeks prior to her graduation.

"I had planned to be at her graduation ceremony so when I opened the letter, I thought pertinent information would be revealed. Seeing her again was my reason for living, but when I saw that she had gotten married without any warning…well, I've had a very difficult time with that, to say the least." Battling with the overwhelming emotions, he paused to moisten his dry throat with a sip of tea before continuing.

"I mentally filed it away where it has pretty much stayed until this trip. I knew seeing you and Hope's old home would bring it all back, but I didn't expect the onslaught of emotions I've had since landing. I'm afraid I miss her as much as I did when we parted."

"I'm so sorry." Odie B was dabbing at the tears in her eyes. Sadness and shock infiltrated her entire being.

"Mr. Drew, I know Mr. Madison wanted to protect his baby girl from ever being hurt, but it still doesn't make it right. I know you've been hurting, but here's what you don't know.

"You feel like you lost her when she up and married before graduating from college without so much as a word to her parents until three days before she married. Her mama wouldn't even go to her wedding because it was spur of the moment. Hope didn't even have a big white wedding dress and Mrs. Madison wanted a proper wedding, with all the people and parties. She told Hope to buy a pretty dress, and they would see her later. His family was at the wedding, a preacher and that was it."

"Do you know why she did it that way? What the rush was?"

"No," she shook her head. "No one knew. We all were grieving. Only Miss Hope knows the reason, but we've never been told. She looks delicate and frail but let me tell you something: Miss Hope has a will of iron and when she makes up her mind to do something, she does it.

"Mr. Madison knew that, so when he told you not to contact Miss Hope, it was because he knew she'd be foolish enough to run off and marry you."

"What would be wrong with that? She did it with someone else."

"I tell you what's wrong with it. Miss Hope wasn't ready to marry anyone when you left for the Navy. I watched her grow up, and those boys..." Odie B paused, took a gulp of tea then leaned over to look Drew square in the eye.

"You know when you catch a fish, you remove the hook out of its mouth then it starts flipping and flopping in your hand."

Drew raised his eyebrows, straining to follow the connection.

"Miss Hope would let boys wiggle, flip and flop around her for a day or two then she'd cut 'em loose and throw 'em back in the water. She was the original 'catch and release'."

Drew chuckled, but he felt dizzy from all the information. Odie B continued talking without taking a breath.

"When I was down in Texas for Mr. Madison's funeral...."

"Wait a minute. Mr. Madison died too?"

"Yes. Heart attack five years ago."

Drew, angry at the loss of time with Hope, threw his head back, covering his eyes with his hands.

Odie B refreshed his tea, then sat back down. "I went back to Texas, so I could help Hope and Mrs. Madison. That was when I saw the envelope addressed to you on his desk"

"I never got a letter from him after he wrote about her marriage and that was several years earlier. I wonder where the letter went."

She hurried to explain. "I put it in the top drawer of his desk. It may still be there."

"How come I never heard about any of this?" he asked.

"I didn't know why you didn't write, nor did Hope. She had a baby a few days after Mr. Patrick was killed and I couldn't see her hurt again," Odie B said.

Drew felt the air leaving the room. Breathing was difficult.

"Hope, losing her husband and being both mama and daddy to her little boy, got back on her feet and started a career, then Mr. Madison's death...well, it was just too much for all of them. Especially Hope. She looked as lost as last year's Easter eggs."

Odie B drank her tea while he reflected on all the suffering Hope had endured.

"After the funeral, Hope whispered to me that the two men she loved with all her heart left without saying goodbye. I looked at her, wondering if she were talking about Mr. Patrick and her daddy, but she wasn't, and I knew it."

Drew groaned.

"Like I was saying, when I went to Mr. Madison's funeral, I met a young man that Hope had been seeing." Odie B's mischievous tone and stifled grin amused Drew.

"He hung around her, followed her everywhere, but that boy didn't have the IQ of a dinner plate." Slapping her knee and grinning, she kept on.

"Yes sir, Mr. Drew, he had never been known to use a word that might send a reader to the dictionary. He was about as useful as an ashtray on a motorcycle."

Drew burst out laughing, while she shook her head and stared at the floor, in pity of the useless boy. Finally, she couldn't contain herself, and they both doubled over in laughter. When she caught her breath, she wiped the tears from her eyes with a tissue she pulled out of her cleavage, before adding,

"His mama should've thrown him away and kept the stork."

Drew strangled on the tea he was trying to swallow. Sprays shot out of his mouth like a cannon ball. Odie B handed him her hanky and glanced at the clock, then she became serious once again.

"Hope never looked at anyone the way she looked at you, and she never felt the same with any of the others, as she did with you. I watched her grow up and I knew you two had something special. When you left, and she didn't hear from you, her heart was broken. She moped around and cried all the time."

A knife penetrated his heart when he heard of Hope's suffering. Fogged mentally, lost in her pain, he tried to absorb Odie B's relentless details.

"Hope went back to college without one ounce of happiness. I knew she'd get through it, but it sure was hard watching her. I didn't know Mr. Madison had told you to stay away from her until she grew up. That just wasn't right. Watchin' her lose her first love and her life change at twenty years old, I knew the good Lord would have to give her a heaping amount of faith and a boat full of strength to get through it. And He did."

She noticed his empty glass and jumped up again.

"Let me get you some more tea."

"Thank you. This is all quite a shock. My mouth is as dry as a bone." Mentally, he wished for a short break, but Odie B seemed to fly without brakes.

She went to the kitchen, refilled the glass, and handed it to him without skipping a word.

"Mr. Drew, did you know Kathryn Madison could start an argument in an empty house?"

He laughed then raised his eyebrows at the insight.

"Miss Hope is a rule-follower, a peacemaker. Miss Riley is like her mama. She makes up her own mind and doesn't listen to anyone."

She leaned forward, and whispered,

"If you want to know my opinion, I think Miss Riley delights in testing Hope."

She leaned back.

"Yes, those two girls are like night and day, but they love each other, even if they're different in their own way.

"In my opinion, Mr. Patrick was able to talk Hope into marrying him 'cause she didn't want to upset him, especially before he left for war. And she also couldn't stand the thought of losing another man and enduring the pain of loss again.

"She liked it that he was going to be a preacher, after he got home from Vietnam, but she didn't feel about him like she did you. No sir. Not even close. After you left, I think she was determined not to feel that deeply for anyone ever again."

Odie B reflected on the grief Mr. Madison caused while she stared at her feet. Then like a ray of sunshine bursting through a thunderstorm, she offered encouragement.

"Miss Hope is a light, even if she's only a speck since her daddy passed, her husband died in the war, and you gone without a word.

Yes, now she's just a speck, but she'll burst into flame again. Yes, she will."

Glancing at Drew, Odie B thought to herself, if brains were leather, he wouldn't have enough to saddle a bug right now.

She had laid it on a bit heavy with him, but she wanted to be sure he would never approach Hope if he weren't in love with her and ready to commit.

"Mr. Drew, we've plowed this road right down to the bedrock. Time to rest the mule."

Standing up, she reached for his glass.

"Did you know Miss Hope taught me to read?"

"No, I didn't know that. When was that?"

"When she was eight years old. I'll tell you about it, but let's have some peach cobbler with a little ice cream first."

"Sounds wonderful." Drew attempted enthusiasm, but he couldn't fool her. She knew he was about ready to cry or put his fist through the wall. Maybe both. And she didn't blame him.

Drew followed her toward the kitchen, but when he saw the size of the small room, he leaned up against the doorway instead. She noticed his reluctance to follow her.

"This space is so narrow I have to go out in the hall to change my mind."

Chuckling, he shook his head as she removed two orange bowls from the cabinet and scooped generous portions of cobbler, each with a big round ball of vanilla ice cream on top. She opened the drawer, reached for two spoons, and glanced at the wall clock. A car door slammed nearby.

"Excuse me", she said, letting the spoon fall onto the floor and almost knocking Drew down to get past him.

"You go ahead and get the spoons," she yelled to him as she headed for the front door.

"I sure will! This ice cream certainly looks good, Odie B," he yelled, about the time the door slammed shut.

Drew stuck a spoon in each bowl, tore off a couple of paper towels for napkins, got out the ice and refilled two Mason jars with sweet tea. A phone, hanging on the wall, reminded him to check with his mechanic. He hung up a few minutes later, feeling a sense of relief. He would pick his car up in the morning.

Odie B went running out the front door with arms outstretched, wearing a smile almost as wide as Hope's waiting embrace. Tears welled in the eyes of both women as laughter burst from their souls. They were finally together again.

"Let me get a good look at you, Miss Hope. You're a sight for sore eyes. Yes ma'am, but I think you're needin' some of Odie B's cookin'. We need to put some meat on those bones and fatten you up!"

They walked arm-in-arm up the groomed path but before they reached the front porch, Odie B stopped to prune a few wilted leaves on the red geraniums.

"Your house is so pretty."

"Thank you. Your Daddy left me stock before he crossed over to glory. Bless his heart. Yes, Mr. Madison paid for this." She made a broad sweeping gesture with her arms in the air. "I invested all the rest with his stockbroker, Mr. Miller, and that man has made me a wealthy woman."

She grinned from ear-to-ear, then lowered her voice to a whisper, "I think the only reason he's so nice to me is because I have more money than God!" They were both chuckling as Odie B opened the door and led the way.

"Come in. There is someone I want you to see."

The Other Part of Her

Hope entered the living room, smiling, taking it all in. Odie B waved toward a brown wooden bench. "Put your purse there," she instructed.

Hope placed her purse on the bench and paused to glance in a wall mirror before turning around. That was when she saw him.

Drew came into the room balancing two glasses of iced tea, his head bent toward the floor. When he glanced up, all color drained from his face and one of the wet glasses crashed to the floor. He stood, frozen. Turning away from Hope was impossible. He feared she would disappear.

Odie B quickly grabbed a towel from the kitchen and bent down on her knees behind him. She gently nudged his legs to move closer to Hope. Drew robotically advanced two steps.

Odie B scooped the ice cubes back into the glass and laid a towel over the river of tea. Backing out of the room with the glass and dripping towel, Odie B waited until she got into the kitchen before softly praising God with unapologetic joy.

"Thank ya' Jesus!" Her hips jiggled in a dance of celebration while she waved her arms high in the air. "Thank ya', Mama B!"

Hope and Drew, unaware of the private celebration behind the wall, stared wide-eyed, in disbelief. He had fought for his life during difficult missions over Vietnam, with traumatic results, but the shock of seeing Hope left him paralyzed. When he opened his mouth, words hung in his throat. He began shaking his head back and forth, as if awakening from a dream, but his eyes never left her. Silently, he began reconciling her image with the photo he had carried, even after she married.

Her skin, the color of cream, hadn't been touched by time, but her cheekbones were more prominent. Her full lips, graced with youth, remained. Her eyes conveyed a library of lessons, he thought to himself, the kind that didn't come from books. He yearned to know each one and in time, he promised himself he would.

Fearful Drew would disappear, as he did in her dreams when she reached out to him, she stood immobile, her eyes widening. His face was tan, and his side grin remained. But it was his turquoise eyes that mesmerized her. They spoke of grief and buried secrets, ones that craved revelation. Did she see a soundless apology, or was it her imagination? Old feelings stirred inside of her, but a gaping wound yearned for healing. The kind only he could provide.

"Hope?"

She nodded slightly. He immediately closed the distance between them. The strength of his tight embrace revealed he, too, had experienced a lifetime of emptiness. A sob escaped from his throat. She pulled back to look into his eyes.

"You're so..." his voice wobbly, "unbelievably beautiful." Tears streamed from his eyes. She held him, clinging, and together, they released years of anguish. Fear momentarily vanished.

Hope pulled back slightly to examine his white uniform, accented by three gold stripes of rank insignia on each shoulder. Flashes of the commissioning ceremony exploded in her mind, as she touched the ribbons on his chest with uncertainty. Each expressed courage and valor. The coveted gold Naval Aviator's wings crowned the colorful display for Commander Andrew Josiah Bartlett, III, United States Navy.

Odie B strolled into the room clapping her hands. They turned to her and exclaimed in unison, "YOU did this!"

"As I see it, you both were needing to have a good talk with each other, so I asked Sweet Jesus to help me. It was clear He sent a few angels to make this meetin' happen."

Then she gave them orders: "You two quit looking dumbstruck and go do some talking. I need to join my Bee Blossoms. So, you go on your way."

Hope smiled at Odie B, picked up her purse and headed for the door with Drew right behind her. Both moved like soldiers who had been given their marching orders. Odie B held the door open, giving each a hug. Then she quickly positioned herself behind the lace curtains, as they strolled down the sidewalk.

She watched Drew attempt to open the passenger door. Odie B shook her head, "He's so confused he doesn't know whether to scratch his watch or wind his butt!"

After they drove off, she poured herself a fresh glass of tea, sat down in her recliner, slipped off her sandals, spread her naked toes wide, and checked the time on the wall clock. Hurriedly, she scooted out of the chair, flipped on the television to watch her favorite soap operas, then made a trip to the kitchen. She returned with a big bowl of cobbler floating in melted ice cream. After repositioning herself back in the chair, she balanced the dessert on her lap while she placed her palms together under her chin and prayed,

"Oh, Sweet Jesus, please forgive me. You know there's not a Bee Blossom meetin'; but those kids needed a shove out the door. No need for 'em to stand around like chickens on one leg and then another, trying to be polite. Lord, I promise I won't tell no more fibs. This situation called for an army of angels, and I gave 'em a little push, but, Lord, I don't tell fibs like those naughty women on soap operas. No, Sir! I promise, Lord. I'm not a vixen. Amen.

TWENTY-TWO

Drew awkwardly fumbled with the keys, before finding the one that would unlock the passenger door. Hope nervously slid inside, staring into the windshield, where her gaze remained, as he clumsily slid the key into the ignition. On the second attempt, he succeeded.

Drew glanced at her out of the corner of his eyes while slowly edging away from the curb. A nervous smile spread across his face.

"I can't believe any of this," he said.

"I can't either," she whispered.

He pressed on the accelerator before realizing they had no destination.

"Where do you…uh…think…Would you like to go to Timber Tavern?"

She nodded.

Disbelief and confusion bounced in open spaces between them, then he reached for her hand, as he had years ago. The feel of his large hand sent chills racing down her spine. Old chills, soothing chills, frightening chills.

He remained silent. Having her beside him was enough.

An attractive, college-age hostess greeted them at the restaurant door. "Pick any place you like. I'll be right back with the menus," she said, smiling at Drew.

He spied an empty table by the window; neither commented on it being the same one they enjoyed years earlier. He pulled out her chair, just as he had a lifetime ago, then sat opposite her. After their drink orders were taken, they glanced around the room and made small talk on how the place had remained unchanged. The brightly lit jukebox, bellowing Elvis' hits from 1959, impacted Hope's mood. Too many memories.

Drew stared at Hope's eyes, noting her doubt and fear. He mentally pummeled himself. How could I have stayed away from her so long, he wondered. *What was I thinking? Why did I let her father deny us years together? How could I have not known how deeply I loved her? And still do.*

Hope turned her focus to the man she thought about every single day; the only man she had truly loved with every fiber of her being. Everything about him made her ache inside. It was the first insight as to how deep the loss had been. Now, she wondered if she could ever believe him. Or turn him loose.

The waitress appeared to take their orders. Relieved by the interruption, Drew raised his eyebrows and glanced at Hope. She grinned and nodded in agreement.

"We'll take a pepperoni and sausage pizza," he said.

"I'll have it right out for you." The attractive waitress offered a wink to Drew before strolling away. Drew didn't notice. He was immersed in how quickly the past had leaped forward. Familiarity flowed, and his side grin spoke.

For a moment, Hope felt as if nothing had changed, then loss and agony began careening through her body. The mere sight of him and the feel of his touch propelled her in a downward spiral; she didn't let her gaze continue. Shaken, she took a long sip of iced tea and stared out the window. He could see the strain on her face, and realized he had to be forthcoming, but she spoke first.

"Odie B never mentioned having contact with you, Drew."

He was surprised by the curtness. She was as distant as a remote island, but he couldn't restrain his own enthusiasm.

"Odie B pulled off the impossible, in my opinion, and I am eternally grateful she did. How do you feel about it?"

She glared at him like he was speaking a foreign language.

"I don't know," she said, flatly.

"I understand," he said.

Hope's doubts, regarding Drew, had been present for years, but today she wondered why Odie B had secretly arranged their meeting. Her face darkened. The peace she had come to feel over the past two days had been interrupted.

Hope had become as intense as the pressure of the cockpit during a pre-dawn mission. He started to speak, but she interrupted.

"Drew, how did Odie B find you?" Her tone, one she didn't even recognize, didn't escape him. Her nerves were frayed, and she was on the defense; he knew the questions would continue until she got answers.

"I asked Odie B the same question before you arrived. She responded that a letter, addressed to me, lay on your father's desk when she was there for his funeral. She secretly made note of my address."

Astonishment looped around thousands of questions in her mind.

"My father wrote you?"

"Yes. That's what Odie B said, but I never received it."

"Unfortunately, it took her five years to contact me," his voice quiet, as he took a sip of tea.

"Two months ago, I received a brief note from Odie B," he explained. "She asked if I were married or had a girlfriend. If the answer were 'Yes', she wished me well, but if the answer were, 'No', she asked when I would be returning to Colorado.

"I responded with a 'No.' Then I told her I would be in Boulder today for Ken's promotion. I questioned her availability, in hopes of getting an update on you. She promptly responded with the time for me to arrive."

Hope's countenance changed. A smile lit up her eyes when she realized Odie B had gathered information about his status before arranging their meeting. Fears of an ill-fated reunion were dispelled, and a deep sigh of relief escaped her, unconsciously.

"I find this almost impossible to comprehend," she said. "I wrote her three months ago and told her I'd be in Estes Park to photograph a wedding this weekend. I, too, asked if she would be available today."

"This is definitely a Divine encounter," he said.

"I went by your home, Hope," his voice low.

"You did? So did I. Sadly, it doesn't look the same."

"I didn't intend to go there, at least not consciously. I knew it would be emotional, but your home and all it represented was so much a part of my life. I'm drawn back each visit, like a moth to the flame. Some of my favorite memories were experienced there."

"I feel the same as you. I re-lived all our times together, one by one. By the time I arrived at Odie B's...," her voice trailed.

Drew clasped her hands between his. She stared at him, but he nervously glanced out the window without letting go of her hand. His eyes twitched. He took another large gulp of tea while searching for the words to comfort her. He cleared his throat then stared directly into her troubled eyes.

"Here's what I want you to know before we go any further," he said. "First and foremost, I never quit loving you, regardless of what you may believe. Every moment we had together is seared in my memory."

She tried to respond, but was too distraught, and could only observe his genuine, visible emotions. Every word he uttered appeared to come from a depth inside of him she understood. It confused her to know this. She pulled her hands from his tight clasp and straightened the napkin in her lap before slowly turning her face back toward him.

Drew wrestled with the increasing tide of her emotions. He saw the questions in her eyes and felt her coolness, again. He took a deep breath and continued.

"Secondly, I know you don't understand why I never wrote."

"You're right, Drew. I don't understand." She immediately felt the sting of tears and turned away. She longed to ask questions, as she desperately needed answers.

Drew charged forward into her maze of confusion like it was the Battle of 1812. Timing was critical.

"I don't have the right to ask you to wait one more hour or one more day," he pleaded, "but if you'll give me until tomorrow, I promise to provide you with an explanation. I didn't know I'd be seeing you today or I would have brought it with me. How long do you plan on staying?"

"I return to Texas in three days."

"Can I see you tomorrow?" he asked.

"If you can come to the Stanley Hotel in Estes Park. I should be through with photographing the wedding around two o'clock. How about two-forty-five?"

"I'll be there."

After waiting eleven years, Drew knew exoneration would come.

Hope analyzed his words, expressions, and gestures for signals of deception. There were none. No hints, no signs, no answers.

The server arrived with their pizza, refilled their drinks, and left them alone. The clock had brought them full circle. Drew, anxious to reveal his heart, stared at the lady who relentlessly inhabited his days and nights. He cut the pizza and put it on two plates while she observed.

"Hope, I have questions. There's so much I want to know."

"I know that feeling. Have you been married, Drew?" Tension filled her voice.

"Yes, a long time ago. It lasted ten months; nine of those I was in Vietnam. When I arrived back in the states, I was presented with divorce papers, and the announcement that she wanted to be free to marry her marriage counselor."

"Her marriage counselor?" she asked, stunned.

"Yes. She went for counseling, while I was away, and came out with her second husband." They both shook their heads in amazement.

"I don't know why I married her." He stopped himself, not wanting to reveal too much.

"Are you dating anyone, Drew?"

"No." He stared deep into her eyes, and with a voice, full of emotion, spoke.

"Hope, you've been the only woman with whom I have ever wished to share my life. I strongly believe our hearts remained joined during years of physical absence. At times, particularly during the night, I felt you knew I was beside you."

Window light emphasized her facial expressions, and Drew saw a woman trying to merge his words with his disappearance. She couldn't and he knew it. He placed her hand between his.

"Hope, you were my first love, and though others have come between us, it is my greatest desire to come to the end of my life with you by my side. I long for the years missed; but I am letting you know that from this day forward, I want us to grow old together.

His voice, his expressions, his eyes, his body language enveloped her. She closed her eyes to absorb each word, each inflection. In some mysterious, inexplicable way, she realized they had remained together and true to his passion for defending his country, he came to her in dreams, so she wouldn't forget. Nor give up.

Drew stared at her with suspended breath.

"How about you, Hope," his voice wobbly, "are you with anyone?" He wondered if Odie B knew the current state of Hope's life. What if they'd come this far and she was unavailable? Hope's silence was his ruination.

She hesitated a moment and their gazes linked together. Then with a broad smile, she replied, "No one, other than my son, Lee. I've dated many different guys through the years and one man hung around for a couple of years. I went out with him for an occasional dose of adult companionship when I wasn't consumed with Lee or photography. Both took precedence over dating. And him."

Relief tugged at the corners of his mouth. He felt the man fit Odie B's description... 'as useless as an ashtray on a motorcycle.'

"Well-meaning friends," Hope explained, "continue to set me up with their acquaintances, but..." her voice drifted off. He waited, unsteadily holding a slice of pizza in mid-air until his trembling nerves were obvious. Then he placed it back on the plate.

"Even though I tried to evaluate other men with full measures of grace, there was never enough to compare with what we had."

Drew dropped his head into his hands while her words raced through his body. He finally whispered.

"I feel the same."

"You do?"

"Yes."

She wanted to believe him. In the two of them. In the future. In the present. But relief had not found her.

Drew grimaced. He wanted to hold her, to kiss her, never to let her go. And to tell her every day, for the remainder of their lives, how much he loved her.

"Why didn't I hear from you, Drew?" Her anguish clawed at him.

He shook his head, wanting to calm her fears, but he knew her father should be the one to explain. In his own words.

Drew reached for her hand, kissed it, and held her with his stare.

"You will have the reason tomorrow. I promise."

They both were finding it difficult to stay composed with the rise and fall of their discussion. Emotions rolled like a ship during a hurricane. Her smile, touch, glance propelled him into an upward spiral. He wanted to consume her.

"Odie B told me of your losses, and I'm so deeply sorry, Hope."

"Thank you. They have been difficult, but particularly devastating was my father's passing. He and my son were extremely close. Pappy, as we called him, was Lee's hero and buddy. He died without warning." She looked away, and in the quiet she mumbled. "He was my anchor, my rock, my confidante, my best friend."

Drew cringed. He paused for a moment without responding, then skillfully changed to another topic.

"Your mother? How is she?"

"She's still strong and determined to make the best of everything. She doesn't have much patience when she sees me sad. Do you remember her saying, 'If you have lemons, make lemonade'?" she asked.

"Yes, I do."

"Well, that's as true today as it was then. Sadness wasn't allowed and still isn't. I avoid her on difficult days. When I told her I was coming to Boulder, she wasn't happy."

"Do you know why?"

"No, I don't. The years in Colorado were the happiest years of my life, but she bristles each time I mention them. However, when I received a contract for photographing a wedding in Estes Park, there was no discussion."

Her eyes glistened with mischief when she leaned over the table and spoke in a hushed voice, "Remember when you and I would talk on the phone late at night, and I would have to quit talking for a minute, so I could stick the phone under the covers when Mother opened my bedroom door?"

"Yes. Quite clearly," he said, grinning.

"I would lie there in the dark, hoping and praying you wouldn't say anything, so she wouldn't hear your deep voice coming from under the sheets. I think she regretted giving me a private phone line, since there was no extension to pick up."

Hope burst out laughing! He couldn't take his eyes off her. Hearing her laughter was like listening to a familiar song. They were the way they had always been.

Hope realized, in that moment, they were talking as they once did, as if time had never passed, nor distance had ever intruded. Surprised, she realized they had remained together, in their souls, and for a millisecond, she trusted him. Then she quickly remembered: he left without a word. Instantly, the hurt returned. So did the shattered trust.

However, there was something different about Drew, something she couldn't identify. Her instincts said his non-verbal communications screamed. He averted her eyes when she asked certain questions, then exhibited a slow, deliberate hesitation when he answered. Her alarm bells reached a feverish pitch when his body language shifted each time she asked about the separation.

"Tell me about your life, where you've been," she said.

"For the most part, I've been flying since I last saw you. After I got my wings, I received additional training before I went to the China Sea, where the ship, USS Ranger, became my home. My dream to be a carrier-based pilot, realized.

"After flying many missions over Vietnam, I became a flight instructor. I also had various collateral duties, including squadron Operations Department head. In addition, I got a Master's Degree in Finance.

She stared in disbelief at the man who had clutched her heart, who had sacrificed his life, who had seen war from the inside, and by God's grace, had returned home. She knew he had always lived life more fully than most, a trait she had found attractive from the beginning.

"That's extremely impressive, Drew." A smile spread across her face, into her eyes. "You've had an incredibly honorable and distinguished career, which is no surprise to those who know you, but hearing your journey fills me with a sense of amazement. I'm very proud of your service, and deeply, deeply grateful. Many times, I wondered if you were. ...alive." She could barely hear her own voice.

Drew stared at her. "Thank you." Humility, gratitude, and sincerity were etched on his face. He took a deep breath and exhaled slowly. Their eyes locked.

"Tell me about your life, Hope."

She responded in a guarded, matter-of-fact tone.

"I live in Fort Worth with my nine-year-old son, Lee. My parents moved back to Fort Worth a few months after we returned home from Europe. After Daddy died five years ago, Mother elected to remain in their home. It's only a few minutes away from mine."

"Do you have a picture of your son with you?"

"I do." She reached into her purse and produced a photo of a young boy who closely resembled her in appearance – wavy hair, full lips, blue eyes, and a broad smile.

"He's the image of his mother."

"Thank you," she said, softly.

"What's his personality like?"

Hope began to relax when speaking of Lee.

"I'm very proud of him, and totally biased so I can't speak objectively, but he's very outgoing. His life consists of school,

The Other Part of Her

church, sports, and he's just gotten involved in Boy Scouts. Seems intent on reaching the top rank, Eagle."

"There's no telling how far he will go," he said. "Most boys that age struggle to find one area that truly interest them."

Embarrassed, she felt obligated to answer truthfully.

"I'm not sure what he'll do, but so far, he's maintained a thirst to achieve. I pray it continues," she said.

"I'd bet my life on it, Hope."

"I've tried to surround Lee with male role models. Many men have helped, but the most influential was my cousin. He lived with us before going into the Army, and under his tutelage, Lee witnessed his innate qualities of honesty and respect every day."

"We were sad to see him leave, but we knew his time with us was temporary. The Army beckoned."

"Sounds like someone I'd enjoy knowing," he said.

"Yes. The two of you have a great deal in common. The same character traits reside in you, as well." Hope felt the pain of what they had missed and changed the subject.

"Your grandmother has had a large influence on my parenting," she said.

"My grandmother? How's that?" Drew asked.

"I reflected on the stories you shared with me that day in the cave, how she kept you involved and supported your endeavors wholeheartedly. I've tried to do the same with Lee. He's the only one, in his circle of friends, who's being raised without a father. I've tried to create a full life for him, just as your grandmother did. I hope he'll focus on what he has, not on what he doesn't have."

Drew nodded without speaking. The emotional impact of her statement affected him in several ways. He turned his head and gazed out the window, briefly re-living the day in the cave when he openly shared his father's rejection, and his grandmother's profound influence. Concerns about how Lee would handle a man in his mother's life came to mind.

"Where's Lee now?"

"He's attending camp in South Texas. I'm trying to prepare myself for when he spreads his wings, but it isn't easy since it's just the two of us. I really can't imagine what life will be like when he leaves home."

"And Lee hasn't been to Colorado?"

"That's right. I wanted to bring him on this trip, but because it conflicted with camp I couldn't." She dropped her head and spoke softly. "I…uh…initially declined my client's offer."

"Why?"

"Memories. I thought it would be too hard." Hope's hushed tone could barely be heard.

"Is it?"

"I'm not sure," she whispered.

He ached when he saw her pain, and desperately wished he didn't have to wait, but he knew it was Mr. Madison who had to reveal the course he chose for his daughter.

Drew paused, signaled to the server, requested two cups of coffee, and skillfully directed their conversation to another topic.

"Did you stay in touch with Sarah Whitmire?" he asked.

She turned her head toward the window, while answering in a tone filled with sadness and regret. "No, I'm sorry to say. After my parents moved back to Texas, we went separate directions and lost touch with one another. I'm happy to hear you and Ken have stayed connected. Did he mention Sarah when you saw him earlier?"

"No, but after the ceremony this morning, he asked if I would hang around, so we could reminisce about old times over a burger at The Sink. I'm sure he would've provided updates about Sarah's whereabouts had there been enough time, but Odie B had made it clear when I was to arrive."

Hope's eyes were wide with surprise, as she leaned over the table. "You almost went to The Sink?"

Drew nodded.

"I had lunch there. We would have probably run into each other."

They shook their heads in awe, wondering how they would have reacted if their paths had intertwined earlier in the day, either at the Madison's former home or over lunch. Both were relieved they had been given the oasis of a protected environment for their unplanned reunion.

Drew gazed at her in silence. His eyes conveyed yearning and loss. His expression told her whatever it was that had kept them apart, had almost destroyed him, as well.

Her heart sank when she realized how much she still loved him. No other man had ever moved her, touched her, or excited her, as he had.

They continued to talk, long after their plates had been taken away. He was curious about the strong connection between her and Odie B, but the main thing he wanted was not the conversation, but simply seeing her, hearing her, touching her.

He had never felt that way with anyone else, and he was determined to absorb the feeling for as long as he could. He decided to pursue why the unusual bond between a girl and her housekeeper, as he asked, "I'm surprised that Odie B didn't return to Texas with your parents when they moved back. What made her stay here?"

"My parents planned to travel extensively, so they encouraged Odie B to pursue interests of her own. She had devoted so much of her life to us. Now, her church, the Bee Blossoms, and working at a library fill her life."

"I bet you've missed her though," he said. His perception came from seeing Hope's lack of sparkle when she talked about Odie B not being with the Madisons any longer.

"Oh, YES! She began caring for me when she was fifteen years old, and I was three. Mama B, her mother, did the housework while Odie B played with me. She was my best friend, and still is."

"Odie B said you taught her how to read. Is that right?"

"Yes, I did," she said.

"I'd love to hear how you became her teacher." He smiled at the mental image.

Hope grinned when she reached into her memory, to the time when she was eight years old.

"I had just entered the third grade when Odie B asked me what was written on a piece of paper by the refrigerator. I told her it was Mama's grocery list. She told me to add 'eggs' to the list. Her face became contorted, and tears brimmed in her eyes. That's when it hit me.

'Odie B, can you read?' I asked.

She shook her head in embarrassment.

'Would you like to learn?' She nodded and wiped the stream of tears rolling down her face with the back of her hand.

"Five days later, after she finished her housework, the two of us gathered in our dining room. Odie B came prepared.

"She had grown familiar with my routine of wearing something new on the first day of school, so she purchased a new uniform, along with new shoes. She had her hair styled at the beauty salon, telling the hairdressers that she was starting school. Mother surprised her with a book satchel, like mine, along with a Big Chief tablet, several pencils, a ruler, and a large eraser.

"On the first day, Odie B's eyes danced with anticipation, as she sat at our dining table, the one she polished weekly. We started with the Pledge of Allegiance. I stood on a red stool while holding the flag, and she stood proudly by her chair with her hand over her heart. Afterwards, I formally welcomed her, as my teachers did when a new student arrived. She beamed like the North Star."

Drew burst out laughing at the image of eight-year-old Hope, the teacher, and Odie B, the student. Hope smiled then added,

"From that moment on, Odie B eagerly absorbed everything I put in front of her. We added math to the curriculum, which stretched our classroom time to a period of two years.

"I concluded my career of formal teaching at the age of ten. By then, she had read almost every book in the library, and I had run out of gold stars. The student had surpassed the teacher."

Drew shook his head, as Hope continued with an update.

"She's working in the Boulder library now. It's my understanding if anyone has a question, she can answer it. She's also read the Bible through several times and most of the classics."

"Today," Drew added quietly, "she became our matchmaker." He stared directly into Hope's eyes

"I wonder where this will lead, Hope. I know where I want it to go. I know where Odie B wants it to go, and after you learn why I never answered your letters, I hope you will be confident of my heart. And our future."

She smiled softly, afraid to loosen the constraints. Pain had been a part of her for so long. To love him, as she once did, was beyond her grasp.

"I think we need to get reacquainted," she said. "The years have changed us; we're no longer the same. Experiences. Life. We're different." The words sounded hollow, even to her ears.

"Hope, my heart never changed. Please believe me." His tone was urgent, his eyes in concert.

She desperately wanted to trust him, but the same question that had plagued her during his absence, of why he lost contact, remained unanswered.

"It is time for me to meet my clients. The wedding rehearsal is in two hours, and I have much to do."

"I understand, but I will see you tomorrow after the wedding. Right?"

"Yes."

They both were reluctant to leave. They were thinking about the future, the past, and the fact that they were inches from each other. Drew reached for her hand; a conversation between his lips and her skin startled her. She knew he felt it, too. Her breath hung suspended, as he held her with his eyes. She pulled her hand from his grasp, and slowly stood.

"I really must go!"

He stood so close she could feel his breath and smell his cologne. The same scent as the last time she saw him. He wrapped his arm around her shoulder, bent down, and whispered in her ear.

"I'm not sure how I've been able to live without you, but now that I've found you, I'm not letting you go," he said, softly.

Hope stared directly into his eyes. Silently, she agreed. A few cautionary flags were waving in her mind, but she ignored them. She knew unequivocally that Drew had consumed her heart. And she wanted more.

The silence was his undoing as they rode back to Odie B's. They both were sifting through the afternoon conversation. When they arrived, he turned toward her. She could see hurt in his eyes. Both remained quiet for a moment; then he spoke with sadness and conviction.

"Hope, since we last saw one another, I've carried your heart with me. I've never been without it. It was your face I saw at night

The Other Part of Her

and every morning. I love you with a depth I didn't know possible. I traveled over seven thousand miles the past few days to be here, at this moment. Do you know why?" She shook her head. "Your face led me home. Being together is our destiny."

Again, she remained quiet. She wanted to believe him, but doubt persisted. In a weak voice, she protested, "I'm terrified of believing you again."

"I understand," he said solemnly. "I will reveal the circumstances that kept us apart tomorrow."

He walked around to her side of the car and opened her door. She felt him, as he brushed up against her. Her breath halted. No other man had ever provoked such a reaction with a mere glance or touch.

When they reached her parked car, he slipped his arm around her and placed his finger under her chin, drawing her face upwards. She felt her stomach tighten. The thought of him kissing her before she knew his reason for leaving evoked a torrent of emotion throughout her body. She needed answers.

He stared into her eyes and spoke softly,

"If I could have one wish, it would be to wake up beside you every morning for the rest of my life and brush the hair away from your eyes with soft, gentle kisses."

Hope realized that the tenderness and love wandering in his eyes was a gentle reminder that Drew was to be her future.

Hope, the same girl, who at the age of twenty looked at him with trusting eyes, was the same beautiful woman beckoning him home again. Her eyes revealed the answer he longed to know.

"I love you, Hope Madison, and I am anticipating ALL our tomorrows."

Dubious, she nodded, got into her car, and began driving the scenic mountain roads, unaware of all the twists and turns. Only the sound and sight of Commander Drew Bartlett remained fresh.

TWENTY-THREE

Hope checked her watch then gasped as she gave Annie Ruth a brief explanation about having another engagement, one that required her to leave. The news brought a curious expression from her close friend but before any questions could be asked, a wedding guest appeared, anxious to talk to the mother of the bride. Hope took the opportunity to make a quick exit.

The antique elevator, sluggishly moving up the floors, gave Hope a moment to reflect on the wedding, especially how the snow-capped mountains and sapphire-blue sky were the perfect backdrop for when Mr. Smith, dressed in a white Navy uniform adorned with medals, escorted his daughter, Laurie, down the aisle. She held onto his arm when a cool breeze suddenly lifted her bridal veil into the air, like a fluttering angel wing. Hope captured the fleeting moment on film. The crowd had gasped.

Drew's impending arrival dominated her thoughts. She rushed to her room and began emptying her photography gear into the narrow closet while imagining his forthcoming explanation. Regardless of what excuse Drew would use for not staying in contact, she couldn't imagine it being plausible. But the thought of a limp excuse filled her with dread, knowing it would make this their final time together.

She couldn't forget his disappearance all those years ago. Nor his eyes, his sincerity, his tenderness from the day before. After years of pain, he had managed to convince her to trust him. Today, she doubted him all over again.

Hope hurried to the bathroom and turned on the bath water. While undressing, she checked the water temperature twice then turned to look into the full-length mirror. So much had changed since she fell in love with Drew in 1959. Her life then and her life now, were distinctly separated. She couldn't be that same person today, not after his absence for eleven years. But her body remained slender and straight, her skin smooth, her waist small. Her ivory complexion, the same as her mother's, and the sapphire eyes she inherited from her grandfather, were a mishmash of family genetics living comfortably in her body.

Hope placed each piece of the clothing she wore for the photo shoot in a laundry bag, then hastily secured her hair so as not to get it wet, before laying a luxurious monogrammed towel on a nearby stool and turning off the faucet. Gingerly, she stepped into the warm water, sinking low into the deep bathtub to relax her stiff shoulders and neck for several minutes. But her bath wouldn't be complete without the bar of scented soap she had brought from home; she carefully unwrapped it, letting the fragrance revive her.

Thoughts of her mother surfaced, just as the soap's frothing bubbles covered her. *What would she think about their reunion? Would she be happy for them?* It didn't make any difference. Not now. Not after so many years had passed.

Finally, Hope emerged from the water, stepping onto the vintage tile floor, knowing she had indulged herself longer than usual. After reaching for the towel, she checked the time and quickly dried herself before going directly to the closet and choosing a red sundress. She pulled it over her head and after looking in the mirror, checking it from every angle, she determined it fit her nicely, but it wasn't appropriate for the occasion. She hurriedly hung it back in the closet and reached for something more suitable: white Capri pants, a navy nautical top and new tennis shoes. She then hastily retrieved a small make-up bag from her suitcase.

Rushing through the routine of applying mascara to her lashes and red gloss to her lips, she removed the clips holding her hair. Instantly, waves of blond hair rested below her shoulders. After a few light brush strokes, she added a fine mist of perfume on each side of her long neck.

The bedside clock revealed Drew would arrive in seven minutes. Her stomach lurched. Her hands grew clammy. Once upon a time, he had presented the sun, the moon, and all the stars to her. Then he disappeared without a word.

Suddenly, while standing in front of the mirror double-checking her appearance, she felt as though a swarm of butterflies were practicing touch-and-go landings in her stomach.

"Why did I leave my new summer dresses at home?" She moaned aloud as words on a page from her youth erupted, ones often repeated by Odie B.

"Hope Madison, pull your dress down!! I can see clear to the Promised Land!"

She chuckled and comforted herself with the fact that maybe the Capri pants were the best option, after all. Then she hurriedly scanned the room, grabbed her room key, trembling as she did, and reached for a light windbreaker, in case of an afternoon shower. Checking her watch, as the door closed and the lock clicked, she ran down the hotel's grand staircase while forming a plan in her mind; she would meet Drew on the outer perimeter of the parking lot, a long distance from Annie Ruth.

Hope reached the lobby area, panting for air after racing down several flights of stairs. She kept her eyes focused straight ahead on the large glass front doors, so as not to be interrupted by the wedding party or their guests. Then she saw him. Her breath caught. He was talking to Annie Ruth, the one person who felt her calling in life was to be Hope's personal matchmaker, though every introduction had failed to take root. Hope never revealed why, but now, unknowingly, Annie Ruth was talking to him face to face.

Drew smiled when Hope surprised them by casually stepping into their circle. Instantly, he draped his arm across her shoulders. Annie Ruth's eyebrows immediately shot up, a glint in her eyes obvious. Hope blushed.

They said their goodbyes, and together, she and Drew strolled across the large parking lot with their arms intertwined.

"I see you met my friends," she said, unable to hide her curiosity.

"Yes, I did." Drew knew a brief answer wouldn't quench her thirst for details, so he continued with the account.

"We started talking when I saw her husband in the Navy uniform. That, along with his gold wings, gave us instant camaraderie. Annie Ruth announced the reason for his uniform was their daughter's wedding. I casually mentioned my purpose for being there was to steal a Texas wedding photographer.

"Her eyes sparkled as she interrogated me, 'Are you speaking of Hope Madison?'

"Before I could respond, she unleashed a boatload of compliments with fiery enthusiasm. I wished to add a few of my own, but it was obvious she knew nothing about our background."

"She's been trying to find me a husband since Lee was born."

Drew stopped in mid-stride. There, in the center of the parking lot, he gently pulled her chin upward, cupped her face in his hands, and stared directly into her wide eyes.

"You can assure her he's been found!"

Not that his statement required a response! He could see in her eyes the same dream, and he knew, with complete confidence, that they would have traveled through galaxies to get to each other.

"My car is right over there," he said, pointing to the corner of the lot.

Hope's mouth flew open in shock. "You STILL have it? This is your convertible! Oh, Drew." She threw her arms around his neck.

Hope, unaware that Annie Ruth had been observing from the balcony, noticed her waving enthusiastically. Hope smiled and waved in return.

"Yes, I kept it," he stated with pride. "Each time I return home, my mechanic performs a maintenance check. I had a rental car yesterday, but I drove up today in anticipation of reliving and making more memories with you." His tone changed, as he put the key in the ignition.

"Since the car was a college graduation gift from my grandmother, I doubt I'll ever sell it. She passed recently. Memories of her seem to grow each day, along with the memories of us, and the car."

"I'm so sorry, Drew. I know that is a terrible loss for you."

He nodded and then changed his somber tone to one with a lilt.

"My last date to ride in it was you."

She feigned skepticism with a roll of her eyes, but her grin couldn't be hidden.

He put on his sunglasses and headed down the winding road, toward the main highway. As he gathered speed, Hope observed him placing papers under his seat.

"I thought we'd go to our familiar place in the Rocky Mountain National Park. I find it reassuring with all its history and time, which is what we have, Hope.

She nodded, as she wondered about a scar on his right temple. As she was trying to think of something to talk about, and nothing came to her, she began speculating on how the scar occurred. Conjecture had been a large part of her life for many years, especially during sleepless nights. *Was Drew injured? Was he alive? Missing in Action? A Prisoner of War?*

She had even wondered to herself if someone wore a Prisoner-of-War bracelet with the name Andrew Bartlett on it. One like the silver identification bracelet she wore for POW, Samuel Johnson.

Fear was tearing through Drew's body as he maneuvered steep mountain roads. The trajectory of his life was about to unfold within the hour.

How would Hope process the revelations? Would she resent him for exposing the person she had trusted most, her father? Would she try to excuse her father's actions since he wasn't able to speak? Would this long-awaited reveal backfire? How would he handle it if it did?

The questions, weighing heavily on his heart, reminded him of the tension when flying tight turns at six times the force of gravity and a simple act, such as looking back over his shoulder for enemy aircraft, or airborne Surface to Air Missiles, was extremely difficult.

Fully aware of the consequences with Hope, he rotated his neck to relieve the strain felt in every cell of his body. His discs and vertebrae had experienced the rigors of combat maneuvering, and the force of anti-gravity, too many times not to be affected, but the enormity of the situation with Hope made the job of being a fighter pilot seem easier.

The car slowed. A strain fell over them when he turned into a parking place. He quickly reached under his seat for a tablet and a large manila envelope; then he grabbed a quilt out of the trunk and took her hand.

Hope, feeling queasy, on edge, and strangely calm as the warmth of his hand threaded through hers, felt the anticipation mounting. Would Drew's explanation provoke more questions or answer all unequivocally? She felt reassurance flowing in the pressure of his grasp. She missed believing in him.

The Other Part of Her

The trail was marked by interweaving patterns of light and shadows, as the mid-afternoon sun streamed through leafy-green branches. Squirrels scurried out of their path while they walked side-by-side. They each were marveling at the turn of events.

Drew was reflecting on Hope's qualities that had engulfed him in the earlier years: her infectious laugh, intelligence, and perceptive heart. All were born out of her unyielding faith.

Mr. Madison's description of his daughter: impulsive, impatient, and a dream-follower, were qualities that Drew found attractive. But her most valuable quality was how she made him feel. She made him a better man.

At that point in their hike, a crystal-blue lake, surrounded by a lush meadow, became visible. The water reflected the clouds in the sky, while sounds of a rushing waterfall flowed through the trees.

They stood silently, holding onto one another among the majestic evergreens and five-hundred-year-old Ponderosa Pine trees. Drew pointed to several deer grazing on the other side of the meadow, then inhaled deeply when he noticed two rock climbers. The dark figures resembled houseflies creeping up a window, as they scaled the jagged mountain. The contrast caught his attention. Quiet serenity with dangerous penalties. His stomach did barrel rolls with the same thoughts.

He brushed his lips lightly across her forehead before scanning the area for a place to sit. He decided upon a small opening in the woodlands, far from the trail so they would have privacy, and there, he spread the quilt, stitched by his grandmother's hands, under a towering aspen tree.

Anxiety surged through her veins when she observed him growing somber, but the scope of what lay ahead of him was the largest task, outside of his military duty he had ever confronted. And the same heightening of tensions that he experienced prior to a launch aboard the aircraft carrier, coursed through him. Except for one large difference, he knew how to handle anticipated disasters in aviation. Training had provided him with skill and an efficient calm in combat. Then he realized another contrast: war identified the opposing ones in battle; he knew where allegiances rested. Hope's allegiance was unknown. A potential disaster had his heart racing; his palms sweating. He possessed no experience in this area, but he knew the truth had to be revealed.

Hope waited with dread.

Drew lowered himself to the ground, and discreetly slid the envelopes and tablet behind his back. She curled up next to him, leaning her head on his shoulder.

He stared quietly at the patterns in his grandmother's quilt, and slowly stretched his legs out, wrapping her closer. Exposing her father was momentarily delayed as he took several deep breaths. The risk seemed too great and the potential loss too severe. He decided to select another route, one that would firmly cement their past. Hope observed him reaching behind his back.

"I have something I want to show you," he said.

He opened the sketchbook and watched her get comfortable.

"This is something I did on the ship. Drawing became my outlet when the waves of your absence were overpowering. It filled many lonely hours while I counted the days until I would see you again."

He opened the first page, to a drawing of Hope in a white coat, her blonde hair flowing past her shoulders.

"Here you are, the first time I saw you." She was stunned at the resemblance, how he captured the emotion in her eyes. They reminisced a bit about their life-changing meeting before turning the page.

"This is of our first kiss, near the waterfall," he said.

She gasped at the emotion portrayed.

Each page was slowly unfolding, allowing them to reflect on each artistic rendering. To her shock and surprise, he had sketched the two of them dancing at the Trocadero Ballroom, hiking in the forest, sitting in Timber Tavern, and her pinning his Ensign boards on his shoulders. She was both moved and amazed at the detail, his recall, and the meaning.

"Here is one of us flying over Colorado, our last day together before I left for the Navy. This is the view of the Sangre de Cristo Mountains, the rivers below, and Royal Gorge in the distance."

He turned the page to a drawing of his arms around her. She, too, had recorded it in her mind's eye when they were in the cave.

Unable to speak, she buried her face in his shoulder. Her emotions couldn't be restrained; tears for lost years fell. Feeling lightheaded, Hope fought for balance as she realized his touch told her she was where she belonged. Memories long denied had been awakened.

Drew braced for the next step. Her tension weakened, and his mounted. He held her close until he sensed it was safe to enter uncharted waters.

In a soft voice, he asked, "Why did you get married just before graduation?"

Hope repositioned herself, so she could look directly into his eyes.

"This will sound shallow, but I was flattered by his interest, since your disappearance destroyed all feelings of self-worth. Eventually, Patrick gave me back my confidence and in December of our senior year, he began talking about a future together.

"We went to his home in Montana, during Spring break, and I met his parents. By then, I realized I couldn't give him my heart, not all of it. I needed more time before making any decision regarding our future together, but I failed to mention it prior to the trip. Once there, surrounded by his family, he got down on one knee, with a ring in his hand, and proposed.

"I was confused. I felt if I declined his proposal, I would experience more feelings of loss, similar as to what I felt when you left. I hesitated. When I didn't respond, I saw the hurt in his eyes."

She stared at the ground and whispered, "So I accepted. When the discussion turned to possible dates for the wedding, the family agreed that in light of Patrick's imminent departure for Vietnam, we should proceed. He was persuasive. Three days later, we married.

"His parents were very supportive. Mine were not. When I called and told them, they were in shock and chose not to attend." She stared off in the distance. "My father surprised me the most. When I returned home, I expected him to broach the subject of an annulment. Instead, there were only two visible responses: a silent track of deep regret streaming from his eyes and…he withdrew from me. We weren't as close after that." She looked at the ground. "I never understood why. I still don't," she said, quivering.

He wrapped her in his arms until she found her voice.

"Six months after Patrick's departure, his letters ceased to arrive. I thought there must have been a change in his routine, until I answered the door one day and a chaplain, along with an Air Force officer, were standing at my door. Their expressions confirmed my fears. I gave birth to Lee three days later."

Drew closed his eyes, unable to voice the pain he felt.

"Daddy persuaded me to move into their home, and it was there the healing of our fractured relationship began. They were wonderful grandparents to Lee, and my strongest supporters. Odie B came from Colorado, until I could get back on my feet. A year later, I purchased a home and started a photography business."

Drew shook his head, and quietly asked, "Do you know what happened to Patrick?"

"Yes. I received a letter from the only survivor. I have it for Lee, so he will know of his father's bravery."

They stared off in different directions while they processed the tragedy. He quietly contemplated what had been Hope's reality: going forward after two deaths. One had been an actual death; the other death was their relationship. Both had died, or so she believed, and the remnants of her heart had blown in the wind like a hurricane. He found the extent of her grief impossible to process.

Hope nestled into him, quietly observing the darting chickadees while two blue jays dove for a morsel on the ground. A gentle breeze blew the quaking aspen branches; he inhaled the scent of perfume on Hope's skin, as it rose to an intoxicating level. He silently prayed for the right words.

"I have some things to tell you, Hope, but I don't know how. I thought it would be easy, but now, I'm unsure of how you will respond."

Drew fought for control, but the pain of remembering years without her crawled into the foreground. The possibility of losing her for the second time gripped him so tightly, as though he were in a vise.

She heard the grave tone in his voice, the reluctance, and squeezed his hand, too worried to speak.

"You want to know why I never answered your letters…"

His tone scared her, but she nodded, hesitantly.

"I have longed to tell you, but after Odie B told me about your dad's death, I wished with all my heart I didn't have to be the one to reveal the answer. However, you deserve to know, even though I'm very afraid of your reaction."

His voice trembled, "Hope, I never forgot you. I tried, but I couldn't, and now that you're here, I cannot bear the thought of living one more day not connected to you. My deepest desire is to have you walking by my side, as my best friend, my love, my wife." Fear flowed in his voice. Hope didn't move, her mouth too dry to speak.

"I want to spend every day giving you the happiness you deserve. I will consider that to be my greatest service in life." He paused to clear his throat.

"Hope, you have been loved and protected. Your parents were doing what they felt best, but what you don't know is they were protecting you at times, without your knowledge."

"WHY? HOW?"

"I'll explain, but I want you to understand a couple of things. First, your parents have always maintained an unquestionable desire for your best interest."

"I know," she whispered.

"Secondly, I want…I want you to know that I never quit loving you." Pain was evident in his broken voice.

Confused, she wanted to scream.

"What I need to tell you may be hard to comprehend," he said in a bolder voice, "but I will try to reveal the hearts involved and the circumstances."

Hope was desperate for his explanation.

"I left to go to the Navy the day after our plane ride over Colorado, which was our last date," he said.

"Yes, I remember."

"But before I left Boulder, I drove by your house to see you one more time. Your mother said you were out shopping. As I turned to leave, she handed me an envelope from your father."

Hope scowled. "You came by my house?"

"Yes. The letter she gave me was to be mailed, but since I dropped by, she handed it to me. I took it and left. I assumed it would say, 'goodbye, good luck', that sort of thing.

"I was focused on meeting the deadline for flight training in Pensacola, so I absently set the letter aside to read later."

"What did it say?" she asked.

"I have it here and you can read it for yourself." Drew took the letter from behind him and with trembling hands, gave it to her. "When you read it, please remember he did what he felt best for you, even though it may not appear to be so."

Hope opened the letter, her brow furrowed. Drew nervously ran his hands through his hair, picked up a twig and broke it, then folded his arms and waited.

Hope gasped, as she read her father's demands. When she finished, she stared at Drew in disbelief. Anger and hurt hung in her throat; her body trembled from shock. The two people she trusted beyond any other had betrayed her.

Unable to find her voice, her face colorless, she spoke in a whisper.

"I can't believe how the ones who kept us apart for years, witnessed my pain. And they did ABSOLUTELY NOTHING! How could anyone do that, Drew? Furthermore, how can you be so generous in explaining their loving protection when they hurt you so badly?"

"I know, Hope. I felt the same. Shock. Disbelief. Anger. Devastation. I didn't know how I could do what was required of me without knowing you were waiting. I needed to be able to tell you my heart and be assured of yours. I understood his intentions, but it didn't make it any easier."

He dropped his head and spoke in a hushed voice, "I wrote you every day, and I planned to personally deliver the letters to you at your college graduation. Then I heard you were married, and I quit writing, but my heart never changed, the emptiness never healed. The loss of you was felt in every fiber of my being.

"Counting the days until graduation had been my survival tools. My desire for you to experience college life was real. I didn't want you pining away during your last two years. That would have killed us both, and perhaps our love."

He stared at the dirt, recalling the agonizing moment when he learned that Hope was married.

"But why couldn't we have stayed in touch, Drew?" Her chin quivered as she swiped the tears rolling down her cheeks.

"Your father felt you would miss out on times that you could never take back, and for what? He didn't know how I felt about you, nor did he realize your love for me. He suspected I would find someone else, and you would get over your schoolgirl crush. Possibly find a nice, college boy."

She threw her arms around him and buried her head in his chest. "Oh, Drew, I'm so sorry."

He held her, stroking her hair. "We're here now. We have our lives back. It wasn't the right time. I didn't know then. But I know it now," he whispered.

"Did you respond to his letter?"

He handed her a copy of the letter.

Hope took the envelope and eagerly opened it. Tears streamed like a broken faucet when she read how Drew intended to marry her as soon as she graduated.

"Did he keep you informed about how I was doing, as you requested?"

"Yes. He responded with a couple of updates, told me you were enjoying your sorority and studies. He said you appeared to be happy, but he also added, 'with Hope, one never knows. She covers well.'

"In May of your senior year, a few weeks before your graduation, I received a letter from him telling me you had gotten married."

Hope bowed her head, trying to absorb all he was saying.

"Here's his last letter."

Drew held it in his hands, trembling from the misery that engulfed him.

"I thought this letter would provide the logistics regarding your graduation. He knew I planned to be there, so I was taken completely off guard when he wrote of your marriage."

The sour taste of those words clung to his throat, untouched by time.

She took the letter, read her father's words, then laid her head on Drew's chest and sobbed. After all the years, Drew was finally able to wrap her in truth, and in his arms. The pain continued to emerge until daylight began to fade. He reached for the manila envelope and the last of the letters.

"Here's the letter I wrote after I got the news you were married, one that was not intended for mailing, unless I was killed or missing in action. I gave instructions to my buddy, Java, to either mail, or deliver a parcel to you that would include your father's letters, and this one from me, in case of my death or capture. I wanted you to know I did not abandon you."

She saw his handwriting and nervously opened the aged envelope.

My Dearest Hope,

If you are reading this, I am either missing or I've been killed in action.

This is a difficult letter to write, but not nearly as difficult as NOT communicating with you. Wherever I am, I cannot be at peace unless you understand why you didn't hear from me during those painful years of separation. I pray you will comprehend my love for you, as I am speaking from my heart with assuredness, confidence, and honesty. I lay it out for your examination.

Hope, a day hasn't passed that I haven't yearned for you, to hold you, to love you. You were, and are, the only one for me.

Loving you has intensified my purpose, even my will to survive. Believe me, when I say, if I've not been killed, I am trying desperately to return to you, even if for a moment.

If I've not survived this war, I am exploring the heavens and navigating lonely seas in search of your face. My peace will come when I feel our souls are blended, as they were when we parted.

I am enclosing a letter from your father, so that you will understand why I've not corresponded since leaving for my Navy duties.

Don't think less of him. I know he had only the best of intentions in placing a wall between us so that you could grow to be the woman I know you have become. Military wives must be very independent and self-sufficient to survive long separations. And though I believe you would have thrived, I imagine you are far more your own person now than you would have been, had I taken you from the University before you had the experiences your father wanted for you.

I don't regret having chosen service to my country. I believe we make a difference in the level of safety and freedom for all Americans by serving. When I chose this path, I wrote a blank check to the country for any amount up to and including my life. I have sacrificed willingly.

Hope, know I've never stopped loving you, and if anything, my love has increased to envelop my entire being. You were and are the stellar light in my life, even after all these years of separation.
My love follows you, my darling.
Drew

Gasps involuntarily burst from her throat. He gently stroked her back, as he spoke.

"While I've journeyed the entire globe, I've carried a desperate longing to see you, to hold you, to laugh with you, to tell you how much I love you. Many times, I stood on the ship feeling your presence. I sensed you were aware of mine. We had our own hushed language, and during those moments, our souls were reunited. Unseen, unheard, but together."

She continued to sob while she recalled him in her nightly dreams.

"Hope, you ignited a flame that has continued to burn in my soul, untouched. It cannot be extinguished. A love like ours cannot die."

Shaken, confused, and angry, she asked an unexpected question.

"Drew, would you please come to Texas with me, so we can confront Mother together?"

"Yes. I would like to get answers. Afterwards, I want to go forward with you beside me."

He took her in his arms and kissed her, as if it were the last.

TWENTY-FOUR

Hope steered the car down the winding mountain road toward Boulder. A cool breeze traveled through open windows, but her father's letter hung over her like a shroud.

She turned on Pine Street and parked in the same location where her life had changed two days earlier. Odie B immediately rushed to the front porch with a luminous smile spreading across her round face. She engulfed Hope into her outstretched arms and Hope clung to her as if she were drowning.

"Odie B, thank you. I have no words."

She buried her head into Odie B's shoulder while the agony of her father's actions, and years of pain, swelled into choking sobs.

"Baby Girl, you've been through so much," Odie B's words flowed like a gentle stream.

Hope trembled in Odie B's tight embrace and together they swayed from side to side, while Odie B softly hummed their favorite hymn. Something she had done many times when Hope was young.

When peace like a river, attendeth my way,
When sorrows like sea billows roll
Whatever my lot, thou hast taught me to say
It is well, it is well, with my soul.

Relentless tears streamed as Odie B held her. In choked sobs, Hope asked, "How can I ever thank you?"

"Your time has come, Hope. You kept the faith. The gift of Drew is not from me, but from our Heavenly Father. He sent his angels to bring you joy. I merely did the delivering."

Hope pulled away to get a tissue.

"Is all well with your soul?" Odie B's concern came from deep within.

Hope's breaking voice reflected the agony of betrayal.

"I'm devastated, angry, and confused by my parents' actions. But I refuse to let them destroy our future happiness. Thanks to you, and all the heavenly beings that helped arrange our reunion, Drew and I will carve out our future together, without any restraints or limitations."

Odie B's large eyes danced with delight as she clapped her hands, and squealed,

"Wonderful! Let me get you a glass of sweet tea 'cause I want to hear all about your visit."

Hope followed her to the kitchen, removed a metal ice tray from the freezer and placed several cubes into tall glasses while Odie B handed her a teaspoon to sample the sweetened tea, just as she had done when she was a child. Hope took several sips to moisten her parched mouth.

Odie B got in the recliner and yanked on the floral dress that climbed above her knees and plunged downward from her ample cleavage. Then she smiled wide, leaned forward, and rubbed her hands together like a sorcerer making a secret potion.

"I want to hear all about it, ever since you left my house."

Hope relished supplying her with rich visualization, but today, her emotions swung like a rickety roller coaster, as she went from tears to laughter. Afterwards, Odie B reciprocated with facts about her visit with Drew.

"Before you arrived, I was telling him all that had happened to you, making it real clear that his vanishing was the worst thing he could have done. He sat there looking as lost as an envelope without any address."

Hope chuckled as Odie B scooted closer to the edge of her seat and whispered, "I didn't know he was following your daddy's instructions until he told me about the letter."

She made a sour face, puckering like she had just consumed a lemon, then leaning back, she proudly declared, "I continued admonishing him just the same 'cause I wanted to make sure there wasn't a possibility of his skittering off. After I pounded into him about how badly you suffered, he looked so dumb, he could throw himself on the ground and miss."

Odie B stared at the floor, trying to keep a straight face, but mischief oozed out of her.

"Hope, his brain was rattling around like a bullet in a boxcar."

Unable to restrain herself any longer, Odie B succumbed to a huge belly laugh, one that came from her toes, all the way up her generous-sized body. Hope joined in with gasps of delight.

When they finally calmed, Hope filled her in on the plans for confronting Mrs. Madison.

Odie B added, "Maybe that letter from Mr. Madison is still in his desk drawer. That's where I put it when I was there for his passing. I laid it in the center drawer, after I copied Mr. Drew's address."

She grinned, lighting up like the moon.

TWENTY-FIVE

Hope drove to her mother's home in Westover Hills. She was edgy, but Drew bore a cover of calm while mentally reviewing their situation. His lips tightened into a straight line when he thought about how he and Hope had been apart for over four thousand days, overly qualifying him for this long overdue confrontation with Mrs. Madison.

"Here we are," she said, as she parked.

"Is this YOUR home?" he asked.

"Yes. Well, it's my mother's."

Drew gasped. "This is reminiscent of the Vanderbilt home I visited in Asheville, North Carolina. What a beautiful mansion this is, and it even has the large circular drive!"

"Really? Mother and Daddy bought this home after they returned from Colorado. I lived in it for a year, after I was widowed, but I was never happy here."

Both took deep breaths and exited the car.

Hope avoided her typical entrance, through the side door by the garage. Instead, while taking Drew's hand in hers, she strolled to the front porch and rang the doorbell. She wanted her mother to see them as a couple, united and strong. The large, double doors swung open.

"Why didn't you come to…?" Mrs. Madison asked, until the sight of Drew registered in her mind, and she went silent and ashen at the same time.

"Hello, Mother. You remember Drew, don't you?"

"Of course …of course, I do. Come in. Why don't we sit in the den?"

Mrs. Madison nervously guided them toward the paneled room where portraits lined the walls. "Would you like something to drink?" she asked.

"No, Mother. We can't stay long, but we have questions only you can answer." The strength in her voice could not be ignored.

Hope and Drew sat down on a velvet sofa, opposite Kathryn Madison, who folded her body into a wingback chair, as if she were hoping the large chair would hide her.

"Mother, Odie B arranged our reunion." Hope gripped Drew's hand so tight her knuckles were white. "Since our meeting, I have been shocked, heartbroken, and confused by who arranged our separation. I have read the letters that Daddy wrote Drew, and the hurt has been unimaginable."

Mrs. Madison, unable to look at them, stared guiltily at the floor.

"Mother, how could you watch me grieve the loss of Drew without ever saying a word about what happened to him?" Hope heard her own voice escalating, as anger welled in her throat.

"Why, Mother? Why didn't you say something? How could you watch me go through that and NEVER comfort me with the truth? How, Mother? How?" Hope's voice was rising to a feverish pitch while Drew observed how Mrs. Madison shrunk under Hope's painful interrogation. Her mother's loss of confidence changed her; no longer did she appear self-assured and poised.

In hushed tones, barely above a whisper, Mrs. Madison spoke.

"I know you are angry, and you have every right to be. I don't know if you will ever forgive me, but I pray so. I was afraid this might occur one day, but since you have read your father's letters, you know why he did it. What he, nor I, ever expected was your marriage to Patrick. We both were at a loss as to what to do when you called to tell us you were married."

"You should have told me!" Hope shouted.

Mrs. Madison replied, her voice full of regret.

"How could we interrupt your happiness with a surprise announcement about Drew? We didn't think the years you and Drew had spent apart guaranteed a future together, and your enthusiasm about getting married, along with the determination in your voice...."

She bowed her head, as she explained how the right time never appeared.

"After Patrick's death, we watched you balance grief and joy day after day. We could see it in your eyes, without you saying a word. We thought the grief was for Patrick, and I'm sure some of it was, but I felt that you were never the same after Drew left for the Navy.

"Eventually, Lee, and a rewarding career in photography, seemed to change your life. We thought you were doing well. The last thing either of us wanted was to bring up the past, since we didn't know if Drew were available, or if your heart would be broken again."

Mrs. Madison turned to Drew, lowering her pallid face when she spoke.

"Drew, your annual letters caused him many hours of anguish. He would read your words, and say, 'I don't know if I did the right thing regarding Hope and Drew. Maybe I should have let it run its course without interfering. I thought I was doing right at the time...'

"He lived with regrets, but he really believed that after your graduation, everything would work out for you two. And then...."

Hope and Drew silently tried to process her words, as the sound of a lawn mower filtered through the windows. Mrs. Madison bounded out of her chair, and strolled toward Mr. Madison's office while she explained over her shoulder,

"He wrote a letter to Drew shortly before he died. I kept it just in case you found each other again."

Reluctance soared through Hope's body. Drew steeled himself for another one of Mr. Madison's letters.

Mrs. Madison held an envelope in her trembling hands when she returned.

"Here you are, Drew."

He nodded, took the envelope with familiar handwriting, and held his breath. His heart plummeted when the date revealed the letter had been concealed for five years. He pointed the fact out to Hope, as she leaned over, reading it with him.

"Drew, can you read it aloud, please?" Mrs. Madison's voice was barely audible.

June 4, 1965

Dear Drew,

I do not know your status, or your wishes, but I am writing to tell you how sorry I am that I interfered with your future, and Hope's, instead of letting both unfold. I now believe that if you two were meant to be, her college experience would not have been threatened with unhappiness due to the separation. It was I who made her unhappy by never being truthful. For that, I have lived with guilt and regret.

Hope's husband was killed in Vietnam in December 1961, nine months after they married. She was pregnant. A few days after she learned of Patrick's death, she gave birth to a fine little boy, Lee. He's four years old now, the center of her life, and ours.

I do not expect you to forgive me. I cannot forgive myself, especially when I look at Hope's eyes and see the normal radiant glow absent or when I observe Lee. I am always reminded of what a fine father you would be.

Should you ever wish to reach her, the contact information is provided below. I want you to know my mistake should not limit you in the future. I pray you navigate through these very complex, difficult circumstances toward the girl who has always loved you, and a father who doesn't deserve you. Having you and my daughter back together would make this family complete. If your heart leads you in that direction, please know it would be our greatest blessing.

Drew, wherever your path takes you, I am sorry that I haven't been able to call you "my son" through the years. You have my highest respect and admiration.
Sincerely,
Tennessee

Drew folded the letter and turned toward Hope with pain etched across his face.

"If this had been mailed, we could have had the last five years together."

Hope sobbed, "I know, I know."

In an unrecognizable voice, Kathryn Madison said,

"I didn't read it. I just left it in the drawer after his death. I'm so sorry."

Time crawled while each agonized in silence. Finally, Hope summoned the courage to respond.

"Mother, I know you are remorseful, and I'm not going to live my life filled with bitterness."

"Nor am I." Drew said.

He walked over to Kathryn, then bending low by her chair so she could see his face, he spoke.

"What has been done cannot be erased; but Hope and I will go forward in faith and confidence that this is our time. From this day forward, we will not look back. Instead, we will seize every moment, knowing that God has brought us together, once again."

 Mrs. Madison bowed her head, unable to restrain the deep sobs escaping her throat. The guilt, pain, and loneliness racked her body, as did her husband's words. Hope took some deep breaths and joined them, as all three wrapped their arms around each other, in a circle of love. Years of desolation were washed away in forgiveness.

TWENTY-SIX

Hope sat wearily in the car. Both were stunned into silence after hearing the confirmation of the truth. The facts were simple: her dad forced their separation and her mother's silence supported it, even after his death.

Drew turned to the woman who had been betrayed by her parents, and by him. The guilt he carried for not being pro-active felt as heavy as the infinite darkness he experienced when Mr. Madison had announced Hope's marriage. Flashes of that day on the ship, and the realization that hope was gone, as far as he could understand, cracked his composure. Now, he swallowed the tears clinging to his throat.

"Would you like to see where I live?" Hope asked, breaking the silence.

"I would like that very much." His voice cracked. "We need an hour alone."

She nodded and turned the car toward her home. Her heart pounded, as she thought about his words: an hour alone. An innocent statement, she thought to herself, but one that shed a broad light on their relationship. They had been in the public arena since their providential meeting three days earlier. Upon reflections, she realized they had rarely experienced time alone, a fact hard to grasp after loving one another for so many years.

Hope opened her front door, and uttered words she never imagined saying to him,

"Make yourself at home."

It was a simple statement. One that had rolled off her tongue numerous times in the past, but now it had a different meaning. She was able to invite the man she loved into her home, a fact that she had not yet fully comprehended.

Hope disappeared into the kitchen and quickly pulled out assorted cheeses, crackers, fruit, and a few of her favorite desserts out of the freezer: miniature lemon tarts and chocolate brownies. She placed them on a table, near the sofa, and added a couple of cold drinks, before she walked over to him. His eyes were misty, as he stared at a wall adorned with framed portraits. He studied each one, then turned toward her. Tenderness filled his voice.

"I'm stunned by your portraits. Each provides an insight into the subject."

"Thank you," she said. "My purpose is for each image to speak, to tell a story."

She stared at the wall and whispered,

"I photograph from a place in my heart where you've resided, Drew."

"How is that?" he asked.

"My desire is to capture a person's uniqueness, so their story will speak silently to their family, and to generations that follow.

"In our case, the stories, years, celebrations, and milestones have vanished, undocumented. Those fleeting moments will never be repeated, which has created a gaping hole in my life."

She dropped her head, and added, "I'm driven by emptiness and longing. My love for you, and the hole your absence created, is in every click of the shutter."

Drew was connecting with her words and realizing they each had been in the forefront of one another's mind ever since they parted.

"Come here, Darling," he said.

She went into his arms and holding her firmly, he spoke with conviction.

"I always felt your presence when I stood on the deck of the aircraft carrier consumed with loneliness. When I learned you were married, I fought a spiral of depression, but I knew if I were to be given one more moment with you, I could not relent to the depression, no matter how difficult. The strength to survive came from the deepest part of my soul. I never quit believing we were meant to be together."

Drew kissed her with the passion of a man who had long been denied the taste of her. When he pulled away, she noticed his eyes were filled with tears.

"I long to wake up with you as my wife. You are my beloved and when you are my bride, you will finally realize how much I love and care for you."

Hope drank in his touch, embrace, and kiss.

Two hours later, he embraced her in the airport terminal as roaring engines lifted departing aircraft into the sky.

"I'm so sorry I must leave. There's nothing I would rather do than stay here with you, but I must deal with my dad's situation."

"I understand. When do you think you will be able to return? I would like for you and Lee to meet soon," she said.

"I agree. The three of us need to spend time together. Since you showed me his picture, I've felt a strong connection with him. Thoughts about what it would be like to have him as a son have filled my mind, along with the deep desire for him to feel like he'll be getting a dad when we marry."

Her face was glowing, as he continued.

"Let's show him your home in Boulder, and the places where we spent so much time. We can do some fishing in the mountain streams like I once did with my father. We can even throw around a football. It seems like I did that for a few years."

"That sounds wonderful, Drew. I would like to meet your father also," she said, smiling.

"He'd like that. I can hear his words now, 'It's about time I get a grandchild'!"

"Really? Has he been asking you about grandchildren and not about when or who you would marry?"

Drew averted her eyes.

"I'll be able to give him an answer soon," he said, softly.

"Is that a proposal?" she asked.

Drew chuckled. "No, but our love story should include a wedding, so I'm planting the idea for when I propose. I want to hear, 'Yes', not, 'Let me think about it'."

"I think I've been given enough time to contemplate my decision, don't you?" Her eyes sparkled, as they hadn't in years.

"We've waited a lifetime, Hope. Our time is *long* overdue."

"United Flight 356, now boarding for Denver."

Drew's penetrating gaze held her as he spoke.

"Hope, please remember I love you. Everything about you and the past few days will remain in the forefront of my mind as I go about the necessary tasks this next week. A day won't go by that I won't be longing for you."

He reached into his pocket for a vanilla-colored envelope.

"Here's another reminder of my love."

Hope held it in her fingers, memorizing the natural scent of him, his eyes, his face, and touch. He walked away, then glanced back at her, knowing she would still be there.

The stifling Texas temperatures and setting sun greeted her, as she walked through the airport doors. She hurried to the car and turned the air conditioner on high before opening the envelope.

My Dearest Hope,

I love you with a fervor that can only come from the One who put us together. Please be certain of this: If I were to pass on tomorrow, which seems early to me, my life would still be complete, for I was loved by you.

Yours Forever, Drew.

The following afternoon, Drew called with good news.

"I found an assisted living place for my dad, not far from where I'll be working, and he seems to be accepting the news of a change quite well. Especially, when I told him about you."

She could hear a smile in his voice.

"This is great, Drew. I can't wait to meet him."

Plans for when she and Lee would travel to Colorado were briefly discussed.

A few hours later, the phone rang while she was preparing dinner.

"Hello," Hope answered.

"Is this Hope Madison?"

"Yes, it is. Who's calling, please?"

"My name is Fiona, but you don't know me. I am engaged to Drew Bartlett."

Hope felt her knees buckle and she quickly sat down to steady herself.

"Who did you say you were?" she asked, again.

"My name is Fiona. Drew and I have been dating for a couple of years. His reason for leaving the aircraft carrier and returning to the States is because we are getting married."

"What?" Hope asked, stunned.

"I know he came to visit you in Texas," Fiona continued, "but I felt you should know about our upcoming wedding, in case he didn't mention it."

"Why are you the one telling me instead of Drew?" Hope asked.

"He has a lot going on between taking care of his father and trying to get settled before his new assignment begins. We are taking off for a few days next week, so we can enjoy a brief vacation."

Hope hung up.

Paralyzed, and in shock, she tried to make sense of what she had just heard. She couldn't. But she knew Drew would alleviate her fears, so she sat waiting for his evening call. When it didn't come, she tried to reach him at the number he had given her. No one answered.

At three in the morning, she threw herself across the bed. Tears soaked her pillow until she fell asleep. Six hours later, her bedroom phone rang while she sat in a hot bath. Unaware she missed the call, her body continued to tremble as if she were in an earthquake; steam rose to the ceiling.

Eventually, she emerged from the bath, wrapped a winter robe around her, though the summer temperature had already climbed to a stifling one hundred degrees. At ten-thirty, the phone rang again.

"Hello," Hope whispered, unable to find her voice.

"Hope, I've been trying to reach you. Where have you been?" Drew inquired.

"I've been here," she said.

"I've been calling since early this morning. I was unable to call last night."

"Oh?" she asked with a whimper of protest.

"Hope, what's wrong? You don't sound like yourself."

Scared, she reached deep inside for the kind of strength only God can provide.

"Who is Fiona?" she asked in a hushed tone.

Drew sat immobile and confused. *How did Hope find out anything about her?*

"How is it you know that name?" he asked.

He didn't wait for an answer, before responding. "She's been the caregiver for my father, but I fired her last night. Dad is now in a nursing facility."

"Fiona called me."

"Fiona called YOU?"

She heard the shock in his voice, as she relayed the conversation.

"Yes. She said you two were in a relationship and the reason you had come home was to marry her." Hope almost strangled on the words.

"She what???" His voice bellowed. In a stern and demanding tone, he ordered, "Hope, listen to me. That is NOT true. How did she get your number?"

"I don't know. I don't know anything," she mumbled.

"Hope, I will straighten this out and get back with you, but before I do here is what you must know. Fiona has been tossing the word 'marry' around since she began caring for my father three years ago. She has hinted, schemed, and coerced everyone into believing we're a couple. My grandmother would fill me in on Fiona's theatrics each time I came home on leave, and we would shake our heads and perform damage control where we could.

"Hope, please believe me. We have never been a couple. She would bring her two young sons around dad and use them as ploys. She would tell him that he'd have two grandsons when we married. I was furious, but I was only home for thirty days, and during that time, I tried to keep friction and disruption to a minimum. Dad and I were finally having cordial visits after so many years of not, and I didn't want to interrupt his care. If she quit when I was in Vietnam, my grandmother would be left with no one to attend to him. Her own failing health would have prevented her from being his caregiver. When I moved him to the new facility last night, he told me he had never liked Fiona, but didn't want to mention it while I was battling for survival around the globe."

"Drew, why didn't you mention her to me, or any of this when we were together?" she asked.

"I thought about it," Drew stated firmly, "but I didn't want to give you any reason for doubting me or my feelings for you. You were already dealing with feelings of betrayal, both from me and from your parents. I didn't want to add irrelevant information. Please believe me when I say, I was trying to protect you, Hope, not hide anything.

"Hope, you have been the only woman to live in my heart. I am so sorry I didn't tell you about her, but I thought I could resolve Dad's situation without Fiona and her manipulating ways interfering. Obviously, I was wrong. You have been through so much heartache and my only mission is to comfort you. Never did I entertain the idea Fiona would seek revenge. I should have anticipated a backlash because of her reaction when I said she wouldn't be needed any longer. She became a spewing volcano and began to yell, 'What about me after all I did? Did you really think I wanted to spend my days giving bed baths to your dad? I did it for us! Mopping up his messes, cleaning toilets, washing soiled underwear... all that was for US! I knew he wouldn't live much longer, as weak as he was; then it would be our time.' She added, like a screeching owl, 'I knew we would travel, stay in luxury hotels, and dine at the best restaurants because you would inherit everything. All I had to do was tolerate him, but now you are just sweeping me aside?"

Hope listened, absorbing every word and nuance in her exhausted body.

"What did you say to her?' she asked.

"I took the check I had written her, threw it in her hand, shouting:

'WE NEVER WERE! FURTHERMORE, WE NEVER WILL BE!'

"I opened the front door, grabbed her by the arm, and pushed her outside. I was so upset; I slammed the door so hard it almost came off its hinges. Then I sat down and tried to gather my wits after hearing such despicable remarks about my dad from the woman who had been hired to care for him."

He paused, remembering the rage in her face, and added in a resentful tone, "Arguing with her was like dueling with hand grenades, but that's why I didn't call last night. It was too late, however, had I known she would unleash her poison on you I would have called at any hour. Why didn't you call me?" he asked.

"I tried, but no one answered." Hope's voice remained devoid of emotion.

"I had gone to get something to eat. Oh, Hope, I'm so sorry. Can you forgive me for not mentioning this messy situation to you?"

"Drew, the last twenty-four hours have been so grueling! The pain and confusion have been excruciating. Let's talk later today. I must process what has happened."

"Hope, forever will I express my love, leaving no room for you to forget, doubt, or anything resembling its eternal character."

Wishing to dispel any doubt in Hope's mind that his love for her was the eternal kind, he said, "I love you, Hope. I cannot have a life without you, my darling." He spoke with deep sadness, then hung up, put his face in his hands, and felt overwhelming fear that he had lost her all over again. Forever.

Hope, shattered, put the phone back on the hook, and fell into a deep sleep for an hour, then awoke to the harshness of reality. She didn't believe Drew, nor was she willing to go through years of doubt and anxiety regarding his explanations. Faced with the question of how to live without him once again, she reached for the phone and dialed.

"Mother, can you come over? I need to talk to you," she said.

Hope had not confided in her mother for years, but they were on different terrain now, after the unburying of secrets.

"Of course. I can be there in twenty minutes if you like."

Hope heard the concern in her voice.

"Okay," Hope muttered.

"Is there anything wrong, dear? You don't sound like yourself."

"I'm not, Mother. I'll tell you when you arrive."

Hope waited on the living room sofa, wrapped in her pink robe, with a box of tissues beside her. When she heard her mother's car in the driveway, she tried to go to the door but was too weak. Her mother let herself in, took one look at Hope, and rushed to her side.

"What's happened, Hope? Is it Lee?"

"No."

"What is it then?" Her mother's face bore grave concern.

Hope explained Fiona's call and Drew's explanation while Mrs. Madison listened with rapt attention. After pouring out all the details, Hope began to weep in anguish. Her mother's arms cradled her.

"I don't know why I can't believe him," Hope sobbed. "When I heard Fiona's words, I felt pain deeper than I've ever experienced, and I'm not sure I can ever love him again, not the way I did. It was such a trusting love, even the second time, after learning the reason for our separation, but when Fiona gushed about their future, I saw my dreams scatter like breadcrumbs in a cyclone."

"Hope, now you listen to me," she said, sternly. "It wasn't Drew that left you in 1959, at least, not willfully so. That was due to your misguided and overly protective parents. And he hasn't left you now. The hurt you are experiencing is the result of a vicious, jealous woman."

Hope saw determination in her mother's face and a resolve she didn't expect.

Mrs. Madison continued without stopping to take a breath.

"I have never observed a more committed, devoted, and faithful man than Drew, one with the same loyalty as your father. Drew's annual letters were indicators of his unchanging heart and his patience. Both worthy of medals. His respect for you was the same.

"Hope, people can say the right things, but it's their actions that speak. Drew's actions have revealed nothing but his love and commitment to you."

"I just don't know if I can put us back together. Maybe, I've mastered the art of losing and I don't know what it feels like to win."

"Hope, having courage doesn't mean you have no fear. It means you walk through fears and doubts with faith and with the man you love and who loves you. Drew's heart and spiritual muscle will carry you. Let him heal the gashes in your heart that were put there by people, other than himself, and place your trust in the Creator who brought you two together. Not once, but twice. Drew has waited for you eleven years, and I feel certain he would wait eleven more, if he had to, but I truly believe you are meant to be together."

Her mother stared blankly at the floor. When she opened her mouth to speak, the words were immersed in the choked tears clinging to her throat. But she was intent on saving her drowning daughter.

"For thirty-seven years, your dad would get up every morning and go to the kitchen to get our coffee. As the aroma filled the air, I silently thanked God that I was being given another day with him. There was nothing I wanted more than another day with your father, year after year."

Speaking in a whisper, she said, "And that is what I want for you."

The ache from his absence could not be restrained, nor her regret that Hope had missed years with Drew. Mrs. Madison bent over and wept uncontrollably. Hope bolted off the sofa to comfort her and together they released grief for the man they both loved and missed desperately, Tennessee Madison.

Hope held her mom, the one who pled on Drew's behalf, while reflecting on her mother's tone and passion; she had appeared like a courtroom lawyer pleading on behalf of an innocent client. A ray of light burst within Hope when the door of truth opened.

"Thank you, Mother, for revealing Drew's true character. I know he is the one for me."

Mrs. Madison, filled with assurance, left the house and drove away.

Seven hundred miles away another scene was unfolding.

TWENTY-SEVEN

Drew realized Fiona's verbal assault had destroyed Hope's trust. All their progress had vanished within a few minutes and now an ocean of emptiness devoured him. He paced back and forth until an unprecedented decision came to life.

Hope was strong, but how strong, he wondered, while he drove the familiar streets. Moments later, he entered his dad's nursing facility. The smell of a potent cleanser engulfed him, as he made his way down the empty corridor toward his father's room.

A temporary nameplate, hanging at an odd angle on the door of 302, welcomed guests to Dr. Andrew Bartlett's room. He knew his father wouldn't like a crooked sign, so he straightened it as thoughts about the other residents roamed through his mind. Many had been his dad's patients, and Drew figured they would continue seeking his medical advice about their ailments. According to the director, all the single women saw him as a handsome catch and wouldn't hesitate to come calling. Drew chuckled to himself, knocked lightly, and entered.

The sterile walls, barren of color and décor except for a nondescript watercolor print, were dimly lit. The kitchenette, tucked into a corner by the entry, had a Formica counter the same color as the bland walls. A couple of matching beige chairs gathered around a brown vinyl sofa near the television.

Drew mentally questioned why older people were short-changed on the ability to choose attractive surroundings, in what would probably be their last home on earth. He reasoned since his father had spent most of his life in a hospital, the change probably didn't appear as bleak to him. But the dissimilarity between now and their family residence, the one where his mother and father lived after they first married, and where his dad had lived for a good portion of his life, was vast.

"Hi, Dad." He forced cheer into the greeting.

Dr. Bartlett peered at his son, then placed a bookmark in the book he was reading, laid it on his lap, and removed the glasses balancing on the end of his nose.

"What are you doing here?" he asked, gruffly.

"I've come to talk to you."

"To what do I owe this visit? Is something bothering you?" His father's gray eyebrows formed into a straight line, while apprehension darted in his eyes like crows investigating the death of one of their own.

Dr. Bartlett huddled under a beige fleece, as he listened attentively to the Fiona story. His alertness astonished Drew, and his occasional nod of understanding gave rise to reassurance. Relieved, Drew felt the vast space that had defined their relationship for years now shrank with every word.

Drew ended by expressing how totally destructive Fiona's actions had been for him and Hope. He paused while his dad turned toward the window and stared at a black-billed magpie perched on a tree branch. The distinct sounds of the bird filled the quiet room. After a moment, his father turned his attention back to Drew and held his gaze.

With a tone of irritation, he asked, "Why are you here, Drew?"

Startled by the question, Drew silently searched for answers. Was his dad's mind unable to retain the conversation? Or worse, did he not care at all?

Drew felt like he had been punched in the stomach. Had he made the ultimate mistake of crossing the invisible boundary that separated them all his life? The line that prohibited the sharing of feelings.

"What do you mean?" he asked, hesitantly.

"I mean, why are you here and not on a plane to Texas, assuring Hope of your love, and your devotion? Why are you talking to an old man who has experienced almost forty years of isolation after your beloved mother was killed in a car accident? Don't let the reckless, malicious act of a raging shrew come between you. Furthermore, don't let any losses deprive you of feeling and giving love, as I did."

Drew sat speechless while his dad's regrets, words he never expected to hear, washed over him. Tears threatened to spill across his face. With trembling voice, he asked,

"Dad, will you be all right if I leave?"

"Yes, I will, and if I need any assistance, there are some pretty nurses around to help me, unlike the one I've had!"

"Dad, why didn't you tell me you didn't like Fiona?"

"Son, you had enough on your mind when you came home on leave. I didn't want to worry you."

Drew stood silent. The comprehension of being called, "son" was beyond the scope of his imagination.

Drew went to him and gave his dad a gentle pat on the shoulder. His father patted the top of his hand in return.

"By the way, Drew, when you stop by the house, there is something you need to pick up."

"Okay. What is it?"

"It's a small, white box in the bottom drawer of my dresser. You'll have to dig in the back for it, because I hid it from Fiona. She was always snooping around! Reach under my sweaters and you'll find it there. It's from your grandmother. I think you're going to want it.

"Thanks, Dad."

His father got up and slowly moved toward the bed. Drew turned to leave, then hesitated.

"Oh, Dad, by the way, do you know how Fiona got Hope's phone number?"

"It was by my bed, on top of the nightstand, and I presume she took it. She was always meddling."

Drew's brow furrowed.

"Dad, did you happen to tell her I was going to Texas to see the girl that I have been in love with all of my life, the words I repeated to you when I left for Texas?"

His father's eyes danced with mischief, as he turned his head toward the windows. "I don't recall. I may have, but my memory is failing me."

Drew realized his dad was teasing but was surprised when his countenance changed.

"Son, I never expected the events to occur as they did. Please believe me and bring Hope here so I can apologize to her."

Drew felt a powerful surge of emotion when he heard words of concern and remorse being voiced by his father. In the depths of his soul, a typhoon of forgiveness swept away years of bitterness and loneliness.

In that instance, fragments from the accident that took his mother's life burst through barriers of suppression. Shadows disappeared, years reversed, curtains parted, and the events began unfolding like a movie. He could see it, finally.

He was five years old, and his dad was on duty in the Emergency Room when he and his mother arrived at the hospital in an ambulance. People in white uniforms began hastily steering his mother in a different direction. After a while, his father came into the cubicle where he lay on a hard bed. Concerned nurses in hushed voices addressed his father's questions. When his dad learned Drew only had a few scrapes and bruises, he gently picked him up and held him close for a long time. Drew felt the tears rolling down his father's face, as they merged with his own.

Drew didn't know why his dad kept repeating how sorry he was, as if he were to blame; now he understood. His dad felt responsible for his mother's death, even though medically, nothing could be done. Not by anyone. But feelings of helplessness and guilt had consumed him. They still did.

Drew took a moment to see if his father was resting comfortably then quietly went to his bedside, feeling humbled by the man who had managed to live most of his life with the worst grief imaginable.

His dad's eyes were closed, and as Drew stared down at him, he realized that after the accident, his father had continued to diligently serve the community in the same hospital where Drew had been born, where his mother had died, where memories haunted him daily.

At the same hospital where life was given, and precious lives were taken away, Dr. Bartlett, Chief of Staff, had carved a successful career.

Drew understood the magnitude of his father's pain and felt a twinge of pride. Choked sobs hung in his throat when he stared down at his sleeping father and softly whispered what had never been said.

"I love you, Dad."

"I love you, too, Son."

* * * * *

Hope was resting on a chaise lounge, enjoying the fading twilight while her mother's encouraging words still rang in her ears. A red-breasted robin calmly sprinkled his wings in a nearby fountain and Zoey found satisfaction in taunting two squirrels.

The sound of the ringing doorbell, and Zoey's incessant barking, interrupted her quiet reflection. She walked toward the front door, chastising herself for resembling the aftermath of a storm. Her eyes swollen, and her ghost-like face was puffy. She threw open the door, and she heard her own shrill voice ask, "Drew! What are you doing here?"

"I came to talk to you. May I?"

"Of course. Come in. When did you arrive?"

"An hour ago. I haven't even checked into a hotel. I picked up a rental car and drove directly here."

Both were feeling strained and awkward. Drew instantly excused himself, went to the restroom to wash his face, and pray again for God to open Hope's heart. A few minutes later he returned to the living room.

Hope distracted herself by leaving to go to the kitchen and pouring two glasses of freshly made tea over ice. When she heard him come out of the bathroom, she invited him to join her in the kitchen. He stood in the doorway while she set their glasses directly opposite one another on the table. She motioned for him to sit.

The extreme fatigue, visually ravaging Drew's face and body, spoke clearly. Despair emanated from every pore, and his typical confident, high spirits had vanished like the morning mist.

Drew took several gulps to moisten his dry throat; then with pleading eyes, he began.

"I have searched for words to beg your forgiveness. You have suffered immense pain by my not actively pursuing you during your college years. I should have done more." Hope listened pensively, as he continued.

"There are no words, only a profound emptiness for the years lost. I do not want that mistake to be repeated. If it means spending eternity earning your trust, I will take comfort in doing so."

"Drew…"

"No, let me finish." He took another long sip of tea to fill his cracking voice.

"From the moment I met you, I knew you were the girl of my dreams. That hasn't changed, but I know my not telling you about Fiona was a grave error in judgment. Perhaps, it was enough to destroy your love for me.

"Hope, if everything you felt is gone, you will not hear from me again. But my deepest desire is to take your hand in mine from this point forward, never to part."

Tears filled her eyes, as she stared at him. Her voice wavered.

"Drew, I realize that I, too, am at fault. I was very frightened at the thought of continuing to love you after her phone call, but I am more frightened of not. I have listened to my heart, and I want to come from a place of love and trust with you."

Drew quickly jumped out of his chair and grabbed her before she could say more. Holding her with a strength she had not known, the fears, concerns, and sorrows were released in a kiss unlike either had experienced. They stood in an uninterrupted embrace as one kiss flowed into another until he pulled back and stared into her deep blue eyes.

"I have more I want to say…"

She interrupted. "I know your heart, Drew. It is the counterpart of mine."

He took her by the hand, led her to the living room, and motioned for her to sit on the sofa.

"Hope, I want you to know the full width and breadth of my love."

He walked to the door and retrieved his flight bag, opened it, and sat down next to her.

"I have a letter I want you to read."

He reached into the bag and removed an envelope.

"I would read it to you, but I lack the composure to do so." His eyes clouded. "I didn't know this letter existed until today. It's from my grandmother."

Hope opened the envelope and began quietly reading her words:

My Dearest Grandson,

Your mother's spirit was full of love. The honor of watering the seeds she bountifully planted in your heart became my purpose in life. You are her legacy, one that would make her very proud.

My eyes are dim and my hands quiver, as I approach my seventy-sixth birthday, but I shall not leave this life until another legacy has been fully revealed. It is the one left to you by your grandfather, a man of great courage.

When I married your grandfather, he slipped a diamond band on my finger next to the beautiful engagement ring he had given me six months earlier. Both are in this box. I was nineteen. He was ten years my senior, a very successful businessman, highly respected, generous in heart and spirit. Travels took him around the world. Friends were made on all continents.

His dream was to participate in all the experiences one could possibly enjoy which eventually led to an adventure that would become a part of history. Passage on the grandest of all ships to sail the Atlantic was booked in honor of our third wedding anniversary. We had our son with us, your father. He was one year old at the time. My friend, Lizzie, the one responsible for introducing your grandfather and me, was there, along with her new husband, and your governess. We stood on the deck of the ship, happily waving goodbye to friends and we remained there until the ship's name became no longer visible to those on shore. The Titanic.

When the unthinkable happened and the impossible became possible, I begged your grandfather to get in a life raft, but he was adamant that your dad and I, along with Lizzie, the governess, leave first. He would follow, after all women and children were secure, he assured.

We stood on the deck embracing, unwilling to let go and strangely, amidst all the confusion and noise, there was a moment of serenity when everything became silent. Chaos did not exist in either of our minds. The swaying, rocking ship stilled. Freezing water relinquished its spraying and the bitter cold evaporated. We were given a moment of peace, as if we were the only ones there and we stood clinging, loving, memorizing, adoring one another. I can still recall the sensation when your grandfather loosened his embrace, and as a final gesture of his love, picked up my left hand and lifted it to his lips. He placed a gentle kiss on my wedding ring, as he had every day since our wedding, and added, 'I will see you in New York. Wait for me.'

Our fingers became untwined, and his grip was gone. I was on the raft, drifting, watching the space between us expand until there was nothing there, but emptiness. His last gentle touch, a caress on my wedding ring, was all I had of him.

Twenty-six years later, your father and beautiful mother married. Soon after, you were born. When you were two years old, a memory was firmly etched into my being. It's a story I've never told you, or anyone.

Your parents were attending a medical meeting while I sat holding you in my Park Avenue apartment. You and I were in the garden room; rays of sunshine were bending around the skyscrapers of New York City, warming us as we sat by the window. You were holding a stuffed bear, but eventually, you grew restless and wiggled out of my arms, eagerly toddling off to play hide-and-seek, your favorite game. Inexplicably, you turned back towards me, and took my hand in your little hands, lowered your head, and kissed my wedding ring. You then gazed up at me with the side-grin of your grandfather. I was speechless. Tears flowed from my eyes.

This same act was repeated many times before you started school. You never offered a reason, but I knew why – a part of your grandfather's loving heart was beating in yours, reminding me of his closeness.

With that said, I am giving you the rings that carry his blessing. They belong on the girl who will give you her heart, who will spend her life loving you and cherishing the legacy of love, courage, bravery, and sacrifice given to you by your grandfather. I am also giving you your grandfather's wedding ring, which was handed to me when I went to identify my husband through the personal items he was wearing when the ship went to the bottom of the ocean. I recognized your grandfather's gold band from the engraving that I had inscribed, 'Love Through Eternity'.

Drew, my beloved grandson, I will always be with you, just as he has been with us. And for the joy you have given me throughout my life, there are no words. Only love through eternity.

Gratefully,

Your Grandmother

Hope sat with tears flowing down her face while he held her.

When he spoke, tenderness streamed.

"Hope, I knew from the first time we met there would be no other woman for me. You came as a gift, bringing life to my non-resonant heart. You were the music I longed to hear; the dream I yearned to see. Though circumstances, distance, and time interrupted us, I have been soaring and searching the heavens for you since we parted. The blessing of a reunion has now been granted; a persistent prayer answered. We are together, never to bear the agony of being separated again. When God calls me home, I will walk beside you through eternity."

He held the engagement ring and slipped to his knees.

"Hope, may I have the honor of being your husband, protecting, cherishing, honoring, and loving you for the rest of my life?"

She nodded, unable to speak. He slipped the ring on her finger.

"I'm aware it's too early, so consider this your first proposal. An official one will come after Lee has had time to adjust. Can I ask him for permission to marry you?"

Hope nodded through a rivulet of tears. The dream that Lee always nurtured, having a devoted father, would finally be realized.

Drew then stood, lifted her off the sofa and closed all distance with a kiss that only those who have been personally touched with loss could understand.

Hope removed the ring before Lee returned home from camp.

TWENTY-EIGHT

"Mom, is Drew coming to Texas?" Lee inquired. "It's been two weeks."

"No. He's taking care of business in Colorado, since he'll be returning to the Navy soon."

Lee mumbled under his breath, "That's a bummer!"

"It sounds like you enjoy having him around." A smile could be heard in her voice.

"I guess."

"You GUESS?" she asked, startled.

"Well, it's not like he lives here, or he's around all the time. What if it all stops, or he's sent somewhere by the Navy, and we don't see him again?" Lee's fears were on edge.

"Are you wondering if he's in our lives temporarily?"

"Yeah," he mumbled while repeatedly tossing a sofa pillow in the air.

He eventually tired, and flopped onto his stomach, resting his forehead on his hands while burying his face in the carpet. She felt certain tears were dropping, and moved closer to rub his back while she shared her previous uncertainties.

"I had the same feelings when I first saw him in Colorado recently. He had been such a strong part of my life in 1959. We were together every day, and then suddenly he left for the Navy, and it was over. I was devastated. But I can assure you, that isn't going to happen again. He will never leave us willingly."

"Well, it still could happen. God took my dad and Pappy."

"Yes. Even though we don't understand why, we know neither chose to leave. The same applies to Drew. He is here to stay in our lives in the same way."

"How do you know? Has he asked you to marry him?"

Hope paused, before answering the unexpected question.

"We've talked about it. We love each other very much, but we don't want to rush. Many things will change when we marry, so how about the three of us working that out later?"

"Okay, Mom." He turned over, threw the pillow back up in the air, and boxed it again while asking, "Where'd he go to college?" Hope noticed his spirits seemed slightly elevated.

"University of Colorado. He attended on a full scholarship and was captain of the football team."

"Really? What position did he play?"

"Quarterback. I heard he was exceptional, but I didn't get to see him play since we met in the spring of his senior year. He was in the Navy ROTC and was commissioned as an officer when he graduated. Then he went to flight training and became a fighter pilot."

"Where'd you meet him?"

"At my best friend's home." She smiled at the memory.

"And you dated after that?"

"Yes. We spent all our free time together, before he left."

"Did you ever see him again?"

"No. I went to college, met your father, and we got married, then I had you. Our paths didn't cross until Odie B arranged a meeting a few weeks ago. Would you like to see some pictures of when we dated?"

"SURE! Do you have some?"

"I do. I'll get the scrapbook I made. It's in the attic."

Hope walked to the garage with her heart racing, excited about Lee's change of mood. As she climbed the ladder, she recalled when Lee arrived home from camp and how the thought of telling him about Drew had filled her with dread. But, like most nine-year-old

The Other Part of Her

boys, he appeared uninterested when he heard the news. Obviously, his views had changed, and she was delighted.

Hope and Drew had decided to spare Lee the details about their enforced separation, and the years of hurt they endured. She never wanted Lee to feel his dad was second choice, or that his grandfather intentionally inflicted pain with his well-meaning protection. They agreed to answer Lee's questions, and to let him become comfortable with the situation before they discussed the future with him.

Now, it seemed Lee was doing the approaching.

Hope recalled Drew's first visit with Lee, as she opened the trunk. It had been a weekend filled with baseball, golfing, and swimming. Lee thrived. Neither Hope, nor Drew knew if it were "beginner's luck", or if their meeting had been especially blessed. They chose to believe the latter.

Subsequent visits also went smoothly. Lee flourished when they flew to Colorado Springs, or when Drew travelled to Texas. This was the first weekend, during the last few weeks that the three had not been together.

Hope returned with the scrapbook and the two intently studied the photos. He drilled her with questions, like there would be an exam afterwards, and she responded with answers. When Lee turned the last page, he appeared engrossed at a photo of her snapping on Drew's Ensign shoulder boards at graduation. More questions flowed.

Finally, they came to Drew's loving messages, each resting in an envelope. Lee inquired and Hope explained, without opening them.

"Drew presented a note to me almost every time we were together. He wanted me to have them when he was gone for long periods. His grandfather had done the same for his grandmother."

"Really? That's cool. When do you think he's coming back?"

"Drew wants us to fly to Colorado next weekend," she stated.

"That's great. We're going, aren't we?"

She nodded with a wide grin.

"I wonder what we'll do. I hope we go kayaking." Lee, fueled with enthusiasm, ran outside to tell his friends.

When Drew called that evening, she gave him a review of her discussion with Lee.

"It looks like our prayers have been answered," he said with a sigh of relief.

"Yes, more than I could have dreamed possible." Her voice cracked with emotion.

"I agree."

"Hope, before we hang up, one of my purposes in calling tonight was to ask you to bring my grandmother's ring with you when you come. I want to have a jeweler check the stones, to make sure they are secure."

"Of course. I'll get it now."

"Goodnight, my love." His voice deepened. "I miss you."

* * * * * *

The next weekend Drew met them at the airport, and over dinner they planned activities for the following day. Hope observed Lee's inner confidence, a direct result of Drew's influence.

"Lee, how about the two of us going fishing early tomorrow morning? We can be back before your mother is up." Drew winked at Hope and grinned.

"Yes sir. That sounds great!"

Hope's heart burst with pride when she saw them side-by-side.

Drew turned to her. "Do you have anything you wish to do while Lee and I are gone?"

"I'd like to visit with your dad, if you think that would be okay with him," she said.

"Oh yes, Dad would love it!"

Drew reflected on the first time he introduced his father to Hope. The meeting had gone well, even to the point that Hope and Drew felt it had been a blessed encounter, but anxiety riddled his confidence when he thought about introducing Lee. Memories of their father-and-son relationship, when he was Lee's age, were agonizing.

The internal debate raged. Should he prepare Lee for his father's austere demeanor before the introduction, or perform damage control later? He made the decision not to inject preconceived ideas into Lee's mind. Clean up could come afterwards.

The next morning, before sunrise, Drew walked quietly down the hall to his childhood bedroom and knocked softly on the door. When Lee didn't respond, he pushed on the door. The room was empty, and the bed made.

He looked around and found Lee sitting at the kitchen table with Hope. Cereal bowls were in front of them.

Drew greeted them, before pouring himself a cup of coffee.

"Would you like to eat something before you go?" Hope asked.

"No thanks. I'll take a thermos of coffee, and when we stop to get bait, we'll grab some snacks. Fishing works up an appetite. Right, Lee?"

"It sure does. Well, I guess it does. I've never fished."

"Well, Lee, we're about to change that." He turned to Hope, "The car keys are on the entry hall table if you want to go see Dad. We're taking my truck."

"What time do you expect to return?" she asked.

"Lee, do you think we'll be done about noon?"

"Sure. After we eat lunch, do you think we can go kayaking?"

Lee's eagerness reminded him of when he and his dad made occasional fishing trips and how special it was to have his father's attention. He wanted to offer Lee the same experience, only more frequently.

"That's a great idea. Why don't we come back and pick your mom up around noon? We can go have lunch, before heading to the river."

He turned to Hope, "Is that okay with you?" He smiled when he observed her contained jubilation.

"I love the plan." Her smiling eyes were like an open highway.

Drew bent over, kissing her gently on the forehead.

"I love you," he whispered.

Lee was already out the door, retrieving the fishing poles from the garage.

When they stopped for bait, they inquired of the shop owner about the best fishing areas.

"Palmer Lake is preferred by most," he said, as he rang up their purchases.

A few minutes later, they were watching a blazing, red-orange ball peek over the mountains in the distance, and gradually ascend into the summer sky.

"There's nothing like Colorado sunrises," Drew remarked.

"I've NEVER seen one like that," Lee replied, his voice brimming with awe.

Drew pulled off the dusty road onto a grassy embankment, but before the truck came to a full stop, Lee jumped out, grabbed his camera bag, the tackle box, and fishing poles.

Drew felt like he was staring into a mirror from years earlier. He smiled to himself and lifted the ice chest from the bed of the truck, then grabbed the bait, along with the snacks they had purchased. Together, they hiked toward the water as sounds of morning birds filled the air and a cool breeze swept across their faces. Thousands of wildflowers swayed at their feet, and ducks were cloistered in the

The Other Part of Her

reeds while the morning fog slowly lifted from the lake's surface. A reflection of the brilliant sunrise swam in the motionless water.

"We may see a bald eagle today, Lee. They nest near here."

"Really? I've never seen one." Amazement resonated in his voice, as he quickly opened a bag holding his Minolta camera, a gift from Aunt Riley.

"I think I'll get some pictures before I start fishing, Drew. The lighting is perfect."

"I didn't realize you were a photographer." Drew's eyes held a flash of surprise.

"I'm not, but I like visual reminders. That's something I learned from my mom. We do photography excursions, just for the fun of it. She taught me about lighting and composition, and we always photograph special events. Today is one of those."

Drew nodded in agreement.

Lee fired off several shots before placing the camera back in its case. While baiting a hook, he casually speculated about the possibility of hooking a rainbow trout.

Drew settled back, quietly thinking about Lee's resemblance to his mother, both in looks and personality. For a brief second, he felt all the past suffering had been worth it.

After a couple of hours, and a string of fish between them, Drew stood up, stretched his long legs, walked around for a moment then sat down on the damp ground. He stared at the lake while biting into a donut. Trepidation coursed through his body. Hundreds of times he had rehearsed how to tell Lee about his feelings for Hope, and the moment had arrived. Unfortunately, it came without one word. He was blank. Lee inhaled two cinnamon rolls and a pint of milk before Drew could swallow a second bite. Clearing his throat didn't help, but a silent prayer did.

"Since your mother and I reunited a few months ago, I've been thinking about the future in a different way." He paused as a Hooded Merganser began splashing in the water. Lee glanced at the duck and said nothing.

Drew shuffled his position as he gulped down his coffee, just as mental alarm bells began clanging like cymbals. He felt off balance, his mouth dry. For the first time, Drew was discovering something that had been overlooked by him countless times. He had never entertained the idea of Lee having a negative response to the idea of their getting married. As a Naval Commander, accustomed to playing every angle, he faltered. His lack of preparation shattered his composure, and doubts raced through his mind. *Is this too soon to approach Lee about marrying his mother*, he wondered. *What if the changes are too drastic for a boy his age? What if he opposes the idea of a proposal? Or a move?*

He fought for control, as he contemplated the fact that there was no Plan B in place. Then, a revelation! There was no Plan B because he could not fathom his life without the two of them in it. Plan A had to succeed.

After taking another swallow of coffee, Drew gently began one of the most important talks of his life.

"Lee, I've been in love with your mother since the first time I laid eyes on her. She had just completed her second year of college, and even with all the years of separation, she has maintained the status of being the only woman I've ever loved."

Lee squirmed, staring at the string of fish, as Drew continued to speak about his mother in a romantic way.

"Lee, this may seem too soon, but I'm wondering how you would feel if we three become a family?"

"You mean you want to marry my mom?"

"Yes, I do. And I want you to be my son."

The Other Part of Her

Drew emphasized his answer by looking directly into the boy's soft, hazel eyes when he spoke. Lee grew increasingly fidgety.

"Does it mean we'd move to Colorado?"

"Yes. How would you feel about relocating?"

"When do you think this would happen, Drew?"

Drew felt perspiration beads forming on his forehead. He hadn't considered the fact that Lee might have a list of specific criteria to address. Drew paused. Was Lee's tepid enthusiasm shielding a lackluster interest in the idea, or was he masking fear? What if Lee couldn't handle a change since he had never experienced a major shift in his short life?

Drew's mouth, as dry as day old cornbread muffins, required him to reach for a cold root beer. He offered one to Lee, then popped the cap, and took a long, cold swallow before answering Lee's question.

"I'm not sure about the timing. You and your mom are going to have a lot to say about that, but I'm thinking we would do it around Christmas."

Drew picked up a long blade of grass, peeling it, as he chose the right words.

"How would you feel about moving in the middle of the school year?"

"Well, I've been thinking about that since Mom told me you two had talked about getting married."

Lee hesitated, looked toward the mountains, and across the peaceful lake before he continued.

"I think I'd like living in Colorado. Can we go skiing in the winter?"

"You bet we can!" Drew's voice reflected an unusual amount of enthusiasm.

"You can invite your Texas friends to come join us, and in the summers, you can go to camp in Texas and hang out with your buddies in Fort Worth. I don't want you to give up anything there."

Lee looked up, staring directly into Drew's eyes.

"I think getting a dad beats anything I'll be giving up."

Speechless and stunned by his words, Drew searched for his voice.

Lee continued, "All my friends will be jealous when they meet you. Mom said you were captain of the football team at the University of Colorado. And on top of that, you're a pilot! They're going to be REALLY impressed!"

Drew's controlled elation set sail, soaring among the clouds.

"I look forward to meeting them, Lee. In the meantime, why don't we keep this discussion about marriage a secret? Especially from your mom."

"Okay, uh…but why?" Frowning and looking perplexed, Lee stared at him.

"For a woman, a marriage proposal is one of the most highly anticipated events in her life. She'll talk about it throughout her lifetime. Even strangers often ask a woman, 'How did he propose?' fifty-years later. A story will unfold as if it were yesterday.

"Some of my Navy buddies went to elaborate lengths to propose and since I've waited this long, I want to do it right! What do you say, we work on a plan together? I'm sure I'll need some help."

The bright orange sun didn't compare to Lee's beaming smile.

"Sure! That's really cool about it being so important," Lee assured. I won't say a word, not even if she asks."

"Great! We have a deal." And they shook hands on the most important contract of Drew's life.

"I think we better head back soon, Lee. Do you want to catch a few more fish?"

"Sure." Then Lee abruptly reconsidered. "Uh… on second thought, let's get back to Mom."

"I think that sounds like a winner."

Drew threw his arm around Lee's shoulder, and they hiked up the hill, toward the truck, both having thoughts of new horizons.

"I have a question." His young voice sounded pensive.

"Okay, shoot," Drew was wondering if Lee were having second thoughts.

"After you and mom get married, do I call you 'Drew' or 'Dad'?"

Caught off-guard by the question, Drew responded, gently.

"Whatever you want."

"Okay." Lee paused to collect his thoughts.

"I'll call you 'Dad'."

TWENTY-NINE

Hope sat at home, in her living room, holding the phone in her lap. Drew had just told her that he had to work all weekend, and he wouldn't be coming to Texas. It was the second weekend in a row. To heighten her disappointment was the distraction in his voice. She felt uneasy and decided to approach Lee.

"How does Drew sound to you?" she asked.

Lee gave her a puzzled look and countered with a tone of defense.

"He sounds fine to me. Can I go over to Robert's house?"

"Okay," she said.

He was on his bicycle before the door slammed. The two boys had been inseparable since kindergarten.

Her anxiety escalated when she thought about how loud a phone is when it's silent, especially, when one is anticipating the sound of a loved one's voice. She picked up her purse and drove to her mother's.

Kathryn Madison took one glance at her, and asked, "You look a little down. Is there something bothering you?"

Hope fought tears, as she revealed how things had changed since her last visit with Drew in Colorado Springs.

"Even his phone calls have slowed down." Her voice, low and unsteady.

"It's probably his work, dear. He's getting settled into a new job, one with tremendous responsibility, and he needs time to adjust. He'll achieve a balance soon and everything will be back to normal," Mrs. Madison assured her.

Hope reflected on the past week, and the rarity of Drew's calls. Thoughts of another weekend alone sent her into depths of despair.

Even worse, she couldn't form the words to tell her mother that Drew's usual loving words were absent from his calls.

"Hope, since your birthday is next week, and Riley will be here this weekend, why don't we celebrate early? How about this Friday night? I can make dinner reservations at the country club." Her mother's eyes twinkled.

"That would be nice, Mother, but I promised Lee that he could go camping with Robert and his parents. Can we wait until he can join us? I'd like him to be with the family."

Her mother stared out the window, as she sipped her coffee.

"Let's celebrate twice," Mrs. Madison stated. "Once with Riley while she's in town and with Lee on your actual birthday. How does that sound?"

"Good." Hope willed a trace of enthusiasm to be heard in her voice.

Mrs. Madison appeared to be debating on whether to say more, while lifting a warm tray of chocolate chip cookies from the oven. After she set them on the counter, she nervously glanced at Hope. A cloud of uncertainty hung in her eyes.

"I have someone I want to introduce you and Riley to. I think Friday night will be a nice time to do so." Her voice sounded tenuous.

"Mother, have you met a man?" Hope's incredulous tone embarrassed her mother. Kathryn shyly nodded.

"Do you remember my telling you about my fiftieth high school reunion?"

"Of course. Mother, is it the doctor? The one you dated, but lost track of when he went into the service?" Hope asked, excitedly.

Kathryn lowered her head as a smile gingerly crept across her blushing face.

"Mother, this is the best news I've heard in a long time. I look forward to meeting him, and YES, invite him to dinner Friday night. I'm sorry Drew won't be able to join us, but having Riley and the doctor there will lift my spirits."

The next day Mrs. Madison arrived on Hope's doorstep with what she called 'an early birthday present', a box from Neiman Marcus. Hope couldn't contain her delight when a white dress, with multiple layers of organza flowing under a strapless bodice, lay under the tissue.

"Mother," she said breathlessly, "this resembles the dress I wore on my first formal date with Drew. I love it!"

"When I saw it, I thought you might enjoy wearing it to dinner Friday night."

"Isn't this too formal? Maybe, I should save it for one of the Fall debutante parties!"

"Nonsense! Wear it Friday night. There will be plenty of parties and you might as well get accustomed to being dressed up now," Mrs. Madison encouraged.

"Okay. I think I will, even though I may be a bit overdressed when I meet your friend," Hope said.

"Not in the slightest. I picked out a coffee-brown, silk dress for Riley. Thought it would be a nice compliment for her dark hair," Mrs. Madison said, smiling.

The two sisters, eager to meet their mother's new gentleman friend, approached the evening with enthusiasm, speculation, and laughter. Kathryn Madison had not given any hints about his appearance or personality, which allowed her two daughters to give birth to wild imaginings throughout the afternoon.

At the appointed time, the girls stood at the entrance of the River Crest Country Club dining room. Their mother waved vigorously from the back of the room, where she stood next to a person they didn't recognize. They both gasped in embarrassment at the scene she was making. It was unlike her sophisticated manner, and they quickly made their way through the crowded room before others noticed her uncharacteristic behavior.

Kathryn began the introductions, her nerves edgy, her smile forced. She had never dated anyone other than Tennessee Madison, and the change in her marital status evoked a gamut of emotions in her, none of which she could control. While the meeting began to unfold, on that August evening, Kathryn Madison's composure crashed.

"Riley, Hope, this is Dr. Murphy...." her voice trembling like a broken violin string.

Riley silently considered his gray hair and distinguished appearance to be a nice compliment to her mother's elegance: an expression of intense confusion was on Hope's face, and Dr. Murphy appeared in shock. Riley and her mother stared at one another, frowning, wondering what had transpired between the two.

Dr. Murphy spoke softly, staring intently into Hope's eyes.

"I've thought about you many times. Your face is embedded in my memory, and I've longed to know how you are," he said.

He shook his head and continued. "I can't believe I'm seeing you again, and to know you're Kathryn's daughter is incredible!"

Kathryn and Riley gawked. No sound would come out of their mouths.

Hope felt submerged in a thick fog, her vision diffused, her hands wet with perspiration, and her brows furrowed. She listened to him. His tone rang familiar, she thought to herself, and there was something about his appearance that brought a vague recognition.

"Have you two met before?" Kathryn inquired.

The Other Part of Her

"I apologize," Dr. Murphy said, as he turned to address all of them. "I know this is confusing, but believe me, this is a wonderful surprise. One I never expected."

He turned to Hope and continued.

"I saw Hope in the Dallas-Fort Worth airport at the beginning of the summer. She was smiling radiantly as she walked down the concourse, and a split second later, all the color drained from her face. Unable to move, she stood frozen."

Hope interrupted with astonishment in her voice.

"YOU'RE the man who helped me!" she squealed.

He nodded, as he explained about the desolation he felt while standing at the window, watching her plane pull away from the gate, and his regret for not being able to follow-up with her.

Hope, overcome with emotion, wiped tears from her eyes, before speaking quietly,

"The events continue to be somewhat unclear, but I have wondered upon occasion, if you were an angel sent to guide me through that maze of darkness. What a great relief to know you are real! Please accept my heartfelt gratitude for your help that day." Her smile came from deep within, and Kathryn sighed a deep sense of relief.

Hope turned to her mother and sister with a thumbnail explanation about the men wearing t-shirts. "They had pictures of the American flag burning on their backs," she said. Dr. Murphy's deep respect for Hope shone in his eyes, as he provided her with details of the moments that followed, ones where her memory had failed.

The story affirmed everything Kathryn had suspected to be true about her former classmate. The assistance he had given her daughter sealed Kathryn's feelings. After they had dessert and coffee, she checked her watch and turned to her daughters with a question.

"Why don't we adjourn to my home and continue our conversation there?"

"Oh, thank you, Mom, but Hope and I had talked about seeing a movie," Riley said.

Kathryn couldn't help but smile with pride at her daughters, who were a study in contrast. They each were loving and respectful of the other, despite their differences.

The four strolled toward the main entrance, until Kathryn stopped by the club's large ballroom and placed her hand on the closed doors.

"Let's see if the manager is here, Hope. We need to make an appointment regarding the debutante party we have agreed to host."

Hope, startled by her mother's inopportune timing, tried to protest, but Dr. Murphy had grabbed the door and was holding it open. Riley fell in line behind her sister, as Mrs. Madison led the way.

A large crowd, seated at decorated tables, began singing, as a band played, "Happy Birthday." Hope felt confident they had intruded on a private party until she heard her name in the song. Her first thoughts turned to sorrow for the absence of Lee and Drew, but her heart happily burst at the sight of many loving friends.

Then the bandleader stepped to the microphone and said,

"Hope, that empty chair in the middle of the room is yours."

Kathryn quickly whispered some instructions into Dr. Murphy's ear. He nodded, then picked up the corsage up lying on the chair. It was a bracelet of miniature pink roses, which he slipped onto Hope's wrist.

Hope, stunned, gazed around the room, waving to friends, as she stared in disbelief at the room's transformation. The ceiling had been covered in white fabric, edged with swags of greenery and pink roses. She marveled at the decorations, and the band, both reminiscent to the Trocadero Ballroom in Denver, where she and

Drew had danced in 1959. A deep longing for him to be present briefly consumed her. As her eyes swept across the crowd, she was surprised to see many friends from church, including Pastor Ted, photography clients, neighbors, and even some of Lee's friends. For the moment, she forgot about Drew's absence.

Then the band began softly playing, "It Is Well With My Soul." Odie B strolled from behind a curtain, onto the stage, confidently taking her place at the microphone.

"Hope, I asked them to play our song, the one that has gotten us through many hard times together."

Hope began wiping the tears away.

Odie B absorbed the moment, smiling at Hope before glancing around the crowded room.

"For the benefit of those I do not know, my name is Odie B Jones. My mama began working for the Madisons when Hope was three years old, and I was fifteen. Mama B, which is what everyone called my mother, took care of the housework, and I took care of Hope. Five years later, during Fort Worth's disastrous flood, Mama B went to be with the Lord.

"For the first time in my life, I was totally alone. One day, not long after her passing, I was ironing, and Hope was sitting where she always did, on a red kitchen stool. She began pelting me with questions about my mama, daddy, siblings, none of whom were still alive, and it became clear, her young mind could not absorb what it was like not to have a family, nor a home."

The ballroom guests sat in total silence, gripped by her delivery.

"That was when eight-year-old Hope said, 'You HAVE to have family!'

"The flood washed away our house," I explained to her. "I'm staying in the basement of the Baptist church. The flood victims are my family."

"Hope jumped down off that stool, put her hands on her tiny waist and made a solid declaration.

'WE are your family, Odie B. You're MY sister!'

The crowd, including Hope, laughed.

Odie B paused, and stared at the floor, as she struggled for control. Then she glanced up, and with tears streaming down her round face, she continued in a breaking voice.

"That was the same day I asked Hope to read Mrs. Madison's grocery list, aloud. I remember Hope quietly studying my expression, and after a pause, she gently asked if I needed to see an eye doctor. I shook my head. Quickly realizing the problem, Hope asked if I could read. I shook my head again. Tears gushed from my eyes when Hope said she'd be my teacher.

"All in one day, this twenty-year-old housekeeper, with no family and no future, was graced by the compassion of a child. My 'sister' would teach me how to read.

"Our school was held at the dining room table, the same table where I served their meals. Mrs. Madison provided supplies and library books for me.

"Once again, my life had meaning, and years later, doors were opened of which I never could have dreamed.

"I now work at a public library in Colorado, and through the generosity of the late Mr. Madison, I have purchased my first home."

The crowd gave a spontaneous standing ovation. Odie B struggled to stay calm.

"So, it is tonight that I want to wish happy birthday to my sister. I love you, Hope."

Hope got up from her chair and ran into her arms, as the band swelled with the chorus of, "It Is Well With My Soul." Odie B held her, and briefly swayed. Then she motioned Hope back to her chair, before taking her own seat beside Mrs. Madison.

The bandleader stepped up to the microphone and announced:

"There is someone else who would like to say a word."

He turned his attention to the band and lifted his baton; music filled the room. Many smiled with memories, as the 1950's hit, "Loving You" drifted in the air. A moment later, Lee, dressed in a suit and tie, walked out. Hope bit her lip, trying desperately to keep her chin from quivering while tears of pride welled in her eyes.

He boldly stepped up to the microphone and apologized for lying about going camping. "Actually Mom, I've been helping with the party."

She chuckled, shaking her head in disbelief. A glance around the room revealed Robert with his family. The two boys were grinning at each other, pleased with their caper. She turned back to Lee. Audible emotion flowed from his voice.

"Mom, you've always been both mom and dad to me. You took it upon your shoulders to do everything, from teaching me to tie square knots, to riding a bike, helping me with Scouts, and teaching me the meaning of documenting life with a camera. You've been my chauffeur, my tutor, and my biggest cheerleader. You even learned all the intricacies of football, so you could help me improve my game. I recall many nights when we sat at the dining table, drawing out different plays, and working on execution in the backyard the next day." He paused for control. Tears blurred his vision.

"But the most important gift you've given me is faith. By your actions and your words, you've taught me that no matter what I will go through, God will give me the strength to endure trials. You're strong. You're brave. And you've given me wings to dream. You believe in me." He shuffled his feet while clearing his throat of the tears.

"For every selfless deed you've done, I cannot thank you enough. I realize now I have taken all this for granted. I assumed everyone's family was like ours, only with a dad. But I see you, and us, with different eyes now. I've come to understand in the past few months that there's nothing equal to a mother's love. Happy Birthday, Mom. I love you."

Music and applause filled the room. Hope ran to him with her arms open wide and they stood in the middle of the dance floor, as the band softly played, "Loving You". After a moment, he wiped his eyes, guided Hope back to her chair, and went to sit next to Odie B.

Hope felt weak from all the emotion and silently prayed they were at the end of the speeches, but the band began playing a few bars of "Anchors Aweigh". Bewildered, Hope glanced at her mother and Lee, wondering if it were a tribute to Drew who could not be there. Their faces didn't reveal an answer.

Hope sat unmoving and tense. Then Drew strolled onto the stage in his white uniform. The audience gave a loud round of applause, along with a few whistles. Hope could not believe what was happening! She wanted to run up on the stage, but she knew it wasn't the right time.

Drew grinned, ducked his head, and in a deep, velvet voice, he responded with a heartfelt, "Thank you." He turned to the band and said, "I didn't expect that one, but thanks, guys."

The bandleader responded, "The boy requested it."

Drew choked for a brief second, and with deep sincerity added, "Thank you, Lee." Then he turned his attention to the girl of his dreams.

"Hope, I feel it is important to give your friends a little of our history, so with your permission I will share it briefly." She nodded, agreeing with a smile brighter than the North Star.

"My name is Drew Bartlett. I'm currently serving as a Commander with the U.S. Navy."

Another round of applause and shouts of gratitude filled the room. His expression and manner gave the crowd a sense of his genuine humility when he lowered his head before responding to their outpouring of appreciation.

"Thank you. It's my privilege to serve."

The crowd roared again, then quickly calmed, as he adjusted the microphone to his height.

"I fell in love with Hope when she was twenty years old. She had just completed her sophomore year of college, and I had just completed my senior year in Colorado. We met at a mutual friend's home, and as crazy as this may sound, I knew during our first meeting that she was the one I wanted to be with for the rest of my life. However, we had only a few weeks remaining, before it came time for me to pursue the dream I had been chiseling out since childhood, to be a naval aviator. In June 1959, after my graduation, our paths separated. But like many, before we parted, we filled each other with faith, dreams, and optimism." He paused.

"Two years later, because of circumstances beyond our control, I received word Hope had married."

He hesitated and shook his head. "I realized it wasn't our time, once again." Tension and whispers floated aimlessly among the guests.

"My primary focus continued with the Navy, and the job that was laid out before me, but I couldn't help but feel the universe was out of alignment. Hope and I were still not together."

He turned to gaze directly at Hope, then spoke with a voice full of conviction.

"Only you, Hope, could make my universe right." He paused before adding, "Earlier this year, I received a letter from Odie B asking when I would be in Colorado, my home state. I wrote that my deployment aboard ship was nearing completion, and I would return on the fourth of June. She instructed me to be at her house on the fifth."

Relief and laughter filtered throughout the room.

He chuckled and added, "Thank God for Odie B!"

A man shouted, "AMEN", and applause followed.

"Odie B had learned through correspondence with Hope that she, too, would be arriving in Colorado on the same day as I, to photograph the wedding of Annie Ruth's daughter. Odie B immediately gave Hope strict instructions on when to arrive at her house. Unbeknownst to either of us, we would see each other for the first time in eleven years." He lowered his head, choking on emotions. "Eleven years of living with a void that no one else could fill."

The pain in his tone did not go unnoticed, but then his demeanor changed, and his countenance brightened.

"Since that meeting, we've spent many hours together. She has shared stories of how Lee's father sacrificed his life for our country, and though I didn't know him, I am deeply grateful for the legacy he left his son, to Hope, and to each of us in this room."

He stopped briefly.

"Hope, we have all gathered here on your behalf, to witness a very important occasion. However, I have a confession. The reason for celebrating your birthday was an incentive to get you, along with all the others, here."

She cocked her head, and asked, "WHAT? Is this not my birthday party?"

He gave her an irrepressible side-grin and answered.

"No, Darlin', it is your engagement party!"

He turned to the bandleader, nodded, then quickly left the stage. The song, "Misty", began wafting through the air, as he briskly walked toward Hope.

When he reached her, he took her hands and stared into her eyes. Stunned, she began to absorb his words.

"The band played this song on our first formal date in 1959. I was on the verge of becoming a commissioned officer, and I recall an older couple coming over to the two of us, beaming while they commented on how we reminded them of when they were young. It was their fiftieth wedding anniversary, and as they had done each year, they were celebrating at the Trocadero Ballroom. A desire for the same took root within me. Silently, I vowed we would follow their tradition.

"I've thought about that evening many times throughout the years and my desire to share that experience again with you never faded. Tonight, with the help of your mother, son, and friends, I have tried to recreate the same ambiance, but this time in the presence of your loved ones."

He paused to let everyone be immersed in his long-awaited dream, as he took her hands in his and continued.

"Misty's lyrics, 'I've been wandering in this wonderland alone', aptly describe my life since we parted all those years ago.

"Hope, my heart has known only one love. I love you beyond reason, and all understanding. Buried deep in my soul are gifts waiting to be unwrapped; each bearing your name."

He slipped down on one knee, and discreetly pulled his grandmother's ring from his pocket. Lee recognized the cue, and subtly moved from his chair with camera in hand. Drew turned his face upward, toward Hope, while placing the diamond engagement ring on her finger.

"Hope, for as long as I live, I'll never quit trying to be the man you deserve. Will you do me the honor of becoming my wife?"

She nodded, unable to speak.

Drew promptly stood, swept her up into his arms, and with a graceful side-bend, leaned her back and briefly kissed her lips. Hope's radiance filled the room.

"There is one more item I need to address," he stated.

Everyone wore a questioning look, including Hope.

"Lee, would you come join us, please?"

Lee, startled, walked toward them.

Drew turned to the young man beside him, handing his camera to Hope and nodding as he did. She read his silent message and backed up a few steps, so she could aim the lens toward the two men she loved with all her heart.

"Lee, you and I have talked about our relationship before," Drew began, "but I would like to ask you a question." An expression of confusion shone in Lee's eyes.

"Do I have your permission to marry your mother?" Lee beamed, but before he could answer, Drew added another request. "And may I have the honor of calling you, my son?"

"YES! YES!"

Drew reached into his pocket and pulled out a custom-made, lapel pin like the gold wings he wore on his uniform. Then he carefully pinned the wings on Lee's jacket, and in a booming voice announced,

"Every pilot needs a good wingman, and you are going to be the best."

Lee threw his arms around him while Hope captured their tender beginning on film. Drew turned to Hope and extended his hand with an exaggerated flourish.

"May I have this dance, my love?"

She smiled and gave him her hand with equal flourish.

The moment was playful, yet so very fraught with serious intent.

He closed the gap and whispered in her ear.

"My dream is to hold you in my arms throughout eternity, after our last dance on earth is finished."

He kissed her engagement ring, wrapped her in his arms, and nodded to the bandleader.

THIRTY

The next morning, Drew appeared on Hope's doorstep. His downcast expression, red eyes, exhausted body greeted her. A knot of anxiety tightened in her throat.

"Drew, what happened? Is it your dad? Let me get you a cup of coffee." Hope turned to go into the kitchen until he caught her by the arm.

"Sit down, Hope. I've something to tell you."

She fell onto the couch with her eyes wide and heart racing. Kneeling before her, Drew took her hand in his. The silence was deafening. Tears blurred her vision.

"Hope, I've flown combat missions, been chased by missiles, tested by nature's fury, and mankind's worst qualities challenge what I'm made of, but now I face the greatest test of all. Leaving you…again."

She stared at him, questioning the direction of his thoughts. *Was he breaking up so he wouldn't have to endure another long absence?*

Her chin quivered.

He stared at the ground.

"Hope, I know we have chapters yet unpublished. Our future is yet to be written…and even though the separation was not of my doing, at least, not intentionally, my deepest regret throughout the years was that I didn't put a ring on your finger before I left. Had I done so, maybe none of this would have occurred. I don't know, but I know I cannot endure another separation in the same manner."

He hung his head, grimacing against the pain.

"Hope, how would you feel if we got married before I leave?"

"We don't have time, Drew. You leave next week. How could we have a wedding in a few days? We just got engaged last night."

Pain ravaged his body as the dire possibility of returning to the ship erupted.

"I've given this quite a bit of thought, Hope. In fact, I've thought of little else the last few weeks. I never want to face the future again without you. As long as I live, I want you to be by my side, as my wife.

"The formal engagement was our first step toward securing our future together." He dropped his head into his hands, unable to find the words.

"I thought it would hold both of us until I return; then we could have the wedding of your dreams. Now, I'm wondering how you would feel about a small wedding. One with your mother and sister, Odie B, my dad and Lee in attendance."

An eerie silence settled over the room. Hope remained mute and wide-eyed, as he struggled to find the words she needed to hear. Words of comfort and reassurance.

"Hope, I know it's not the vision you dream, but if I have to leave, which I do, I want us both to have the assurance that regardless of what the future holds, we are husband and wife, holding one another at the forefront of all we do."

He couldn't even glance at her after realizing he was ruining the dream she had nurtured for years, the one of her walking down the isle of a large church toward him.

"Hope, I apologize for springing this on you immediately following our engagement party, but only one week remains before I leave."

He ducked his head, knowing he had destroyed the dream she'd always nurtured.

"I know this isn't fair, but I had to know what others thought about our having a small private wedding ceremony before I approached you with the possibility. Your mother, sister, Odie B, and my dad agreed to stay for the wedding. I also spoke with your minister."

Shock filled every crevice in her body while Drew exhaled deeply.

"After talking with each one of them, their enthusiasm and excitement swelled. Now, it's up to you, Hope. Are you able to find it within your heart to make this change"

Still as stone, she stood there!

He ducked his head and whispered, "I also have something else to confess."

"What?" Her voice trembled in fear.

"With regard to another decision I've made, I apologize for not asking your opinion about this."

He took her hand in his, as a broad grin travelled into his eyes.

"I'll be submitting the required paperwork to leave active duty as soon as I return to the carrier. It will take a while for it to be processed, but I'm coming home. To you and to Lee. And to the family we hope to have. I'll serve in the Navy Reserves so that we might build a life together."

She threw her arms around him with tears streaming down her face.

"Drew, when you stepped into the Whitmire's home, I knew I would love you for as long as I live. Oddly enough, through the years of absence, I continued to fall more deeply in love with you. Though I didn't realize it at the time, I know your frequent appearances in my dreams were a constant reminder of a love so strong nothing could separate us. You are now, and have always been, the other part of me."

He took her in his arms and kissed the pain of the past away.

EPILOGUE

I stand at the window of my photography studio, gazing out at the lawn. It seems years have passed since I last stood here. The small, lush garden Lee and I created in the spring has yielded its last bounty of fresh vegetables and the vast array of blooming flowers are now bending their heads under the last days of summer sun. The rattling air conditioner remains temperamental, but the clock continues to chime. Pristine white shelves are now showcasing photographs of Drew and me at our engagement party. A wedding album rests on the coffee table.

The memories of our wedding evoke an overwhelming sense of joy. I chose to stroll down the aisle in a white silk suit, one that Miss Bain personally selected, along with a matching hat and sandal-strap high heels. In one hand, I held a lush bouquet of white roses and lilies of the valley. The other hand was intertwined loosely in Lee's arm.

Drew brushed away tears as he stood proudly at the end of the aisle. The sight of him in his medal-adorned uniform took my breath away.

Lee placed my hand inside Drew's, smiling as he did, before taking his place as best man. A small pin in his lapel, the gold wings Drew had given him, sparkled like Mother's eyes. Odie B's smile dimmed the sun.

Dr. Bartlett rested his hand on Lee's shoulder, like a proud grandfather, and Lee promised Drew he'd take care of me while he was away.

Drew's quaking voice and moist eyes revealed his promise to officially give Lee his last name. Adoption would soon be realized.

Our honeymoon was everything I could have dreamed.

Peace. Wholeness. Sanctified by God. I am now, and forever, Mrs. Drew Bartlett.

The anticipation of his glorious return, and the beginning of a new chapter as husband and wife, makes this last separation bearable. My heart is racing with a waterfall of excitement for what lies ahead. One week remains until he returns home from duty, but I must admit to unstoppable tears on that warm, summer morning he held me in his arms for the last time. I crawled into bed that evening, aching from loneliness, and was warmly greeted by a note he had secretly placed under my pillow, prior to leaving. His words continue to comfort me, in the light of his absence. Soon my world will be complete.

June 22, 1970
Darling,

You are my before and after, the only one I've loved with my entire being. I believe God guided me to your side in 1959 and He has kept us together over the years. Now, I eagerly approach another role, one I cherish more than all the rest. The one as your husband.

Opening this door will allow me to demonstrate my love to you in unparalleled ways: to provide light where there is shadow, faith where there is doubt, hope where there is sorrow, and love to last through eternity. That, dearest Hope, is my highest calling.
Forever Yours,
Drew

In Memory

of

Shelly Lashley
For three short years, you brought us indescribable joy then God gave you wings to soar among the angels. A reunion is coming!

Connie Frady
My fiercely devoted older sister, you are probably asking God for a copy of this book, the one you so desperately wanted to read before leaving this earth. I heard your whispers. I felt your hand guiding mine. Your influence is in every word.

Genny Smith
I'm filled with gratitude for all the joy you added to my life. You were a radiant light, full of fun, laughter, and love! When thoughts of quitting this project would occur, your words of encouragement took me over the finish line.

Travis Vardell
My beautiful friend on earth and my encouraging angel in Heaven. You were the inspiration for Hope Madison.

Jene Maag

My dear friend, as well as my biggest cheerleader! The fun and laughter we shared is missed every day.

Ray Turner

My Wonderful, Loving Husband, you left us with the strength and perseverance to go forward, but we sorely miss your encouragement. Whether you were cheering for our family, friends, ministers, co-workers, the Texas Rangers, or the Dallas Cowboys your words of support made us all believe we were winners. Thank you for giving me the privilege of being your wife.

Paul and Connie Turner

Connie, your heart of gold is sorely missed, along with your passion for a good time, good friends, good food, good slot machines, and a good book. If you were here, I have no doubt that you would share this book with everyone in New Jersey. Thank you for blessing me with your unconditional love and support! (Please give your sweet husband, Paul Turner, a heavenly hug from me.)

My Mother, Edythe Frady Childs;
Dad, Bill Frady; Stepfather, Dr. Tilden Childs;
Mother-in-Law, Sybil Lashley

The blessing of a loving family made this book possible. Your faith, love, and encouragement travelled like a winding river through the creation process. I miss all of you terribly!